Palo**|||||||**ul

Richard Gill

Bolotti

Paloma Azul

This novel is entirely a work of fiction. The names, characters
and incidents portrayed in it are the work of the author's
imagination. Any resemblance to actual persons, living or
dead, events or localities is entirely coincidental.
Trademarked products are acknowledged and used fictitiously.
Warning: Graphic adult content.

Bolotti Press
An imprint of Bolotti Limited
This paperback edition 2022

1 3 5 7 9 8 6 4 2
First published in Great Britain by
Bolotti Press, an imprint of Bolotti Limited 2022
www.bolotti.co.uk

Copyright © Richard Gill 2022

Richard Gill asserts the moral right to be identified
as the author of this work.
A catalogue record for this book is available from the British Library.

ISBN: 978-1-7397438-0-2

Printed by kdp.amazon.com

All rights reserved. No part of this publication may be reproduced, stored in
or introduced into a retrieval system, or transmitted, in any form, or by any
means electronic, mechanical, photocopying, recording or otherwise, without
the prior written permission of the publisher. Any person who does any
unauthorised act in relation to this publication may be liable to criminal
prosecution and civil claims for damages.

This book is sold subject to the condition that it shall not, by any way of
trade or otherwise, be lent, re-sold, hired out, or otherwise circulated without
the publisher's prior consent in any form of binding or cover other than that
in which it is published and without a similar condition including this
condition being imposed on the subsequent purchaser.

Contents

1   First blood

J udy Madden knew she was in trouble. Frozen fingers ready for keystrokes she would never execute. The mugger sat down opposite her and held the blade up to her nose.

She was late this morning on the 11:41 tube from Leytonstone. An empty carriage rattling westwards into central London. Next stop, Mile End. Judy was a young lawyer, well dressed in a neat business suit which complemented her dark shoulder-length hair and green eyes. She had been intently revising a corporate acquisition document.

Now it didn't matter.

The mugger swapped seats and squeezed up next to her, keeping the knife close to her left eye. He grabbed the laptop and briefcase, sliding her possessions into a striped laundry holdall. Her D&G handbag was wrestled off her, exploding its contents on to the carriage floor. He'd done this before and he enjoyed it.

'The rings, Tag Heuer, mobile, and necklace, love,' he hissed.

'The ring was my grandmother's!' Judy lied, handing over her Samsung.

'Too bad, lady.'

She fumbled with the necklace and surrendered it, leaving her diamond engagement ring till last. She glanced up at the emergency stop-handle, well out of reach.

He grabbed her wrist, and menaced her with the large serrated hunting knife. An eye, a nose or an ear? he thought to himself.

First blood.

Mr Knife smiled, revealing dirty teeth that had never seen dental floss…waxed or unwaxed. The nose hair wasn't too good either. He liked using his survivalist knife; it would cut nicely through cartilage. He might get to skin a whole deer with it one day.

'It's precious ring time!' he taunted, moistening his index finger provocatively in his ulcerous mouth.

'Move it…rich bitch!'

Judy blanched at his foul breath of bile, coffee, sulphur, and rotting gums, and attempted to lunge upwards at the red handle. He ripped the arm off her mauve bouclé jacket, revealing a white short-sleeve blouse, and pulled her back down into the window seat.

Judy would normally get off at Chancery Lane, walk east down High Holborn and into Fetter Lane.

But not today.

'The ring I said!'

Judy made a play of trying to twist the ring off, but Mr Knife knew this one. He tightened his grip on her wrist, digging his dirty nails into her skin. He lowered the sawtooth edge and sharply grazed it over her knuckles, drawing blood immediately.

That normally did it.

'No!' she screamed.

Thomas Bell slumbered in the late morning sunshine at the other end of the carriage, listening to music. A merciful late start to a Tuesday in the office. The door slam must be a ticket inspector working his way down the train. He relaxed with his eyes shut, deeply immersed in track five, 'Cocaine and Cognac', from Para Noya's third album.

Thomas Bell, outwardly a well-educated city worker, wore his profession's standard attire: dark suit, Italian shirt, silk tie, and expensive shoes plus laptop bag.

Judy's second scream bypassed his headphones.

Bell sat up immediately, fully alert.

The train slowed into Mile End. An empty platform.

'This is my stop,' said Judy, as if this constituted permission to go.

'Yeah, love, you stop here till we've got everything.'

Judy twisted off her priceless ring with bleeding fingers. To her horror, Mr Knife swallowed it, blood and all, poked his tongue out, and belched into her pretty face.

'What else you got?' he grinned, raising his eyebrows, tugging at her blouse.

'You've got everything!' she screamed.

Mr Knife was becoming agitated.

He was getting too far away from the safety of his home territory, the East End. He didn't want to go beyond Bethnal Green, but this bint was a plum.

Mr Knife noticed Thomas Bell standing there. The mugger assessed this good-looking city boy in shining armour, and released Judy's hand. He knew how to deal with people like this. Oh dear, the deer is here! First blood. Flesh, bone, and cartilage.

'Can I help you, pal?' he sneered.

Bell looked him over. Slipknot chic in a heavy leather jerkin, on a warm day. Hot shivers and the need to feed the habit, sweating body odour, flaking skin, and yellowing ferret eyes. Needle scratches and scabs told their own story. Steel toe-capped boots, shapeless tattoos up his calves, and greasy hair mostly hidden by a tight-fitting baseball cap.

The girl was beautiful and in big trouble. Definitely his type, though. Bell glanced down at her bloody left hand. This arsehole really meant business; he would have to be careful.

Her earnest green eyes pleaded with him to do something.

'Bella, you're late in today, aren't you?' he bluffed.

'You don't know her, you dumb arsehole!'

'Come and sit with me,' smiled Bell.

'Piss off will yer, pretty boy?'

Mr Knife was right, he could piss off back to his seat or…

'Help me, David,' bleated Judy, playing along.

She tried to rise, but Mr Knife held her down and drew the holdall closer to himself.

'We're just having a little chat, okay?' he spat.

The hunting knife was the only weapon Bell could see. It surely had fish hooks, line, and a compass in the handle. This guy had happily sliced it across the girl's knuckles, so he would no doubt be more than delighted to split open Bell's scrotum with it. The girl just sat there looking pathetically paralysed with fear, nursing her injured hand.

'…looks like you dropped something,' said Bell.

Bell shrugged and made to walk off back to his seat, to Judy's instant dismay.

Mr Knife relaxed enough for Bell to aim a long punch, but Mr Knife was ready for him. He had anticipated well and was up on his feet in a flash, dodging the blow. He countered with a slash of the knife, missing Bell's gut by a few inches.

Bell landed his second punch on the side of Mr Knife's head who, in return, caught Bell with the butt of the knife, grazing his temple. Then, a violent scuffle up against the double doors. Mr Knife kneed Bell in the stomach, and landed another two blows to Bell's skull.

Bell countered with an elbow strike to the face, and the knife went skittering across the floor. Despite a decade of drug abuse, Mr Knife was still strong and had a lot of practice under his belt. This was his day job and he grappled Bell's neck into a sleeper grip, but failed to squeeze the carotid artery shut.

At least Bell knew that one.

Mr Knife's speciality was biting off a piece of ear or nose. Bell could smell the foul breath panting next to his face. Mr Knife released his grip and head-butted Bell just above the nose. Bell hit the deck. He could taste the sickening, metallic taste of the blow, but was able to protect himself from the heavy boots pounding mercilessly into his stomach and ribs.

The train slowed into Bethnal Green and came to a halt. Judy grabbed her chance, and the laundry holdall, frenziedly stabbing the 'open' button. The doors drew apart and she ran, as fast as her heels would take her, to the exit.

Mr K was taking deep breaths, beads of sweat on his grimy forehead. Before Bell could leap back into action, Mr Knife had retrieved his weapon and made it to the doors. He hawked up the contents of his lungs, prepared the oyster of taut phlegm into a ball with his furry tongue, and expelled it across at Bell. After a momentary lament for his lost swag, Mr Knife disappeared, hoody up, trying to work out how it had all gone wrong.

Don't hang around next time! Just cut 'em up and cut 'em good. Learn your lesson. Mr K gobbed some more on the tarmac platform, as the train pulled out.

Next stop, Liverpool Street.

Bell slowly pulled himself up on to a seat, gasping.

Hmm…that could have been better.

As a rookie MIX agent, still in training, Bell resolved to have his advanced unarmed-combat modules brought forward and intensified, with a special emphasis on street fighting and unholy tricks. However, to take a beating, no matter how unpleasant, was still a valuable lesson which contributed to his grounding.

Don't let it happen again!

Blood seeped down the side of his face. His tongue was also bleeding a little, and his face was swelling up nicely.

He'd live.

Status report: teeth, nose, eyes and testicles still intact...the delicate bits that were difficult to mend. He committed Mr K's face to memory, just in case there was a next time. Jesus, his ribs were on fire! Did he have a punctured lung?

He bent over in agony and retrieved a handful of her belongings, including Dior eye shadow, moisturiser, and some tweezers.

The Harvey Nicholls store card appeared to be in the name of 'J. Madden'.

Yeah, maybe not Bella, after all.

***

Bell emerged from Liverpool Street station, walking westwards down Sun Street. After Finsbury Square, he headed north on City Road towards Cyventure House, just beyond Old Street tube station.

He entered the offices of his employers, Charles Carrington, accountants and registered auditors. An ugly building, on ten floors, which might just as easily have been occupied by an overseas development agency or Her Majesty's Revenue and Customs.

Reception was starkly decorated in sterile whites, greys, chrome, and marble composite. The ex-military man on the desk, in a white shirt with blue epaulettes, glanced at Bell and continued to sift a pile of junk mail. A coffee table littered with trade magazines, topped by the Investor's Chronicle, stood next to a black leather sofa and a hollow glass sculpture, illuminated with crystalline balls.

Bell stepped into the body mass scanner, then pressed his left eye against the state-of-the-art, iris-recognition machine. The glass airlock hissed open and he took a lift to the third floor.

To the outside world, Charles Carrington was a specialist London accountancy practice. It supposedly had a select group of clients in the music, property and leisure sectors. CC, nicknamed 'Carbon Copy', had a respected presence in the City, its bland website bulked up with press releases on recent financial directives.

Cyventure was Charles Carrington's management consultancy arm. The work was sexier and you got to travel more, working in places like the Seychelles, Bermuda, and the British Virgin Islands. Places you could jet off to, and mix international tax planning with sun and cocktails.

London is a hotspot for dirty money, corporate fraud, and money laundering. The only law not being broken was that of supply and demand. Accountancy was a lucrative and dangerous profession.

Charles Carrington was no ordinary firm of accountants. It was a front for MIX, a branch of British military intelligence so hush-hush that no one knew it existed.

MI5 and MI6 had gradually become compromised with exposés, ex-spy memoirs, and kiss-and-tell leaks.

Both intelligence agencies had their own websites, and well-known London buildings which came under mortar attack from time to time. They openly advertised for operatives in the national press, as if you were joining a national supermarket chain on a management training scheme.

Nothing was really covert anymore.

The time had come to form a new organisation, which would be truly clandestine.

MIX had an unlimited budget and a global brief. It was the new instrument of state to excise persistent security cysts on the UK's exposed arse, in absolute secrecy.

It drew on the best expertise and equipment, supplied by allies and foes alike from around the world, to train its agents to the highest level of spycraft. It had a particularly generous arrangement with the US Central Intelligence Agency, who were knee-deep in advanced military technology.

An accountant can go anywhere in the world, with a briefcase and a calculator, without arousing suspicion. Audit review, systems analysis or due diligence work? No problem, this way please. The perfect cover for highly trained agents to carry out dangerous missions.

In order to make the pretence absolutely watertight, all operatives had to be thoroughly trained as real accountants, learning all the principles of accounting, alongside those of spycraft, explosives, weapons, hand-to-hand combat, and advanced military training. The entire set-up had to be plausibly accurate right down to the finest detail, so that their cover would never be blown, even under torture.

Bean counters with balls.

The lift doors opened on to a hot desking area, and private office suites furnished in creams and limed oak. It looked like the interior of any one of the top twenty accountancy practices based in the City.

Bell headed for the kitchen and rest area, complete with pool table. Blood was still busy oozing, necessitating immediate attention for his swollen face. He almost broke the first aid cabinet off the wall, spilling bandages and antiseptic cream everywhere.

I need ice, ice, ice.

He raided the fridge and tended to the blood, bruises and swelling with ice cubes in paper towels. His stomach, ribs and head still hurt like hell and he looked like shit, but he'd recover. A visit to the medical officer was borderline; we'll just see how we get on.

Bell was still mastering the basics, in the first phase of his career, drummed in with intensive training. He would have to get to grips with the advanced topics in due course.

Aged twenty-seven with a degree in Economics and English, he was sporty, six foot tall, slim but muscular, with short dark hair. Judy had remembered the clear blue eyes and ready smile, just as Bell had filed away the features of Mr K.

Every week since he had started had been a typical week. The grinding repetition of spycraft, bookkeeping fundamentals and MIX operational guidelines.

He fixed himself a strong cup of tea and sat down at his desk, switching on his computer. He spread some papers out and started clicking. He hoped he'd be in good enough shape for intermediate aikido, part of his unarmed combat module, that afternoon.

***

2pm. Bell pressed minus three and descended seven floors into the basement of Cyventure House.

He entered the dojo.

Danny Wilson stood there relaxed and warmed up, ready to give a two-hour martial arts training session. He wiped his ears with the towel wrapped around his neck and grinned at Bell.

'Allo mate, fit then?'

'All set,' replied Bell.

As sensei, Danny was stripped to the waist in black silk shell-suit trousers, with a red sash wound three times around his waist. An interior mock-up of the Blind Beggar pub stood at the far end. Danny's barrel-like torso sported a myriad of distorted tattoos that would make a Yakuza blush. He was a forty-seven-year-old hardened criminal and ex-gangland enforcer.

A copy of the one hundred deadliest karate moves lay on one of the benches. The double ear-clap, which would burst both eardrums, was Danny's favourite. Bell changed into a similar outfit to his teacher, but with a white sash.

'Been in the wars 'ave we, son?'

Danny gently cupped Bell's face and studied the patched-up injuries.

'Look's like someone's been taking liberties, my old china.'

'It's just a scratch.'

'Tut, tut. You've been slapped good and proper. Was there a young lady involved?'

'Yeah.'

'Thought so. Looks like I need to teach you everything I know. It'll take a little time but we'll go easy on you today. Are you still up for it?'

'Sure. I hate being scratched,' grinned Bell.

A while later, as they finished their session and towelled off, Bell pointed at the fourteen-inch, angry red scar slicing across Danny's muscled back, made by a carpet knife.

'How did you get that?'

'Not at a West Ham home game, that's for sure!' replied Danny, laughing.

'...In a pub in Romford, two years ago. I got slashed by this geezer who said I'd been eyeing up his bird. Maybe just like you, my young friend.

So, I walk over to the ice bucket standing on the bar, take out the ice pick and put it straight through the side of his face. Kind of acupuncture for beginners, if you know what I mean. That would've been fine, just to be done for affray or ABH, but this guy catches a bug in hospital, and gets eaten alive by the Ebola virus...'

Danny took a moment to look at his watch.

The rest of the Romford story would have to wait till next time.

***

Friday. An exhausting week.

After a lunchtime drink in the Artillery Arms in Bunhill Row, Bell ambled back through the warm haze of London traffic fumes. He slumped back in his chair, and thought about going home for the weekend, heading due south to Brighton.

He idly turned the plastic Harvey Nicks store card in his hand, admiring Bella's signature on the reverse.

J. Madden.

Julia...Jane...Joanne or Jasmine?

He ran his finger repeatedly over the raised gold letters. He thought back to the vision of her, pressed up against the train window, pathetic and vulnerable in her ripped jacket, her green eyes looking into his. On a whim, he decided to locate her and headed for the fifth floor.

He sat at a semi-circular desk on a plush, leather swivel chair and stared at the forty-inch flat screen. A cable as fat as a baby's arm led from a grey distribution box on the floor.

The air-conditioning in this small, quiet room cooled him, his white shirt quickly separating from his skin. He had authorisation-level six access to both Aurora and Echelon.

Aurora is Britain's internal citizen database which links together data stored by government departments, supermarkets, credit card providers, banks, CCTV archives, hospitals, telephone companies, and others. It provides a three-dimensional data life profile on anyone living in the UK.

Echelon, on the other hand, is the US National Security Agency's global spy system which captures and analyses virtually every phone call, text, email, and telex message sent anywhere in the world. It is controlled by America's NSA, its National Security Agency, in conjunction with the UK, Canada, Australia and New Zealand, through a series of intercept stations which trap satellite, microwave, cellular, and fibre-optic communications traffic.

Bell clicked on Aurora.

The cursor tripped across the screen and came to a halt, blinking impatiently over 'Data source'. He changed the dropdown selection to 'Store cards'. The system processed the sixteen-digit number in seconds and a mass of information appeared.

Judy Rachel Madden.

Judy!...he should have guessed.

Address in Wimborne Minster, Dorset.

Part of the address must be missing, no street name or anything. No London address given. Date of birth...January...age…twenty-five. Other store and credit cards were listed. Bell ascended to a higher menu level, and multiple page tabs appeared. He clicked on 'HMRC' and browsed her tax returns and income.

Employer: Falcon & Falcon, corporate lawyers, Fetter Lane, London, EC4. Mergers and acquisitions. Other tabs: NHS, directorships, shareholdings, bank accounts, terrestrial, and mobile phone numbers. He had it all now.

Finally, a high-resolution UKPA digital photo of a beautiful girl centred the screen. It had been taken two years ago. Her hair had been longer then. He sat back for a moment and admired Judy's enchanting eyes.

A chance meeting, perhaps?

2   Gone fishing

Arturo Cardona stood in the wheelhouse of his trawler, the Maratiaga. Unlike other fishermen, he dared to go out further from San Antonio harbour to trawl the richer, deeper waters north west of Ibiza. Their nets ought to be full by now.

April 7th 1966: light wind, calm sea.

Nearing the end of an unproductive day in early spring conditions. He and his two-man crew would carry the disappointment all the way back to the cofradia de pescador, the fish market, in San An. All that unused crushed ice and empty fish trays.

They would cast the trawl-net one more time, and carry out a controlled pass, just like the abnormal number of American warships threading their way up and down his patch. He normally had the place to himself, but the bastard Americanos were frightening the fish away.

The truth was that the US Navy had lost something and it had to find it, no matter what.

Jesus, he was sick to death of hacking fish guts into grubby plastic buckets. Despite all the modern navigational aids and fish finders, there was little payback from trying to catch elusive marine life. Any mistake you made out here was severely punished. He couldn't stand it any longer and wanted to retire. He gently touched an illuminated icon of the Madonna and child, affixed next to the wheel. He closed his eyes and said a little prayer. What could he sell the Maratiaga for?

'Bastardos Americanos! What the hell are they doing here?!' he screamed, thumping the main instrument console.

Romero and Silvio overheard the captain's expletive, and jumped back to it amongst the netting and the marker buoys. They could not know that Arturo's vitriol was evenly split between the cruel fates of the sea and the swaggering Americanos. As usual, their voyage would yield only a pittance for a day's effort.

An American ship bore across the port side, a large grey phantom making twenty knots. A super-sized, silhouetted number 83 was painted in white on her bow. Romero marvelled at the vessel's complex superstructure, as Arturo steered quickly to starboard, straining the hawsers of the trawl net as they went. The Maratiaga shuddered as Cardona clung to the wheel. What are they up to? Do they think they own the bloody place?

For ten days now, a special US Navy task force had been hard at it with sophisticated sonar equipment rushed over from the United States, in response to some kind of emergency. Large vessels with A-frame steel girders and stabilisers. Dual hull ships, like dredgers, working in rows, mapping the seabed and trailing finned torpedoes on wires. At intervals, they halted and launched remotely operated vehicles, small unmanned craft attached by twisting umbilical cords which dived down to the seabed.

Cardona chuckled as he recognised a Russian trawler which had been monitoring the labours of the US Navy. A break in the boring routine of their normal game of cat-and-mouse played out on the world's oceans. The Kremlin would be revelling in schadenfreude at this latest nautical accident, gleaning data from the frenetic activity.

Until it was their turn.

***

Eighty days earlier, Gary Dowie sat in the navigation bay of a US airforce B-52G Stratofortress, flying high above Spain's Costa Almería.

A USAF KC-135 jet tanker is to rendezvous in nine minutes' time to refuel air-to-air. It was one of seven hundred jet tankers that were always airborne somewhere in the world. Up here on the flight deck, the smell of hydraulic fluid and sweat always lingered in your nostrils. The roar of the B52's four Pratt and Whitney engines vibrated continuously in your eardrums.

He looked at his watch and turned to speak to Hicks, the cool, detached, electronic warfare officer who was checking gauges: needles trembling at a quarter-to.

'The Kaycee will be here in a minute…'

A nod.

The sun inched around the fuselage as the plane lined up, causing sunlight to blind him momentarily through the Plexiglas. Dowie slipped on his Polaroid aviator sunglasses, and subconsciously gripped the star buckle which held the webbing harness of his ejector seat. In the back of his mind, he was aware that this silver bird, the Carol-Ann, carried four B28 RI hydrogen bombs which would each produce a yield of 6.5 megatons. He did not like to think about it. The sooner he left the employ of Strategic Air Command, the better.

Over-ocean refuelling should be routine, but today the repeated drills practised high over the Nevada desert would lend no assistance. Human error, a lapse of concentration, and the sudden realisation of impending doom would take over where the textbook left off.

If it can go wrong, it will.

Murphy's third law of physics.

The vapour trails of the Carol-Ann and the tanker closed quickly, high up in the sky. The captain of the Stratofortress prepared to receive forty thousand gallons of jet fuel through the metal proboscis protruding from the nose cone. As he turned to port, he saw the KC coming on to them too quickly and at a strange angle.

'Jeez, what the...'

The last words from a decorated Korean veteran.

Sudden impact.

Metal, rivets, components, and human flesh fused in a ball of incandescent heat generated by the tons of highly inflammable liquid. The burning fuselages of both aircraft spiralled downwards in a gruesome embrace into the Mediterranean, south of Palomares, in the province of Almería.

Two of the four high-yield thermonuclear devices, which had landed to the east and west of Palomares, had ruptured on impact, their chutes failing to open. It allowed radioactive particles to disperse over farms growing tomatoes and oranges. A radionuclide cocktail of caesium, plutonium and boron showered the pristine agricultural landscape.

The radioactive plutonium metal was instantly transformed into insoluble plutonium oxide, not an ideal substance to ingest. Pu-239 attaches itself to your bones and cannot be excreted from the human body during the rest of a person's lifetime. Fifteen hundred tons of Spanish soil, used for generations to grow fine produce and venerated by the locals for its fertility, would now be shipped in fifty-five-gallon drums to the Savannah River nuclear dump in Aiken, South Carolina, USA.

One of the bombs landed intact near Palomares, in the dry Almanzora river bed to the east. It prompted further panic and the arrival of the dry cleaners: a specialist USAF team, armed with space-age vehicles and radiation suits, directing the clean-up. The fourth bomb was lost at sea, many miles off the coast. The Americans searched for it twenty-four hours a day. Seventeen naval vessels and twelve thousand personnel combing the seabed systematically in a controlled sweep.

***

The captain of the USS Petrel, Edward Kurtz was sick of it all too. Another goddam fuck-up! They were gonna have his balls on a stick if they didn't find this mother. And that was just for starters.

That reminded him, he needed to go take a dump. At least it would get him off the bridge for thirty minutes, thumbing through unsanitary mags in the head. He might as well have a wank in there while he was at it. That bitch firecracker must be down there…somewhere! At least they weren't looking in the Mariana Trench.

Kurtz chewed nervously on his half-smoked cigar, trying to visualise a twelve-foot metal tube lying on the seabed. He reported directly to Rear Admiral Guest, who had been appointed by the US Defense department to sort out this sorry shit. He had been resting behind a desk at the Pentagon, nursing his ass, when he'd been hooked out to deal with this one. All that Guest could do was chain-smoke up on deck in that brown leather coat of his, screaming fuck at everyone.

Kurtz's close friend Jack Daniels was going to get him through this. Those cocksuckers monitoring the sonar readings had missed something; this was the third time they had blanketed the primary crash area. Holy shit! It should jump off the screen like a branded mustang! Where the fuck is it? He would give anything to be back in Nam right now, anchored in the Mekong delta with the NVA throwing everything they had at him.

***

Arturo Cardona was completely unaware of this. The setting sun marked the end of a wasted trip. Silvio and Romero set the winches running to pull in the last trawl of the day. The steel cable strained, as the neck of the net emerged from the deep, tiny quantities of silver fish clearly visible in the failing light.

They did occasionally bring up some odd things: strange jellyfish, a human torso, oil cans, a revolver, a cannon ball…things which usually tore holes in the nets. Never caches of 22-carat gold doubloons.

Cardona looked dolefully out of the wheelhouse, as the pathetic catch was hauled in. Seabirds circled looking for scraps, the Russian trawler still visible in the distance. The winches squealed as the hawsers tightened.

'Stop, stop, stop!' screamed Silvio, as wood splintered on the transom. Arturo ran down from the wheelhouse to take a look. At first, he thought it was a giant squid, but he quickly realised it was sodden parachute material and multiple strands of nylon cord. It was all attached to a shiny, stainless-steel tube, two and a half metres long, with busted fins and warhead. The whole lot lay entangled in the ripped trawl-net, bunched up against the side of the Maratiaga.

They had no idea that this was what the Americanos were searching for. Cardona looked at it carefully, studying the cream-stencilled markings and the USAF white star motif on the tail. Romero and Silvio attempted to lever the object over the gunwale and on to the deck, but it was far too heavy.

'Leave it Romero, we'll lash it tight where it is and head for home.'

'Si, capitano. Is it a bomb?'

'Si, Romero. We have a good catch at last.'

The skipper decided to cover it with a plastic tarpaulin and get moving quick. The Ruskie was too far away to have seen anything.

Cardona could sense money and an end to all his problems. If they wanted it back, they would have to pay Señor Arturo Cardona many pesetas. The Americanos would cheat him, cheat him out of his peaceful retirement. They had clever maritime lawyers.

Abogados malvados!

There was no choice. He would have to speak to a person many people were too afraid to deal with. It had to be done. Then he would never need to fish ever again. The Maratiaga swung to port, engines at full throttle, and headed home. First stop, to unload the deadly cargo unobserved in a deserted cove.

He cupped the illuminated Madonna and child with his good hand, leant over, and kissed the plastic icon.

'Gracias...muchas gracias,' he whispered.

***

Captain Kurtz studied the naval communiqué carefully. The US Secretary of Defense had ordered the end of the search. Dozens of vessels and thousands of man-hours had produced nothing.

Zippo.

The USS Petrel would rejoin its battle group in the Philippines and head back to Vietnam.

Tortured wreckage of both planes was now in their hands, on a highly radioactive inspection barge. Men in clear plastic suits walked the decks, nervously measuring radiation levels in millisieverts and kilobequerels.

But no bomb.

Maybe the commies had taken it from under their noses with a goddam grappling hook and line. The reds would gleefully strip it down in one of their remote Siberian facilities, and play catch-up with Uncle Sam.

Yep, it would have to go down as an unsolved mystery, one of the many unfathomable riddles of the deep. Kurtz adjusted his sweaty nether regions in the high captain's chair, and stared out towards the horizon. He lit another cigar.

Cocksuckers! Just give me Agent Orange and a cold Bud for Chrissake!

3 Valhalla

Ilya Pago emerged from the pool and wrapped a white monogrammed towel around his portly figure. The sort of figure you develop by eating forty pieces of sushi at one sitting. He casually wiped his bald head with a matching hand-cloth and adjusted one of his titanium nipple-rings.

Standing on the top of three decks, he surveyed the shimmering coastline running north to Cala Vadella, Sa Conillera and beyond to San Antonio. Three hundred and twenty five feet of ocean-going yacht beneath his feet and a crew of fifteen. Hardcore pornography had been good to him. The pool at the stern of the Valhalla was still now, its bottom entirely adorned with a vivid bull-beast mosaic. The image had been faithfully replicated from the original in the Cretan palace of Knossos, home of the Minotaur.

He lifted a miniature bottle with oriental writing, from the ice bucket, snapped off the lid and drank the milky contents down in one. Secretions from the larvae of the giant wood hornet. Part of his carefully controlled diet and fitness regime. Immense wealth meant that one could happily indulge in faddy healthcare products manufactured in the Far East.

He lay down on one of the teak sun-loungers, closed his eyes and awaited his daily zoku-shin-do foot massage. The serenity of the huge sundeck, and the exquisite pleasure from the Japanese girl's fingers, would allow him to focus his thoughts on the day ahead.

Dressed now in a shorty wetsuit, he ran down the main spiral staircase, pounding the gold-plated banister as he went. Out on deck, he ordered the Kawasaki two-man jet ski to be launched immediately. A crewmember jerkily operated the hydraulic controls and eventually managed to get it into the water. Pago glowered with irritation at the klutzy sailor, who quickly adjusted his sailor's cap and jumped to attention, eyes dead ahead.

The Valhalla comprised a steel hull and aluminium superstructure on three levels including an atrium, a spiral staircase and a helipad. Pago had made other modifications, including a missile detection system. The vessel had eighteen guest staterooms, each air-conditioned, with en-suite Penteli marble bathrooms. The intimate 'Rose and Crown' English pub was decorated with timbers salvaged from a Spanish galleon, and the bar stools were covered in whale foreskin. The sanctuary of the azure lounge, with its iroko panelled library, was definitely his favourite place to relax. Twin diesel engines delivered the power and range he might just need for a quick getaway.

He nestled his ample buttocks on to the plastic seat of the Kawasaki, clipped the control cut-out to his wrist and gunned the marine engine. With his Oakleys pressed tightly to his face, he raced off at full speed over the mirrored surface towards the shore.

The craft pulled up sharply at the deserted beach and he hooked it up to a red buoy in the stony shallows. A wooden sign announced 'Playa privado, Eintritt verboten', suggesting World War One minefields and barbed wire. This was a beach to die for and not a soul on it.

A quad bike awaited him in the shade of a cluster of pine trees; a few minutes later he'd powered his way up to the top of the cliffs. From this high vantage point, he stopped and turned to admire the Valhalla. Its snow-white hull, topped with a funnel sporting a bull head motif, pulled gently at her anchorage in the blazing sunshine. More than satisfied, he accelerated away into the thicker pine forest.

Ibiza, the pine island. One of the four main Balearic islands seventy miles south of mainland Spain. Also known as the 'White Island', said to be called that because the ladies ritually whitewash their houses to cleanse away impurity; supposedly an ancient Punic ritual designed to exorcise all that is sordid. Pago also knew about impurity and why, for him, this was La Isla Blanca.

His thoughts turned to the business of the day as he bowled along over the rough track.

The Mexicans.

It was his custom and practice to lay on a welcome his guests would never forget, or take to their grave. Ilya Pago was highly intelligent and able to focus all his effort on a specific goal, without deviation. He was also sadistic, cunning, dissolute, sordid, and capable of any excess but, when it came to his own skin, he was a complete coward.

The forest thinned and human cultivation became evident. Windmills with billowed sails turning slowly in the light breeze, giving the area its name, 'Puig des molins' or 'Hill of windmills'. The long grass concealed entrances to dozens of Phoenecian tombs dotted around the hillside. Pago continued past acres of sunny orchards of oranges and apricots. Olive, fig and carob trees stood in rows, shrouded in the heavy scent of mint and jasmine. He approached the traditional finca at the centre of the Dos Lunas estate, flecking up a plume of red dust as the bike hit the neatly raked gravel drive.

He dismounted and stood before the massive, savin-wood double doors of the main building, flames of bougainvillaea licking the walls. An ex-French Foreign Legion paratrooper stepped out on cue and stood to attention.

'Bon dia, Pierre,' Pago whispered, kicking off his pink flip-flops.

'Bona tarda, chef,' replied the young trooper.

The bodyguard slapped the heavy riveted door behind them, as Pago strode through into the air-conditioned hallway, over cool white marble tiles, to the main lift.

Helmut Kranz, a pharmaceutical scientist, stood by the workbench, two floors underground, looking over a complex set-up of laboratory glassware. Pago stood back as Kranz, in his clear protective glasses, was about to repeat the process a gifted chemist from the Cali Cartel had carried out on a hunch...and which led him to strike pure gold. Kranz dissolved cocaine powder in ammonia, added water and bicarbonate of soda, and heated it till the liquid boiled off. What remained were magnolia-coloured rocks of...crack cocaine.

'This is one I did earlier,' beamed Kranz, one hand thrust gamely into his white lab-coat pocket.

The trooper stepped forward with a plastic bottle, some pipe, foil, and a spoon. He followed his orders without question, taking one of the dull crystals and heating it up, which filled the plastic bottle with smoke vapour. He then inhaled it deep into his lungs in one gulp, slumping back into a lab chair.

The drug targets his stomach first, a warm, buzzy glow that spreads through his body like a hot shiver. Then it hits his head and everything explodes, firing off all that dopamine.

'What's it like?' asked Pago.

'It is everything,' gasped Pierre, 'Sex, power, winning the lottery, all the drink, all the chocolate in the world. I am alert and powerful and I can take on the universe…I…I can accomplish anything.'

Pierre sat up suddenly, every negative thought banished from his mind. He had never felt so alive before, driven by raw energy pumping through his veins. Kranz looked on dispassionately. Pierre was like so many white rats, monkeys, and pigs he'd experimented on in Switzerland. Never be tempted to give them pet names, he mused to himself, as he selected a paragraph from his written notes.

'The subject experiences forty to fifty seconds of instant euphoria. It is a high with no parallel, culminating in eighty percent addiction within two weeks.'

Pago nodded approvingly, his menacing eyes magnified through the protective lenses, worn like designer sunglasses.

Kranz continued, 'In contrast, one can achieve thirty minutes with cocaine. Three to four hours with heroin.'

Craving…action…emptiness.

'Magnificent! Full production can commence as soon as deliveries from South America arrive. Do you foresee any problems, Kranz?'

The scientist felt Pago's cruel pupils boring into his head.

'No…no Herr Pago. Everything is in order, alles klar. Not a gram of das weisses Zeug will be wasted. We have all the facilities we need here at Dos Lunas.'

'Excellent…' replied Pago, glancing at his Rolex,

'…we will make it as chic and desirable as our existing product offer.'

***

'The people I represent can offer five hundred kilos per month, the cocaina to arrive by sea, in a manner of our choosing,' explained Dario Hernandez, chief emissary for the Alacrán cartel.

Dario and his bodyguard, Diego, sat in strategically positioned chairs opposite Pago in his wood-panelled office, a picture window looking out over the western Mediterranean. Traditional oil paintings furnished the walls: Jesuit monks burning screaming heretics at the stake, battles fought with sword and musket. Portraits of the Spanish conquistadors Pizarro and Cortés looked down solemnly upon Pago and his Mexican visitors. When Cortés landed on the Yucatán peninsula in 1519, he held two clear advantages. Guns and smallpox.

Dario was more used to open-sided huts, makeshift facilities deep in the jungle, rather than air-conditioned laboratories.

He had attractive, South American features and cropped stubble, complemented by his finely cut, thousand-dollar suit, fresh white Ferruti shirt and gold tie pin. A silver briefcase, with combination locks, containing two million dollars in cash, rested against the leg of his chair.

As a teenage wildcat smoking basuco under the flyovers in Medellin, he had swiftly graduated to administering quick deaths for easy money. He had risen quickly through the ranks to become a stylish foot soldier feared by many, working exclusively for the big people. He had learned the whole production process. First the coca leaves, then the processing of the cocaina in pop-up factories perched over streams in the jungle, dumping tons of toxic chemicals into once pristine streams and rivers. Paraffin, sulphuric acid and calcium sulphate, some of the forty-one chemicals used in three phases of production to manufacture el blanco.

'What are your terms and conditions and can you guarantee the quality of your product, Mr Hernandez?'

'That is a large quantity of cocaine to be delivered every month,' smiled Dario.

'So, what is the price?'

'That depends, Señor Pago.'

'Depends on what, exactly?'

'On the alternative proposition I have for you.'

'Go on.'

'We will purchase your business. We like your operation and it will be an additional entry point into Europe for us. Galicia is very hot right now, so we can step into your shoes here, as it were.'

Pago looked both puzzled and alarmed.

'...and what makes you think I'm up for sale?'

'You will want to sell! There are certain...how you say...synergies, common links of language and culture.'

Dario waved his hands carelessly and smiled with assurance. Never let us know who you are or where you live, he thought.

'That is no real reason but, I am curious, what price do you have in mind?'

Pago raised his finely clipped eyebrows and glanced down at his sweaty, upturned palms.

'For your entire business we offer you one of your Euros...the cartel believes that is a fair price.'

Dario and Diego drew their handguns from their loose-fitting suits. Pago had anticipated treachery such as this. A move into crack and cocaine had its inherent risks, relying on outsiders to supply the main ingredient. Perhaps he should have listened to Kranz after all, and chosen something else.

Methamphetamine.

A psycho-stimulant drug which triggers a cascading release of dopamine. It induces intense euphoria, with a high potential for addiction. Kranz had assured him that the manufacture of crystal meth, by the reduction of ephedrine using red phosphorous and iodine, would have been simple, despite the high fire risk. They could easily have installed an effective extraction system to expel the phosphine gas and other noxious fumes which were synthesis by-products. Now it may be too late.

Pago squirmed uncomfortably behind his desk, thinking quickly. His mouth was arid dry, not helped by the barrels of the two firearms pointing directly at him. He leant forward awkwardly and reached for his mineral water. It would seem that he was alone in his own office with two ruthless killers.

'We...we can discuss this...it is the start of our business relationship, after all,' blurted Pago, offering the glass up to his lips.

'Instruct your guards to disarm immediately, and then rise from your desk...por favor,' ordered Dario.

Pago had considered various ways to cater for a situation such as this. Hidden machine guns, flying knives, poisoned darts, and many others. He had assessed all the options, his foot now hovering over the red foot-pedal underneath the desk.

Ultra-powerful industrial scanners in the entrance lobby, delivering an absorbed dose equivalent to twenty-five back X-rays, had revealed everything about these men. All except the contents of their mysterious, silver metallic case, which was lined with lead. With that amount of ionizing radiation, Mr Hernandez would not be producing any more children...that is, if he had any, and ever got to try again.

'I also have an offer that you cannot refuse,' said Pago, recovering his composure.

'And what is that?' laughed Dario.

'I offer one of your Mexican pesos for your life.'

'One peso...but that is truly worthless!'

'Precisely!'

Dario and Diego had no time to react as the trap door gave way and they tumbled into a void, chairs and all.

***

Pago bit into a scented marzipan ball from the dainty selection box, poured some Laurent-Perrier pink champagne into a crystal flute, and surveyed the bloody face of the Mexican.

He swallowed a Selenium vitamin pill, placing the flute carefully back on the desk. Anatoly Kadic wheeled in a heavy, dark green box on screeching castors containing primary and secondary copper coils and connected all the wires. It had two large bakelite dials marked with Cyrillic characters and slatted ventilating grilles.

Dario fought against his bindings, straining his eyes round in their sockets in horror. A distended maroon flex now led over to the control box on Pago's desk. The generator hummed quietly, a ruby bulb indicating its readiness. The Russians always excelled at this sort of thing. Think young sailors, nuclear submarines and freezing seawater. Kadic, head of security, threw a bucket of cold water over Dario, naked, bound and gagged in the same chair he had relaxed in so comfortably earlier.

It cleared his face, making him look curiously refreshed, as though he had just emerged from a power shower. Blood continued to drip from his broken nose and vitreous humour seeped steadily from his collapsed left eye. He sat in exactly the same spot as before, Cortés and Pizarro regarding the scene with approval.

'Do you like cooked meat, Mr Hernandez?'

Dario tried to answer but the gag was too tight.

'The powerful current that will soon flow through your body will cook your internal organs...and it may hurt a little, of course. Such is the power of electricity. But I do not expect you to understand this, being merely a Mexican peasant,' taunted Pago.

Kadic opened the atrium windows and attached the sharp, serrated clips to Dario's testicles and neck. He nodded when all was ready.

'Chef.'

'...and now...,' said Pago.

Pago's puffy right hand picked up the control and flicked the cable nonchalantly, like a buggy whip. A platinum ring, mounted with sapphires in the motif of a blue dove, adorned the flesh of his pinky finger.

He sucked the remains of the marzipan from the gaps in his back teeth and turned the dial. Hairline needles shot to the right as Hernandez writhed and arched in the chair, straining against the ball and leather gag. Snot, sweat and blood streamed down his face, as the burst of current coursed through his body. If he could have sucked the gag down his throat and choked on it, he would have done it gladly. Relief at any price to escape from what was coming next.

Back in Mexico City this would be a natural death. Everything in Mexico had to be strong to live. He had thought that all Europeans were pussies, but this was the old world, the world of the Inquisition and centuries of perfected cruelties. He had been wrong, inexacto.

Now his whole life played out before him. How, as a young narco from a poor barrio, he'd been on dozens of Cessna drops. Shrink-wrapped bricks of cocaina destined for so many noses. Sitting in the cantina in his iguana skin boots, drinking tequila, laughing at the Federales. Sweat, flies, salt, and girls in tight white jeans. Chicas calientes. Hot girls. Chicas offering company and intimate night entertainment.

He thought back to the high sierra, and realised that he would never see the Rio Grande again. He thought of Gina. Lazy afternoons in bed with her, with the sun dappling the eucalyptus trees in the courtyard, flaking shutters, half open. Their bronzed bodies fused in perspiration and ecstasy. His silver Beretta, the handle inlaid with mother of pearl, and a fresh pack of Mustangs on the bedside table. Adios Gina, I will not see you again. For I have lived by the sword.

Kadic, with long experience of torturing prisoners in Bosnia, knew when the end was close and the spirit was broken. He nodded to his boss.

Pago spoke again.

'Mr Hernandez, what will your people do if you and your er...colleague do not return?'

Kadic removed the gag, Dario tried to answer...

'C...c...ca...cart...'

'Mr Hernandez, what will...?' pressed Pago.

'Cartero.'

'What is he saying?'

'El...c...cartero,' repeated Dario.

'It means...the postman,' replied Anatoly, looking unsure.

'Mr Hernandez, who or what is the postman?' asked Pago, with growing impatience.

'He will come for you. You...you are a dead man.'

Dario and his superiors also expected treachery. He would die but the cartel would never forget. There were certain niceties to be observed in this business.

'Who is El Cartero?' quizzed Pago.

In his frustration, Pago jacked the power up to ten, the highest level. Without the gag, Dario unleashed a piercing, unearthly, childbirth scream, and collapsed back into his bindings. With superhuman effort, he raised his head for the last time, forcing a wretched smile.

'El...cartero...el...s...siempre entrega!'

Kadic darted over and checked for a pulse.

'Your visitor is bien hecho, probably a heart attack, there's only so much the human body can take.'

Kadic released the clump of matted, bloody hair and Dario's head fell forward again.

'What did he say?'

'The postman...he always delivers.'

Pago turned away and grimaced to himself.

He should have left well alone. Ecstasy had worked so well for him, but he had been tempted by new markets and new products. Now, his whole enterprise was at risk. What chain of events had he set in motion which could destroy him? Once things started to unravel, when the threads came loose, everything would fall apart. Pago consoled himself. If it did come to it, if he couldn't staunch the haemorrhage, he was fully prepared.

***

Stephanie Walters peeped through a crack in the door to see the body of the man she had been made to sleep with dragged past by two guards.

He was naked save black plastic ties eating into his bound wrists. So that was the scream, she thought. The guards had a leg each and pulled the corpse along face down, leaving a bright trail of blood on the white marble tiles. She could hear Dario's nose, jaw, and skull bouncing and splintering each time they went down a set of steps, disappearing off into the distance.

Jesus! She had to get out of here!

It was worse than she had suspected.

Stephanie had been approached in the Labyrinth Club with the promise of easy, well-paid work. Glamour photography. She'd been skint, utterly desperate, and had managed to lose her passport somewhere.

The work was, in fact, hardcore films and performing sex acts for the web in accordance with the strict instructions of online clients. Lesbian girl-on-girl action, bondage, rubber and asphyxiophilia. She immediately discovered that she was now a prisoner and slave with a load of other girls, held in some sort of isolated, concrete complex. They had taken her new passport and beat her if she didn't do as she was told.

She couldn't be sure that she was still in Ibiza but knew that this place had many underground levels, and was near the sea.

Anna Lanika controlled this 'cover' operation for Pago, which cleverly concealed the true purpose of Dos Lunas from the outside world.

She was a pitiless, dragon lesbian with short blonde hair and a fetish for military uniforms and young girls. She took pleasure in breaking in, beating and humiliating the ones that did not submit to their new circumstances.

Anna had knocked Stephanie around when she had first arrived, softening her up, crushing her spirit. They had told her that if she tried to escape, she would be fed to the sharks.

For all that, they ate well and were encouraged to use the sun terraces like so many birds in a gilded cage. Escape was always on her mind, a thought sustained by the scrap of paper with her true passport details, concealed in the lining of her denim jacket.

So much for living and working in Ibiza indefinitely. She'd been forced to resort to petty crime just to stay alive. Her finest prize, stalking the nightclubs and the strip, was a new Gucci bag complete with credit cards, cash and a British passport. She'd looked so similar to the girl in the photograph, she had been able to assume a brand new identity.

1:00a.m. Stephanie skilfully picked the lock of her room again. She and her friend Mia were now in the corridor listening for footsteps. All quiet.

Plan: Get to the top floor, quietly submerge themselves in the indoor section of the main swimming pool; careful, no splashing, then silently swim out through the plastic curtains to the open-air pool area; head straight for the far edge, climb over the lip, scramble down the outer wall and run like hell through the pine forest towards the sea. No problem, dead easy.

Stephanie knew that all doors to the outside were secured by swipe-card locks. One day it had dawned upon her that the route to freedom was provided by the main pool. Only a few more metres to go and they would leave the corridor behind, be through a glass door, past a few rows of sunbeds, and be lowering themselves into the water.

Footsteps.

Maybe a guard on his rounds.

Stephanie pressed a door handle and dragged Mia with her into a large office. The sound of footsteps receded, and it was silent again.

A reading light was still on, illuminating Pago's desk.

Stephanie scanned its surface for anything useful.

Just a half-empty bottle of Laurent-Perrier, a box of chocolates, and various packets of tablets. On a whim, she decided to scoop up anything with a blue dove on it, and stuffed them into her jacket.

'Can we go now Steph? I'm scared.'

'Yeah, let's get out of here.'

Stephanie opened the heavy door a little.

All clear.

They scurried over an expanse of teak decking, slipping into the water, swimming slowly and silently across to the seaward side of the giant infinity pool. Up over the edge, they scraped their way down rough Ibicencan stone, breaking nails and scraping knees.

Finally landing on dusty red earth, crouching down and soaking wet, they caught their breath, ready to make the one hundred metre dash to the tree-line.

'Left or right along the beach, it's all I can think of; but if we stay here, we're shark bait.'

'Don't say that, Steph!'

'Just stick with me and do what I do.'

'Run!' gasped Stephanie.

The moonlight kindly helped them in the gloom. They could hear the soothing crash of the waves in the distance. They were half way now, offering the tantalising chance of freedom. The girls stopped for a moment, heaving with nausea.

'Steph, do you think we've done it?' wheezed Mia.

Anna was doing her rounds, checking the girls' quarters, considering which one she would choose as her playmate for tonight. As head jailer, she could take her pick from the smorgasbord of young female flesh. The cocktail of over-the-counter Viagra and anabolic steroids gave her a permanent hard-on. Show us your cock Anna, they taunted. She rubbed her groin in anticipation. They weren't far wrong. Her libido and sexual ingenuity knew no boundaries.

Anna pushed the bedroom door open. The little bitches. She would teach them a hard lesson when they were caught and brought back to her, weeping and pleading for mercy.

She thumbed her walkie-talkie. No matter, Kadic already had them on infrared, sector K. The security lights went on, the whooping alarm sounded, and the dogs were unleashed from their compound. Kadic and six guards with quad bikes and halogen searchlights, followed the barking Dobermans out into the night.

Stephanie looked up, fear gripping her stomach like a balled fist. She wrenched Mia's damp 'Aloha from Hawaii' T-shirt.

'Come on, keep running or we're dead!'

'I can't! We'll never get away now!'

Mia never sensed the red laser dot on the back of her blonde hair. Another millisecond and all her youthful dreams were to become so many brain cells and skull fragments, spattered in all directions.

Stephanie knew she was close now. She was running on a surge of pure adrenaline. Her legs were striped with grazes and cuts, but she felt nothing. She knew that the dogs and the bike units were gaining on her. She had heard the shot, but she was going to make it. She would swim for it, lose the dogs and melt into the darkness. Just get to the beach, dive in and disappear.

The cliff edge was quickly coming up to meet her, the waves crashing on the rocks one hundred and fifty feet below.

In the final strides, as she cleared the last of the pine trees, the moon shone brilliantly on the surface of the sea. She tried to adjust her eyes, dazzled by the bright sparkles in the distance.

All of a sudden, she was running in mid-air, flailing in the blackness. Stephanie fell like a stone into the waves, staring into the lights of...Valhalla.

Disbelief, impact and oblivion.

***

Anna looked back at Pago and Kadic with the unwavering gaze of her big brown eyes. She tightened her US Marine-issue belt, and tensed her stomach muscles under her vest. Her soft, husky voice broke the incident room silence.

'We need more girls.'

4 Pretty in pink

The blonde Hutton sisters emerged from customs in a blur of pink, Prada and white. Armed with two matching Samsonites, they made for the terminal exit. The front doors of Ibiza airport opened to a blast of midday August heat.

They were soon in a hire car heading east past San Jordi on the dual carriageway towards Ibiza Town.

'Well, thank the fuck for that!...It's finally over,' screamed Sienna, devouring the screeching clutch.

'I'll drink to that!' shouted Amber, punching the roof.

'Say bye-bye to the exam room, sis!'

'Our BAs are behind us, girl…now, we're bad asses!'

The Playa d'en Bossa junction blurred past on the right, as Sienna precariously skirted a line of bollards.

'I'm first in the pool!'

University was over. Three years of hard work and harder play. Their eight-week revision nightmare had been excised in a ten-day burst of booze, marquees, stretch limos, and karaoke. That was enough Malibu for now. After a short period of drying out and some frantic packing, they were ready for a change of scenery. Four weeks at their parents' luxury villa in S'Argamassa to chill, check out the party scene, and see what happens.

Amber eased off the air-conditioning and jacked up Para Noya's classic: 'Dreamday Lover'. She just loved their second album. Sienna accelerated through the truckstop of Ca Na Negreta as Michael Kroll, the band's exotic frontman wailed:

'I wake up crying all night long.'

Can't sleep alone, I did no wrong."

The band would be playing a massive final gig on the island in a week's time, the closure of their world 'Blowout' tour. Amber could visualise Kroll strutting the stage, bare-chested in taut jeans, drawing back his mane of long, wet, blonde hair, taunting the crowd. Can't wait! They had managed to get tickets before the website had crashed.

'They say that Johnny Lazzara will marry Pixie!'

'What a gold digger!' scoffed Amber.

'So, will you be seeing Karl again?' asked Sienna, interrupting Amber's reverie.

'I've been forced to have a deep think about him.'

'The 'L' word?'

'I'm here to unwind and enjoy.'

'It's over, then.'

'He says he's not looking to get serious.'

'He just wants the sex, and saying that means he doesn't have to worry about how you feel.'

'I guess.'

'You should be angry you wasted so much time on him, but you still love him, don't you?'

Amber nodded slowly.

Sienna overtook three vehicles on the raised stretch to Santa Eularia. Keep driving on the right, girl, we're getting there, not far to S'Argamassa now.

'He thinks a clitoris is a rare Peruvian flower, but he has a washboard stomach and staying power.'

'And just how many thongs did I see you chucking into your Sammy?'

'A month's supply, but there's a doctor out there who says that women are suffering from friction problems!' laughed Amber.

'That doctor is a man who's never heard of VPL. He'd have us all wearing big pants. Tosser!'

'As long as they stick when I throw them at the wall, then I know I've had a good time.'

'Yeah, time to party and may the devil take us.'

Finally, a straight blast down towards Es Canar, then a tricky jink left and right past abandoned windmills and a tract of virgin forest. Sienna pulled the car up to the heavy wrought iron gates with a scrunch of fine gravel. The large traditional villa was set in its own grounds with pine and carob trees. The thick walls were laced with spiky bougainvillea, a driveway curving round underneath to a massive subterranean garage.

The villa was pleasingly overgrown, which made it more secluded, with a view out to sea and Santa Eularia just visible out to the west. Rough-cut tree trunks protruded from the whitewashed masonry over the shady terrace, Ibicencan style. Two circular towers, cladded with sandy stone facings, defined the style of the property, cornering the building on the seaward side. As they approached the mahogany double doors, a green lizard, clinging to the wall, tilted its head slightly then spun off into the shrubbery.

Soon they were laughing in the pool, then San Miguels and crisps, followed by a tapas order delivered by motorbike. Sienna and Amber continued to laze on the giant loungers into the late afternoon, smoking menthol cigarettes and listening to the cicadas invisible in the trees. Super-size cream umbrellas with hardwood struts creaked in the warm breeze, the taut fabric protecting them from the sun and pine needles. Amber was busy painting her toes by the pool using a foam toe separator.

'I thought polish was passé this year?' said Sienna, studying the UV details on a tube of L'Oréal. She threw it on the lounger and picked up her Stila lipgloss.

'It is, but to hell with it. I'll do the naked pedicure when I'm good and ready.' snorted Amber, applying cerise nail polish.

'How are your ski toes now?'

'Like a baby's. You should try him.'

'At Claridges?'

'Just make an appointment with Mario, it's an intimate experience. He cuts away the dead skin, exfoliates, moisturises and polishes them with a dentist's drill. It's so exquisite, some handsome guy playing with your feet, buffing your toes till they come up conch-pink and shiny. It sent me all dreamy and I wished he'd never stop.'

'Dreaming about Karl?'

'Maybe,' smirked Amber.

'So, you're ready for your Gucci toe-job sandals instead of ski boots?'

'...and not to mention the leg and foot massage with his strong Italian hands.'

'I can't bear anyone touching my feet, how do you do it?'

'Huh? You're kidding?'

'Slicing off my dead skin with a scalpel makes me cringe!'

Sienna drew thoughtfully on her Kool Ultramint, exhaling slowly. Maybe she would try fuchsia pink instead. The Plexiglas finish would give her lips a polymer veneer and a satisfying bubblegum plasticity, just as the ad had promised.

'So, is she a lesbian, then?' inquired Amber, changing the subject.

***

The iron gates were still shutting behind them, as the sassy and stunning pair were back on the road again. First stop Ibiza Town and two expensive cocktails.

'El Divino to start?' quizzed Sienna.

'Let's try the Esclavo instead.'

'What?...in San An?'

'Just drive Sienna, I'm thirsty. We can dump the car and pick it up in the morning.'

***

Anatoly Kadic, aged thirty-six, charming, spontaneous, enigmatic, petulant, and a psychotic heartless killer leant back from his rustic Ibicencan desk, closed his eyes and cast his mind back to Bosnia. A Turkish cigarette and a strong coffee steamed alongside a flat screen displaying eight CCTV feeds. A collection of rare samurai swords lay nursed in a black lacquered rack on the opposite wall.

He smiled at the memory of emptying a clip into a crowd of innocent civilians, standing naked, freezing in the snow. The time when he made a prisoner gnaw off and eat the genitals of a fellow inmate. The sheer ingenuity of it! He started sniggering to himself and broke out into an uncontrollable belly laugh, as he reached for his fast-burning Samsun. I caused all that pain and I am totally alone.

He killed for fun; he made the grim reaper look like a game-show host. As a section head of security in the Balkans, he was known as Black Death, due to his jet-black hair held back in a ponytail.

He had used the war and the chaos to traffic drugs across the snowy mountain passes in Eastern Europe, and had consumed vast quantities himself. He still needed a full load of the white stuff each day, the only snow he got to see now in the fragrant heat of this Balearic island. He was pharmaceutically sustained, and it was nearly time to take his tablets which controlled his psychotic cravings.

Were they still necessary? he wondered.

He slothfully scratched the razor-wire tattoo round his left upper arm, as he nursed a live Czech anti-personnel mine. Its exquisite design and ability to amputate a man's legs just above the knee fascinated him.

Ilya Pago had found him by accident, recognised his talent for unalloyed brutality, and dragged Anatoly back from the abyss. Kadic could now face reality again, physically and emotionally, in a stable role as head of security at Tagomago S.A. It promised to be another quiet night at the finca Dos Lunas.

Ilya Pago unexpectedly burst into the smoke-filled office and dropped a file on Anatoly's desk.

'When I eat something...I never want to see it again!' Pago screamed, standing like a baying colossus before him.

Anatoly stubbed the foul-smelling Samsun in the cavernous terracotta ashtray and read quickly.

'Sienna Hutton! She's back!...b...but it can't be!'

'Well, it is!' replied Pago.

Kadic studied the data in disbelief, squinting at the grainy digital mugshots of two girls. Dos Lunas had been hacking into the Balearics' inmigración system for years. Special software scanned all departures and arrivals at Eivissa airport against a monitor list of names, passport numbers and foreign airports.

Yacht and ferry movements were all handled in the same way. Pago's security team had also been on special alert to look out for anyone who might conceivably be El Cartero. Perhaps a professional assassin in the pay of the Mexican Alacrán cartel. A needle in a pile of needles. Pago was justifiably nervous.

'She's just flown in from London with what must be her sister!'

'I don't get it. It was rough weather that night. The rocks would have split her open like pulled pork. Her remains would have been flushed out to sea as fish bait.'

'Did you check?'

Kadic stayed cool, although he wanted to tear his boss's tongue out with pliers.

'No one could have survived a cliff fall like that...she should be dead.'

'She should be! We now have the opportunity to make it happen this time. No more mistakes!'

Kadic retrieved a large pile of passports from his wall safe and flitted through them like playing cards. He found Sienna's original passport with a grimace.

'You recall that some of our stock was pilfered off my desk that night, including our new product line. I want them brought in alive for questioning. Understand, Anatoly?'

'Yessir.'

Ilya moved forward menacingly.

'Remember that I pay you very well to maintain total security here at Dos Lunas...otherwise...'

'We will find her,' promised Kadic.

Ilya leant in closer, two inches from the head of security's nose, like an obscene gargoyle.

'I know you will.'

Kadic was unaware that the body of whom he thought was Sienna Hutton was in the island morgue. The Dos Lunas security systems benefited from neither Echelon nor Aurora, whereas MIX in London did. Kadic couldn't possibly know that the reason for Sienna's miracle jump was to be found sewn into the lining of Stephanie Walters' denim jacket.

***

San Antonio.

Amber and Sienna downed the second of their vodkas and Red Bull.

'Ready for your first Malibu?'

'Don't, I'll be sick,' grimaced Amber.

Jack Daniels and Cokes, and a bowl of marinated olives were delivered to their table, sticky with spilt tequila shots. They rocked to the heavy beat, as clubbers in zipped leather shorts and all things black minced past in groups. A wall of flickering crimson posters advertised Tiesto, Paul van Dyk and Jacques Lu Cont.

'I love the Esclavo!' screamed Amber, above the music, downing the JD & C in two gulps.

'I hope that's Diet Coke, Amber.'

'Like, are you a slow drinker or what?!'

'Let's go somewhere else.'

***

'It's three for one or try a bluey,' the barman explained, pouring a line of Black Russians. He handed the girls some Blue Lagoons - a lethal mix of blue curacao, vodka and gin, while a couple of Pago's men in their twenties studied them from a distance. The sisters knocked them back, slamming the empty shot glasses down on the bar.

'There she is. It's her, our person of interest,' whispered Dino.

'Who's the other one, then?' replied Andy.

'That's her little sister.'

'People getting tanked in here generally move on to the Labyrinth. Let's hope we're in luck.'

'Yeah, if they do it'll be easy.'

'All you have to do is try to be charming and debonair. Do you think you can manage that?' joked Dino.

'Hmm, very funny. I'll do the younger one and she's going to love it.'

Sienna and Amber staggered out on to the San Antonio Boulevard, carefully shadowed by Pago's well-trained enforcers. The inebriated blondes clacked in their high heels past the sling-shot bungee machine, and headed towards the illuminated bull-head sign of one of Ibiza's most exclusive clubs.

They arrived at the Labyrinth in high spirits ready to boogie, only to have their hopes dashed. A long queue of clubbers was corralled by a thick velvet rope, looped on chromium stands, which ran alongside a red carpet. The hopefuls were being rigorously policed by surly bouncers with walkie-talkies. 'Extreme Euphoria week', proclaimed the PVC hoarding.

The Labyrinth Club was owned by Tagomago, a Pago front company. The Lab lived up to its name. Dedicated to the Minotaur, the bull-beast which roamed the labyrinth of Greek mythology, the club was a warren of bars, dance areas, chill rooms, and lounges, all decorated in the neo-Babylonian style of Nebuchadnezzar's palace. Tonight was Baal night, dedicated to the Ibizan storm god, and included a live sex show.

Clubbers would witness girl-on-girl action, naked wood nymphs in a trance, pleasuring each other, fondling and fingering. Then the man-beast himself would be fanfared on to service the queen of the nymphs, on her back, legs spread apart, her body anointed with baby oil by her handmaidens. He would penetrate her slowly at first, masterfully, then faster and faster, the clubbers chanting in unison, till they finally climaxed together. The lights would be extinguished and they would be gone. Well, it got the punters in, anyway.

'Shit, look at this queue…we're not gonna get in!' screamed Amber.

'I'm pissed and it's only our first night. Call me a lightweight if you like…let's pull the plug.'

'What? and miss Baal night? We'll just have to join the line, that's all. How about we slip the doorman a hundred Euro note?'

'…or magic up a couple of Labyrinth season tickets? I'm not joining the bloody queue! Anyone in a Chanel LBD should get straight in, come on Amber, let's taxi back. I'm looking forward to enjoying a leisurely breakfast.'

Pago's accomplished predators had overheard the exchange and moved in swiftly. The girls turned to focus on the not unattractive duo.

'No season tickets? So how about complementary VIP invites which include your first drink? It would be a great honour to escort two lovely ladies into the Minotaur's lair.' grinned Andy.

'Wow! Just like magic!' whooped Amber.

Before she knew it, Andy had his arm around her, leading her to the front of the queue.

Sienna looked at Dino in disbelief, she was to be his by default. The part of her brain which processed risk had been neutralised by the surfeit of alcohol, pills and nicotine. What lay ahead was by no means inevitable. She fumbled for a Koolmint and lit it, trying to decide.

'Come on, sis, let's do it.'

'Amber!…what happened to the taxi idea?'

'You're kidding kiddo, we're in.'

Arms interlocked with arms, the magic rope is unhooked, and the two couples enter the Labyrinth.

***

The drinks arrived. Two Estrellas, and two cocktails laced with liquid ecstasy and rohypnol. The foursome had subtly paired off, Amber responding to Andy's ready humour and charm.

Dino sat as close to Sienna as possible in the crescent-shaped banquette.

'So, what do you do?' inquired Sienna.

'We deliver yachts all over the Mediterranean.'

'A girl in every port or any port in a storm?'

Dino waved his hand with a dismissive smile and put the chilled Estrella to his lips. Amber and Andy seemed to have gone off for a dance or something.

'You're not drinking your Blue Lagoon. Bottoms up…'

At that moment, a procession of nymphs, guarding their sacrificial queen, passed by enroute to the stage for the main event. A spectacle titillating enough to distract Dino for a moment, during which Sienna poured most of her drink on to the carpet. So, where the hell has my sister gone?

Amber held on to the washbasin in the Ladies as she frantically splashed water over her face. Someone who resembled her stared back from the huge mirror. She felt really weird and it was getting worse. In a panic, she staggered uneasily out of the toilet, and a nonchalant Andy snaked his arm expertly around her slender waist.

'Hey babe, maybe you should sit down for a minute.'

Amber eased herself backwards into the comforting embrace of Marilyn Monroe's mouth. Andy nodded skywards, and the wall-sofa lips rotated abruptly in on themselves. Amber's drugged reactions failed her and she was gone. The hydraulic lips rotated back to their start position, ready for the next kiss.

Sienna's legs started to feel like jelly. Dino's face gyrated in front of her on the dance floor. The alien chemicals relentlessly tightened their grip, melting her vision, unbalancing her mind. Why had she said yes?

'W…what's happening to me? Where's Amber and Andy?'

Sienna longed to be back at the villa, fast asleep, safe between starched cotton sheets, her body preparing itself for fruit muesli and mango juice. Dino just smiled back at her. Strange, she had held out longer than expected, he would give it a few more minutes. Then a peck from Norma Jean.

Something tripped the club emergency lighting and fire alarms. The music stopped and roaring carbon dioxide down-vents filled the place with a chilling, dry ice fog.

The crowd surged towards the exit in a screaming stampede of panic. Sienna's heel snapped, so she ditched the shoes, only to be swept away, barefoot, in the crush. Dino was nowhere to be seen. She fought with all her fading strength not to be trampled to death by the hordes clawing to get to the emergency doors. She was finally disgorged out on to the pavement with hundreds of other clubbers, as fire engines and police cars arrived.

Close to losing consciousness, she caught sight of a vending machine in the distance and went for it. Fresh water, I need cold, fresh water now! So thirsty, head swimming, burning up inside, a bad dream not really happening. Amber where are you? Made it. Sienna pressed her forehead to the glass, weeping. Bottles of chilled Evian stared back at her. No bag, no euros…no drink.

'You're wasted, love,' a passer-by shouted.

She startled and moved on quickly. Did we come by car or taxi? In the darkness, she stumbled blindly towards the edge of the open, concrete-lined storm drain which funnels rainwater out into the bay. It's mostly dry during the summer months. Sienna's fall was only broken by the tall rushes and reeds growing on a bank of silt. She lay concealed, half submerged in a standing pool of swampy water full of larvae, beer cans and bottles.

Sleep at last.

5 Dodo island

Thomas Bell stood inside a dank, slate-roofed boathouse which looked out over the lake. A sash window, densely woven with cobwebs and dead bluebottles, let in the first shafts of morning sunlight. Split cane rods and fishing lures testified to decades of balmy summers messing about in boats. Brackish water lapped the rotting timbers, the smell of which was the cure for any hangover. Judy Madden broke the silence.

'Let's sail away for a year and a day...'

'...to the land where the bong tree grows?...,' continued Bell.

'Why don't we go to faraway places, exploring?' joked Judy jauntily, pulling up her little black dress.

'Exploring what?' said Bell, steadying the rowing boat in the gloom.

'Each other of course!'

Bell took Judy's arm and she plumped herself down amidships, dropping the rowlocks firmly into place.

'So, where are you taking me?'

'To ecstasy,' winked Judy, with a smile.

'I've heard a lot about ecstasy... it's everything they say...and more,' he grinned.

He undid his bow tie, as the clinker-built craft emerged out on to the lake, plying its way through the early morning mist. Judy, still in her evening wear, had insisted on rowing. She braced her impractical Jimmy Choos against the bulkhead, as the boat headed towards Dodo island.

Her father owned one hell of a place down here in Dorset, paid for, no doubt, by the vast wealth he had accumulated in the Far East.

Bell could sense a kind of detached uneasiness in Judy which he had not seen before.

He sat at the stern pressed up against a hamper which contained full English breakfasts in foil containers. He could feel the warmth glowing through the wicker slats, as he let his hand run lazily in the cool water. He admired her shapely legs and the flash of white gusset, every time she pulled the oars through.

A Japanese pagoda towered above them as they moored up. After a short walk through long grass they were soon comfortably seated eating their food.

'Why's it called Dodo island?' asked Bell, busily devouring eggs on toast.

'Damned if I know. The house and grounds have been in the Nazelle family for generations,' replied Judy, absentmindedly.

'Hey look, no grilled tomatoes!' said Bell, rooting through the aluminium trays.

'I have something I must tell you, Tom.'

Bell turned to her slowly in the full knowledge that it was over. All that sex, laughter, and kind, loving words to each other soon to be consigned to the wonderful memories archive.

'You're pregnant,' said Bell, knowing it wasn't true.

'No, Tom, we were too careful for that.'

'Don't sugar-coat it Judy, just tell me.'

Judy looked away, tears running down her cheeks.

'I'm engaged to be married...I...I...should have told you before.'

'To whom?'

'He owns a hedge fund based in Mayfair. Dad says you've got a big hat but no cattle. Anyone who marries his precious little girl has to bring something to the party.'

'I guess I'm not good enough, then,' smiled Bell, ruefully.

'Dad's business empire is built upon strategic alliances. I regret to say that I'm part of his grand master plan. I'm afraid that we'll have to stop seeing each other.'

'I suppose one last shag is completely out of the question?! I openly admit that I've never tired of lying naked next to you in the darkness,' chuckled Bell, lightening the mood.

'Tom, I know you would happily fuck my brains out any time, anywhere, and I concede that you taught me a couple of things in the bedroom that I didn't know,' smiled Judy, signalling a negative response with her wide green eyes.

The sun was up now and it had become quite warm. Bell produced two padded sun-lounger mattresses from somewhere. She turned her back towards him so he could unzip her. After her underwear had made its descent, Bell laid down beside her, kissing her voraciously. He moved his hand up her silky inner thigh to seek out her moist labia minora, and gently pressed her legs apart to heighten her pleasure.

Just as he had never become weary of holding her tight, she had never tired of feeling his naked, muscular body interlocked with hers. Judy arched her back up off the mattress, as she had done so many times before, as he placed a loose cushion under her behind. He was braced on his elbows directly above her, face to face. They French kissed deeply with tangly tongues as Bell breathed in her delicious scent. He broke away and kneeled back for a moment as her prepared to enter her, savouring the sight of her in a state of full arousal. Then they were one again, Bell breathing rhythmically into her ear as they approached the finale together for what would probably be the last time. The final kiss, leaving me alone like this.

After it was over, he tenderly cradled her beautiful head, cheek to cheek, next to his, for a few, closing, exquisite moments, and then rolled off to one side. Judy turned to him as his phone bipped.

'I'm still not sure how you accidentally bumped into me in Prêt à Manger. Anything you would like to tell me? Mmm?'

'Just blind luck, I guess...serendipity,' smirked Bell good-naturedly, as he read the text message and noted the grid coordinates. She gradually arched her body into a bridge, pulling her knickers back to their starting position, then stood up.

'...and what exactly do you do for a living, Mr Bell?'

Bell ignored the question and got to his feet. He hugged her close and kissed her lightly on the forehead.

'We have to get back. A chopper will pick me up in thirty minutes. He's a lucky man, this fiancé of yours, but I will treasure everything we did together...always. I'll row this time.'

***

Ryan Madden, Judy's father, sat in his sumptuous office, and stared out of its huge windows to reset the focal length of his eyes. He admired the genuine Egyptian obelisk, the centrepiece of the south lawn, which had been transported back to England from Philae in the 1820s. He had acquired the entire estate, which included a listed main house, outbuildings, and farmland, on the back of a dubious property deal in Macao.

When not in London, he could control his worldwide interests from this sleepy rural setting, down here in Pamphill in Dorset. He hadn't acquired his immense wealth without some considerable effort, and took great pains to protect it and himself. That still allowed him a little time for the occasional guilty pleasure which had become rather addictive.

Ryan Madden alt-tabbed on his keyboard, and his favourite porn site burst into life.

A dominatrix, with jet black hair, dressed in leather and high heels, stood in a dungeon behind a girl wearing only a pair of pink panties. The girl was shackled at each wrist and was being coerced, with a cruel hair-pull, to stare directly into an HD camera. Ryan's pulse raced as he typed the instruction on the task bar. Mistress Raven smiled and stepped back, raised the leather cat-o-nine-tails and whipped the blonde filly's buttocks. She yelped and strained against the chains, as the lashes alternated between her back and behind.

A military helicopter flew unusually low overhead, but Ryan Madden failed to notice.

He zoomed in on this beautiful new girl, and typed another command. Mistress Raven dropped the whip immediately, and bear-hugged her captive wench fiercely from behind. She kissed her on the neck, licking her ear while fondling the girl's nipples. She squeezed them expertly between her finger and thumb, twisting them painfully. The girl yowled, arching her head back. Mistress Raven smiled at the camera. The blonde leaned forward, her tearful eyes imploring anyone who might be getting off on this...

'Help me!' she screamed.

Mistress Raven quickly pulled a rubber, zipped mask down over Amber Hutton's head, stifling her screams and the live broadcast abruptly aborted to a blank screen.

Ryan Madden headed off quickly to the smallest room in the mansion.

6   A place in the sun

Thomas Bell sat in his boss's office, on the top floor of Cyventure House. It was decorated like a Napoleonic Parisian boudoir with ornate furniture and tapestries. It felt curiously intimate for a secret service office. One would half expect to find French cavalry officers in here, relaxing, drinking brandy, and entertaining ladies of the night.

MIX had an unlimited budget. They got whatever they needed and did whatever they wanted…with impunity. The broad frame of his section head, in a Pink shirt and braces, was seated opposite Bell, behind a large mahogany desk. It was buttressed by gilded eagles, and adorned with rich, 'pietre dure' flowers, fruits and insects. It was more than likely that it had belonged to Napoleon himself. Codename: Lambda, had started his illustrious career in MI5.

'How's the accountancy, Bell?'

Lambda moved several NCIS reports to one side, and picked up a large pair of stainless-steel tweezers.

'Hell, sir.'

'We all had to do it. Some clever bastard at the Treasury came up with the idea. I begrudgingly get it now,' he chuckled.

Bell sat back and focused hard on his boss's facial expression. He searched for clues which might indicate what all this was about. Lambda noticed Bell's appreciation of his surroundings.

'Most of it comes on loan from the bowels of the V&A, spoils from the golden age of British rule that wouldn't normally see the light of day.'

Lambda's generous smile flashed for a second, as he pincered a small, pale blue object from a Petri dish.

'Ecstasy…' continued Lambda reverently, rotating the pill.

'…ordinarily cut with the likes of baking powder, aspirin, rat poison, or anything that takes your fancy. Chemical name MDMA. It was discovered by Merck Pharmaceuticals as a by-product of their search for an effective blood-clotting agent. They patented it in 1912. The compound is a member of the amphetamine class of psychoactive drugs. Designated a class 'A' drug here in the UK, and a Schedule 1 controlled substance in the US. The example I have here is the black market gold standard...Paloma Azul.'

The pill escaped the grip of the tiny metal jaws and shot across the desk. Lambda took no notice, instead he produced a slim, anorexic file with a buff cover and pushed it across to Bell.

'Tried it yourself, Bell?'

'The most valuable thing I have is my brain, sir.'

'Very wise, but if you were tempted, this is top drawer.'

'Looks like a pack of Ibuprofen or Advil to me,' said Bell.

'Exactly...Paloma Azul, or Blue Dove, is high grade ecstasy of consistently superior quality. It's manufactured to full pharmaceutical standards not unlike the output from companies such as Ciba Geigy or Bayer Roche. Twenty-four tablets, two hundred milligrams sugar coated, 100% pure MDMA...Methyl...'

Lambda's eyes turned skyward looking for the word.

'...DioxyMethAmphetamine,' assisted Bell.

'...and not a hint of adulteration with such as MDEA or MDA. It's caused a huge surge in demand since it first appeared. One has a grudging admiration for whoever's behind it. A sophisticated operation is producing this stuff.'

Lambda pushed the silvered packet over the burnished leather surface. He relaxed back in his leather chair and lit a cigarette. As he luxuriantly exhaled, Bell carefully studied the sturdy box with its stylised Blue Dove logo.

'...quality retail packaging, bar-coded and full product information. Impressive,' said Bell.

'Note the batch number and the expiry date. We've been tracking this product across Europe for several years now. Its origin is unknown, despite our best efforts to trace it. Paloma Azul pills are sold in their millions. It knocks the back street stuff into a cocked hat.'

'Has the European Drug Enforcement Agency got anywhere?'

'They impound caches from time to time, but the actual source remains a mystery. The European commission wants it stopped.'

'So, what's new, sir?'

Lambda flicked open the file and thumbed through a couple of pages.

'Two girls getting into trouble, crack cocaine and the Spanish island of Ibiza.'

'Not unusual for sunny Ibiza at this time of year,' observed Bell.

Lambda raised an eyebrow and continued.

'The evidence indicates the likelihood of a manufacturing facility concealed somewhere within its shores. There is also an indication that full production of Paloma Azul crack cocaine is about to commence. They do say that this small Balearic island is the best stocked pharmacy in Europe.'

'Do the girls know anything?'

'We've got two Sienna Huttons, one in the local morgue, the other virtually comatose in the San Antonio Galeno Clinic. It's your riddle, I'm afraid.'

'Do we have any faces on the island?'

'Just the usual timeshare barons, bullion robbers, pop stars, European royalty, and pornographers. Shadowy men in sunny places.'

Lambda stood up abruptly and walked across to the bulletproof window. The Old Street traffic crawled slowly through East London in the late afternoon heat. Bell took the opportunity to edge his chair away from the icy chill flowing from a ceiling vent. Lambda picked up his putter and dropped a new Callaway golf ball on to the carpet. He drove the ball across the room to a waiting Putt-O-Matic machine, which swallowed the ball up into its gullet with an audible click. It then spat it out forcefully back at him. Lambda trapped the speeding ball under his brogue and sat down again.

'Of course there may be nothing in it, but at least you'll get some sun,' grinned Lambda, brightly.

'…get out there, find the factory…if it really exists, destroy it and whoever's making the stuff.'

'Yessir.'

'Ibiza airport security is known to be compromised, so you'll have to go via the back door, if you forgive the expression.'

'Understood,' smiled Bell.

A cream Bakelite telephone burred lazily on Lambda's desk. It signalled the end of the briefing. Bell walked back over the thick carpet to the door and made his exit.

***

The following day, Bell had taken off from RAF Mildenhall, in Suffolk, onboard a USAF C5A Galaxy military transport aircraft destined for Iraq. He now sat shivering in its cavernous cargo hold clutching a disgusting cup-a-soup. The engine noise was unbearable. After a while, a flight officer came up to him and handed him a sheet of paper. Bell nodded and the guy disappeared.

Bell surveyed a curious array of vending machines, cocooned in bubble-wrap, lined up at the top end of the cargo bay. Motivated by a mixture of boredom and stiffness, he stood up to take a closer look.

Twenty brand new vending machines were strapped to the deck eyelets with heavy duty webbing. Each offered a mixture of Coke, Sprite, Minute Maid, M&Ms, and a whole load of other types of sugary tooth-rot. He inched past heavy wooden boxes labelled 'DU', each one etched with serial numbers and radiological warnings. Maybe he now felt like a Coke, but he didn't have any coins on him; they weren't switched on anyway.

'IVMs,' barked sergeant Schultz, with a slow, Alabama drawl.

Bell, startled, jumped backwards. He hadn't noticed the big guy creeping up behind him. Better sharpen up, thought Bell to himself. The puggy face told a story of too many helpings of waffles and maple syrup.

'Intelligent Vending Machines.'

'Yeah?'

'I'll show ya, buddy.'

Schultz produced a credit card of input codes, and proceeded to type in a series of digits on the hexadecimal keypad. A to F, 0 to 9.

'Never occurred to you, did it? Courtesy of DARPA, Arlington, Virginia.'

'Amazing,' replied Bell.

'Good evening, what is your command?' asked the machine.

Schultz followed with more key punches, blocks of two characters entered in sequence, B7, 1F, 77…

'Delay is set to one hundred and twenty seconds,' cooed the soothing female voice, from a hidden speaker.

'Let's log off, buddy, before we turn this flying whorehouse into a fireball!'

Schultz punched in the abort sequence in a trice.

'Have a nice day,' ciaoed Candy.

'Twenty pounds of C4 in the dummy condenser unit. Take out half a city block. Here, have one, might save your life one day.' Schultz handed Bell a credit card mini-guide.

'How do you know it's an IVM?'

'Simple.' Schultz pointed at the maintenance contact card wedged behind the glass.

'Oh, I get it.'

'We've got 'em dotted all around the Mediterranean and the Middle East…worldwide to be honest…loads of 'em. We leave them on street corners, public places, and offices. Self-destruct is not all they can do. Check it out, man.'

Schultz tapped his ear-piece.

'You're on in twenty,' and gently punched Bell's black HALO suit.

High Altitude Low Opening.

AHLO. A Happy Landing Ok?…Hopefully.

The Galaxy C5A banked slightly and throttled back; the pitch of the engines mellowed, lining the lumbering workhorse up at a steady twenty thousand feet just to the north-west of Ibiza. They were approaching the Ibiza coastline, Cap Nuno and Cala Salada, the main C-731 road from San Antonio to Ibiza town

heading east. Then, south-east into the distance, the island of
Sa Conillera with its automated lighthouse. The hydraulic rear
door of the flying juggernaut lowered partially, and Bell
clambered along the guide-rails up to the lip. He could see the
coastal lights shimmering below. A cruise ship bore out to sea,
heading in the direction of Formentera.

Bell jumped on green and adopted a skydiving position, his
altimeter glowing a warm orange on his wrist. The rush of air
buffeted his face, as the land mass rushed up towards him.
Finally, he pulled the ripcord and the black silk canopy burst
open like a popgun and trembled in the slipstream. You could
make a thousand pairs of panties out of this directional chute
or a considerably larger quantity of thongs, mused Bell. He now
focused in on the northern curve of San Antonio bay. He had
to land on the flat roof of the Hotel Palmyra.

Hey, buddy, no mistakes!

He was getting closer to the landing zone now, and used the
chute cords to alter his alignment and rate of descent. This was
where all the practice with the Parachute Regiment would pay
off. Car headlights, like lines of fireflies, picked out the roads
flowing out from this popular resort. The Hotel Hawaii, with
its huge green neon roof sign, was the best marker beacon and
reference point. The Hotel Palmyra stood on the busy
Avinguda Dr Fleming.

Bell controlled the steering lines expertly as the hotel building
rushed up at him. He locked on to the rectangle of hotel roof
which was his LZ. An approach length-wise would minimise
the risk of an overshoot or a delightful slam into the side of the
building.

Music from the pre-club bars and the hum of traffic was
clearly audible now. Jesus, he was going to have to land on a

sixpence! The prongs of the slingshot bungee machine whizzed past to his left as he came in to land. Shit! Satellite dishes and rows of solar panels! Wait!...and some hotel laundry hung out at the far end. To hell with it! thought Bell as he crashed into layers of fluffy towels and came to a dead halt.

Welcome to the White Island.

7 Not exactly quidditch

Bell stood on the flat roof of the Hotel Palmyra, gathering up his chute, looking out over the dark water that was San Antonio bay. At the port, a large Balearia ferry could be seen disgorging its human contents on to a concrete causeway. Thankfully, no one had spotted a dark bat plummeting from the sky.

The American aircraft carrier USS Indianapolis with her escort ships, the USS Curtis Wilbur and USS Farragut, were clearly visible at anchor in deep water, further out.

The Indianapolis was on leave from the Middle East and formed part of the American sixth fleet. The giant Nimitz class nuclear-powered carrier had a crew of over three thousand, and bristled with F14 and F16 fighters, tomahawk cruise missiles, and ground attack helicopters. Her uranium fuel provided enough power to sail around the world for three years.

The island now had hundreds of horny marines running around getting drunk, smoking hash, and taking pills. Anything to forget the likes of Baghdad, Basra and Kabul. Rest and recreation European style. Yup, they got it all on this liddle ol' island, here.

Bell descended the service stairwell, and gingerly opened the metal fire door into an empty corridor. Next stop...room 414. The rhythmical throb of music shaking the foundations indicated that Club25 activities were in full swing. Holidaymakers preparing to test their metabolism at Privilege and Amnesia. Drink as much as is humanly possible, roast your eardrums, consummate a brief relationship, and lose consciousness. Then do it all again the next day. Sex, San Miguel and sick.

Wish you were here.

The three star hotel backed on to the Playa Arenal which was a sandy bay lined with bars and restaurants. The paved beach walkway wended its way round to the port past the Bay bar, Manumission bar, Nandos, and over an open storm drain containing brackish water, rushes and rubbish. You could buy useless trinkets from the lookie-lookie men, or get a henna tattoo applied to your vulnerable skin with a toxic, permanent dye.

The hotel frontage overlooked the main road from the south of the island, called the Avinguda Dr Fleming. Bell's room faced the roadside, the tops of mature date palms brushing the edge of his balcony on the fourth floor. At this time of night jeeps, taxis, and motorbikes crawled up the strip, past supermercados and clubs churning up dust and fumes. The Secret Garden, The Labyrinth, Es Paradis, and Eden lined the way to the main San An roundabout, its centre adorned with an egg sculpture. From here, the Avinguda de Portmany went all the way south east down to the capital of the island.

Bell used the key he had been given and let himself into the darkened double room. The balcony doors were slightly open, and the evening air rippled the net curtains. Cream and Pacha stickers were affixed to the glass in an attempt to prevent the intoxicated from severing an artery on jagged glass. Better to head-butt the wall instead.

Bell could hear groups of people shrieking and running up and down the corridor. Distant doors constantly slammed. The usual rosy-cheeked fun for a club hotel like this one, he guessed. The borrowers had left three black combination lock suitcases. He checked the contents of each in turn. There was also something important to pick up from elsewhere.

Bell retrieved the telescopic sight from the gun case, and stood on the balcony watching the traffic and the revellers go by. Two Humvees crept past, with US Marines in search of I&I onboard. Bell focused in on the young Americans peering out of tiny rocket-proof windows. He could only assume that the US Navy was loath to rent a fleet of pink Twingos. The brass hats preferred their grunts to drive wide, heavy-duty personnel carriers on the narrow Spanish roads.

Bell checked his watch: midnight. All set now, time to get the head down after a long day. He broke the seal of a large bottle of Granini juice, and took a long slug of coctel de frutas. It quickly flushed the dead starling from his parched throat.

He took time to refold his parafoil chute, compressing it carefully back into its pack. Discarding it on the roof was definitely not an option. The noise in the corridor was intermittent now. Heat, hedonism and hijinx. Drunken football clans cat-calling obscenities to innocent holidaymakers from balconies draped with team-branded towels and rancid trainers.

He closed the last of the MIX cases, and slumped in a chair for a moment. Maybe he could get a shitty snack from somewhere to tide him over till morning. He'd only been seated for a few moments when he became aware of a scraping sound at the door. He concentrated his hearing, holding his breath. Again a scratch, metal on metal, and then the gradual insertion of a key in the lock. The door handle turned slowly. Bell leapt across the room like a gazelle and took up position, ready. A figure crept warily into the darkness only to find themselves in a professional headlock, with the door slammed firmly behind them.

'What the!' the girl screamed, dropping her bag, choking with flailing arms. She fought like a sewer rat on a hot plate. Nails, elbows and fists. Bell tightened his grip and pinned her down easily.

'Get off me you bastard or I'll kill you!' she screeched.

'How did you get in here?!'

'I stole a maid's pass key, i...it's a game of kiss-chase we play at night.'

'A game?'

'You have to give a blow job if you get caught, now let me go for fuck's sake!'

'Not exactly quidditch, eh? So you owe me a blow job, then,' taunted Bell, playfully.

'This room should be empty, what the hell are you doing in here?!'

She struggled ferociously and Bell held on, levering her face down on to the bed.

'None of your business.'

'Let me go before I scream!'

'That was the idea.'

'Like, I don't think so!'

Bell allowed her to twist around so she was face up to him on the bed. He had her arms pinned back, and was hit by the potent aroma of perfume, moisturiser and alcohol. He could make out the glint of her teeth and her fiery eyes in the semi-darkness.

Was this young lady just a chickenhead?

She was only wearing a thong and see-through top. He now knelt astride her, holding her down, not daring to release her arms, wondering where the stalemate would go from here. Bell felt aroused by the fight in this plucky girl and the smell of her.

If you don't drop them right away, I'm going to report you to the management and the Spanish police. You'll be arrested for theft and sent straight home, do you hear?' warned Bell, chuckling to himself.

'Hey, this is the start of my holiday, you evil bastard!' she screamed, her voice rising an octave.

'Do it or you're on a plane back to England.'

The struggling stopped immediately and a long silence followed. A simple, stark choice. Sucking this guy's cock or the next flight back to Gatwick.

'Okay, so long as you don't tell anyone. I've spent ages saving up for this.'

Bell was amused that she had surrendered to his idle threat. He withdrew his grip and she sat up on the edge of the double bed. He switched on the bedside lights and caught the first clear glimpse of her face.

An attractive girl about nineteen years old, maybe. She hung her head in resignation for a moment then looked up, and flicked her dark hair defiantly to one side. Now she had a better view of her tormentor who was already down to his Calvin Kleins. Her spirit rose in tandem with Bell's hard-on. Maybe this wasn't going to be such a bad thing after all.

'Got any booze?'

Bell indicated Smirnoff Ices, vodka, and mixers lined up on the writing table. She retrieved her handbag from the floor and removed a packet of Paloma Azul ecstasy tablets. A painted nail burst one out of its blister pouch into her cupped palm. Bell caught sight of a very familiar product logo. She neatly clipped the top off a bottle, and glugged half of it down with the pill. Bell preferred to abstain, not wanting to dull the nipple-chilling excitement of exploring this girl's body for the first time.

'I'll be coming up by the time we've finished, whatever you want me to do.'

'Like timing an egg, eh? How do you know it's going to be crap?'

'Always is, I never get to climax, whatever happens. Show me something I haven't seen before...perleeze!...or let me go, will you?'

'You broke the eleventh commandment.'

'Which is?'

'Thou shalt not get caught.'

'Switch the lights out and let's get on with it,' replied Becky, slamming the alcopop down.

'The lights stay on...it's a man thing,' said Bell, kicking his CKs away.

Becky stood up and removed just one item of what you could call clothing, to reveal her perfect, dark nipples. Bell leaned over and inserted his finger inside her thong elastic, pulling it and letting it twang back against her flesh.

'Yow!' she exclaimed, in mock pain.

'Let's have this off, then.'

'Get it off yourself!'

She laid right back on the bed, as he followed.

Bell could sense that the drug and vodka mix was now taking effect. He kissed her slowly, breathing in the scent of her hair, laced with her perfume. She responded for the first time with what appeared to be any kind of willingness and kissed him back. The cool breeze fanned the fresh cotton sheets, and Bell moved his hand and felt her breasts. He fondled each of her nipples in turn which responded quickly to his skilful touch. He ran his hand down over her flat stomach to meet the resistance of the top of her thong.

Once inside, his fingers met with her warm frictionless juice. She gave a sharp intake of breath, her panting shorter now as he rubbed her engorged clitoris. He could stand the constriction of the thong no longer, it was making his gun-hand ache. As he tugged off the moist apology for a garment, she arched her rear up off the bed slightly. Now he could penetrate her with one and then two fingers, feeling round to her G-spot with a rhythmical pumping. He quickened the pace, building her arousal. She had his penis in her hand now, teasing the skin back and tensioning it, pulling his frenulum tight, glistening with precum, it would not be long now. She ran her index finger round his taut glans and traced her lips with his juice.

'Lip gloss!' she laughed.

Their bodies were now hot and sweating with the exertion.

'I'll put something on,' he whispered.

He didn't fancy the prospect of a necklace of herpean sores or an honourable discharge in a few days time.

'Do it!' gasped Becky, grateful that she didn't have to mention it.

Bell tore open the square foil packet, then the age old conundrum...which way does it unroll? He didn't want to contaminate the outside, so ran a quick test in each direction. Satisfied, he squeezed the air out and rolled his own, as it were. Bell spun round on to his back and pulled the willing Becky over on top of him, sliding deep inside her for the first time, caressing both her breasts. Soon, they rolled over, their faces pressed close together, bodies fully engaged. The smell of her perspiration drove him on harder.

Her eyes flashed wide open, the dark pools of her dilated pupils fixed upon him. He signalled to her to turn over. Bell puffed the hotel pillows underneath her stomach as she brought her knees up and spread her legs outwards again. He pressed his hands over her buttocks and pulled her apart gently. He entered her easily, while idly massaging the outline of the Celtic tattoo on her lower spine. She moaned with pleasure as he thrusted into her repeatedly, caressing and teasing her sheriff's badge with his index finger. Bell held back his own climax till she came in a rising whirl of juice, moaning and muscle spasms.

They lay there panting in each other's arms, coiled up in the cotton sheets, exhausted.

Bell woke up with a jolt, completely disorientated after nodding off for only fifteen minutes. Becky lay wide awake beside him, staring dreamily at the undulating net curtains.

He dragged himself off to the ensuite and switched on the harsh strip light. A groggy MIX agent with dark hair and a hard, muscular body stared back at him from the mirror. This dude might just qualify for the Diet Coke break ad. Maybe he'd better start thinking seriously about his crazy assignment.

The clean-up starts here, especially when you've just had the type of sex where you have to number your fingers. He ran the chrome mixer tap, and squirted some citrusy shower gel on to his palms. Would he really be up for another game of hide the penis? The question split into two parts, firstly whether he actually felt like it, and secondly whether he should be conserving his energy for this pharmaceutical bug hunt.

Bell turned to see Becky leaning dreamily in the bathroom doorway, a bunched Kleenex stuffed between her legs. She smirked at him confidently, as he marvelled at her firm body which looked fantastic even in the unflattering light.

'What's your name?' said Bell, rinsing off the pale green lather.

'Becky, what's yours?'

'Thomas, but call me Tom.'

Intimacy, then the introductions. Bell moved away from the basin and approached her with a new hard-on. He ran his left hand round the back of her neck, and kissed her once more. She tilted her head in response and pressed in closer against his naked body, spreading her legs a little, the sticky tissue curiously defying gravity.

'You think I'm a slut, don't you?'

Bell ducked the 'no, no, not at all' with a relaxed laugh.

'Well, Tom, can we do that again?'

He looked at his watch.

'I thought you were going clubbing?'

'Something changed my mind.'

'What do you do back in dear old England?'

'I work at Knickerbox in Basildon.'

'What do you really want to be?'

'A fashion designer or a porn star, maybe.'

'Estrella del porno...no more knickers, eh?'

Becky ran her fingers wistfully through Bell's hair.

'I suppose I'll have to stick to selling them instead of taking them off.'

'We all have choices to make.'

'So Tommy, what do you do, apart from kidnapping, blackmail, and having safe sex with young women?'

'Finance and stuff. The City.'

'A man in a sharp suit and a silk tie.'

'Yeah, international travel…things to sort out.'

'So is this business or pleasure?'

'Without doubt, a great pleasure,' he grinned,

'…but I may have some business to attend to.'

'So, you're not an accountant, then?'

'Not really.'

'Okay…enough talk. We'll definitely meet up and do this again. I'm off to Es Paradis.'

Becky grabbed her few items and popped another tablet, handing Bell the half-used blister-strip.

'Hey, don't take too many of those!'

'Like, you're not my mother, yeah!'

'So, where do you buy these?'

'Anywhere…don't fret, I'll get you some. Promise.'

Becky broke their cuddly embrace and stared him straight in the eye.

'Look, there's a guy in the hotel who thinks I'm his girlfriend.'

'He's a boxer isn't he?'

'Kick.'

Bell feigned unease.

'Mmm...that's comforting.'

Becky blew him a kiss, and tossed the box of MDMA on to the bed.

'Here's the rest of them…don't overdo it, remember! See you later.'

The door slammed behind her.

Bell studied the serial number and expiry date with renewed interest. Yeah, probably nothing in it, he thought to himself.

He lit a Silk Cut on the balcony, the one cigarette a month he allowed himself, and looked out over the bustling avenue. He glanced down at the stark health warning on the crush-proof packet, 'fumar puede matar'.

Give death and take death.

8   Emporio Mare

After a shower, Bell's clammy skin was pleasurably warmed by the golden orb rising above the hotel palms. The sun god Ra was bathing him in celestial light; it was like being reborn. Sunday 31st July, another glorious day on the White Island. He stood on the balcony, with a towel almost wrapped around his waist, drinking a melon iced tea. He was hungry as hell and urgently needed a big breakfast. At nine o'clock he would get a look at Sienna Hutton number one...or what was left of her.

Bell strode through the Hotel Palmyra public rooms on the ground floor, past the subdued pool area of umbrellas and sun-loungers. Most people were sleeping off hangovers, dehydration, and sunburn.

Becky was probably in the building somewhere, perhaps wrapped in someone else's arms...and maybe hating every minute of it. He really hoped that he would see her again.

A pool attendant was busy spraying down the concrete flags with a hosepipe, as groggy sun worshippers unrolled their towels. All they had to do now was drag over an Amstel parasol on a concrete base, and they were all set for the day. He walked past a slim girl sitting upright, knees up, engrossed in a Danielle Steele, a wing of her panty liner peeping out from her bikini bottoms. A nice touch, thought Bell as he approached the Club25 reps.

JJ and Linzi gulped down Bloody Marys, and gnawed at bacon butties as they consulted their guest lists. They dished out high-fives and called everyone 'you guys' but wished they were still in bed with whomever they'd pulled last night. JJ drew hard on a Fortuna, her hands shaking from a summer season of tequila shots and vodka spritzers.

'Where's Janine for fuck's sake?' grizzled JJ.

'Dave got lucky this time, didn't he?'

'She's a lazy cow!'

'This is the last time I'm covering for her.'

'She can sort these party games herself, next time.'

'I bet she's got a migraine and won't be able to walk,' winced Linzi.

The thought of another three Miss Wet T-shirt competitions this week depressed them both, too many to contemplate by the end of the summer season.

Bell jogged down the hotel steps on to the beach promenade and took a right. He smiled to himself as he headed for the Passeig de Ses Fonts. So agreeable not to be in Central London.

Bar owners were busy unstacking aluminium chairs and placing menu boards in the way of pedestrians. A group of yobbos were hard at it dragging a small fishing boat off the beach. They were headed across the main road and into the grounds of their one star hotel. In a few minutes, it would be floating in a cloudy swimming pool.

The bay was totally still. Yachts lay motionless at their moorings, just the tiniest waves licking the water's edge. Bell could feel the heat rising, prompting him to adjust his cap and mirrored Oakleys.

As he approached the quayside, the burble of diesel engines from glass-bottom boats disturbed the early morning calm, casting a toxic haze over the water. Later on, they would be fully laden, leaving the madness of San Antonio behind, heading off for exotic beaches like Cala Bassa and Cala Comte.

Bell selected a restaurant at random, and slumped himself into a seat next to a stack of empty beer crates. What the hell, I'm running a bit late, he thought, let's eat. At least there were large awnings which protected diners from the glare of the blazing sun. He could relax for a moment, watching revellers staggering back from a long night out.

He ordered the full English and placed the greasy menu back in its holder. 08:36. The food was delivered just as a youth vomited up kebabs, lager, and bile into a nearby flowerbed. It amused Bell that a group of older Spanish ladies, in traditional black garb, wasted no time in berating the puking partygoer.

ABBA hits, synchronised with the line of fountains, played as he ate. Knowing me, knowing you. Bell mentally prepared himself for what he was about to see that morning. He wasn't sure whether lining his stomach with this chow was necessarily a good idea. Whatever happened, he didn't want to see this meal ever again.

The vision of a pathologist sawing off the top of a girl's skull overwhelmed him. He tried valiantly to suppress the sight of a grey brain held in a latex glove, dripping with shiny mucus. Gulping hard and drinking tea now, he only just managed it.

Sienna number one had probably known the answers he was after. There was no guarantee that the other Sienna would ever wake up to tell her tale: then what? Unless her remains and possessions contained any clues, Sienna numero uno had taken the only key to the puzzle with her. No more chataloola from her.

'No more carefree laughter,
Silence ever after,
This is goodbye.'

***

The stainless-steel trolley was wheeled to one side. The pathologist stared back at Bell across the autopsy table, his tired eyes distorted by a hemispherical, plastic visor. Dr Miguel Sanchez stood in plastic overalls and rubber boots, holding the first of a number of implements which would anatomise this young girl's body.

Bell tapped his own headgear with a rubber-gloved finger, the air supply making a sad, rhythmical noise at every breath. Despite the high-tech apparatus, he could still smell the antiseptic, formaldehyde, and decaying, human flesh. Bell studied the girl's grazed legs first, then her feet, to steady himself. Chips of magenta nail polish were still visible on her toenails.

'She's been in the water for nearly a week. We'll start with the pulmonary cavity,' observed the Valencian patólogo.

Bell looked down at what was once a beautiful young woman.

'You can go off and inspect her possessions while we open her up, if you like.'

'I'm okay,' smiled Bell, lamely.

'We've X-rayed her of course, nothing internal. You can see she has a piercing through her clitoral hood.'

The pathologist placed his finger between the labia and snipped it off using a pair of surgical nippers. The external examination came first, the obvious broken neck, a check of all body surfaces with an ultraviolet light wand. Visible details were all carefully noted before a body block was placed under Stephanie's top half, which pushed the chest upwards. A large Y-shaped incision was then made from behind each ear, running down the sides of her neck and meeting at the breastbone.

'You can get a lot of bleeding in cases of drowning, but her neck may have been broken before she entered the water,' said Sanchez, continuing with the Stryker saw, to open up the chest cavity.

Bell nodded as blood and bone fragments flecked upwards. Sanchez decided to switch to hand shears, and finished off all the way down to the pubic bone. The evisceration complete, he examined the main organs and took tissue samples, finishing by weighing the heart. Sanchez sawed a cap off the skull, just as Bell had feared. The brain was then checked in situ, before its connection to the spinal cord was cut. Sanchez continued to speak into his microphone, bent over the dissection table.

'...the subject's pubic area and mons Veneris are smooth shaven, armpits have underarm hair, no disfiguring marks of any kind...'

'Don't often see that, the armpits I mean,' said Bell.

'Anything goes on the White Island, Señor Bell.'

'Did the genetic tests reveal anything?'

'The DNA we analysed is South American.'

'She's from South America?'

'No...the last man to screw her.'

Bell took the ring over to the examination desk which displayed two Paloma Azul packets and a white-gold bracelet. He sat down and studied the jewellery under intense light with a powerful magnifying glass. In microscopic letters it read: 'SW', a heart, and 'JL'. He thought of the pleasure that this simple piece of jewellery must have witnessed. Bell turned the bracelet over which read 'Sienna Hutton - No penicillin'. There was no other identification to be had.

The pill boxes were slightly different from each other. The first one was the all too familiar MDMA 15g tablets, but the other one was different. Same logo, silvered foil, and the flying blue doves. On the reverse it stated '…contains benzoyl-methyl-ecgonine'. Bell squeezed the blister strip and a perfectly formed crack-cocaine crystal dropped out.

He examined all the seams of her denim jacket, slitting it open where the stitching seemed to have been tampered with. The effort was not in vain. He held the hand-written note up to the light, a short message in biro torn off a nightclub flyer.

'My real name is Stephanie Walters. I don't know where I'm being held, but I'm still alive. If you're reading this, I'm probably dead.'

***

Bell emerged into the late morning sunshine, gulping in the fresh clean air. The smells he had just encountered clung to the back of his throat and the very lining of his lungs.

He entered the double doors of the Galeno clinic, and presented himself to the bored receptionist. Thankfully, the next one is alive, but only just: the real Miss Sienna Hutton. He was led into an interview room and offered a plastic stacker-chair. King Juan Carlos of Spain glared at him from the wall, as he took a moment to enjoy the delicious air conditioning. As he drew a second cup from the watercooler, Dr Sofia López, already developing the air of a senior consultant, entered the room.

'Mr Bell, you are from the British Embassy, I understand.'

Bell showed his credentials.

'Where was she found?'

'In a storm drain, not far from here, heavily intoxicated.'

'So, what is her condition now?'

'She's sedated and very lucky. The stagnant water in the flood channel cooled her body down, and probably saved her life.

She should recuperate quickly now. Physical recovery may include some memory loss, however.'

'Not what I wanted to hear,' grimaced Bell.

'It's the pharmacologic effect of benzodiazepines.'

'Intoxicated with what, exactly? '

'Tests reveal the presence of rohypnol, MDMA, and a high level of alcohol. She will have suffered confusion, delirium, and disorientation which led to her fall...'

'...or push...'

'...over the rail.'

'How quickly? '

'She's on a saline drip and some other drugs. Give it twenty four hours.'

Bell pondered how the Hutton girl had managed to consume such a noxious brew. She'd obviously been out on the lash, maybe with some pals. Liquor and ecstasy: self-administered, probably. Rohypnol, a fast-acting date-rape drug, taken voluntarily: definitely not. Someone had deliberately presented her with the cup of Beelzebub.

The doctor read out a carefully prepared list of important facts, translated into English. Her body temperature had registered over one hundred and four degrees when she had been brought in. Drowning in your own vomit was the most popular way to die around here, apart from falling off balconies. The lethal cocktail of exhaustion, sun, alcohol, and recreational drug use was endemic. Fingers crossed, any memory loss would be short-lived, with a low probability of brain damage. Bell needed a full recovery so she'd be fit enough to answer some questions. He hoped he'd get lucky.

'May I see her?'

Bell pulled back the plastic curtain and peered in at sleeping beauty, as Dr López kept her distance. A couple of medi-tags adorned the girl's left wrist. He noted her encrusted eyelashes, a nasal oxygen catheter, and her long blond hair which was matted and unwashed. Despite that, she still looked like an angel immersed in a deep sleep.

What poisoned apple had she bitten into? He felt like the prince standing over Snow White, ready to kiss her on the lips, with all the forest animals looking on. The animals had probably put her there in the first place.

So if Stephanie Walters had stolen or found Sienna Hutton's passport, the real Sienna was just an innocent tourist who knew absolutely nothing. For how long had Miss Walters been using a valid alias? If only he knew where Walters had been held. It seemed likely it was the very place he'd been sent out here to find. He would return the instant the clinic contacted him.

***

Near the junction of San An's Carrer Vara de Rey and Carrer de L'Estrella, Bell arrived at an unmarked garage door. He twisted a security key in the lock and let himself into a cool, cavernous space. A dusty Seat Leon Cupra R, with special MIX modifications, awaited him. It had been superficially distressed and busted up to blend in with the rest of Ibiza's road-hardened traffic.

He drove southeast across the island on the C-731, past Sant Rafel and into Ibiza Town, parking near the docks, not far from El Divino. He entered the old quarter on foot and ended up in a deserted side street. He was now standing outside the sun-bleached frontage of Emporio Mare, the Marine Emporium. He was buzzed in immediately. Inside it was hot and oppressive, stacked to the ceiling with tinned fish products which were now no longer produced.

A bald man, with a pitted face, sat behind the hardwood counter reading El Mundo. A globe-shaped glass vessel, containing preserving fluid and the body of a large octopus, occupied the space next to the till.

'Bon Dia,' said Bell.

'Bon Dia,' came the uninterested reply.

'¿Quiero algo vegetariano?'

'Le recomiendo mariscos o sopa de pescado.'

He handed Bell a slip of paper with a bin reference, and continued to read his newspaper.

There was nothing vegetarian in here. Bell walked through to the warehouse, past aisles of overfished sea life. Salmon, sild, herring, squid, anchovy, and much more...all preserved in sunflower oil, tomato, or sweet chilli sauce. Rack upon rack of the stuff on pallets, right up to the roof. The intense smell of old cardboard soaked in brine prickled his nostrils.

He now stood before a box the size of a cereal packet, at head height, which he lifted down. This was what he had driven here for. It carried the logo of the US Defence and Research Projects Agency and at least half a dozen bio-hazard warnings. It cautioned 'To be opened by authorised personnel only' and 'Handle with care'.

***

Back at the Palmyra, the party games were in full swing. The murky pool was now alive with humanity. Lines of blindfolded girls and boys were passing fruit from one person to the other, neck-to-neck, oranges and bananas, egged on by a screaming rabble.

JJ, Linzi, and a hung-over Janine were sick to death of it all. Roll on the ski season. The hotel bar was seething with drunken red lobsters gyrating to the thumping music; smoke from the barbecue going everywhere. Hair of the dog, thought Bell as he slipped unnoticed back up to the fourth floor.

He soon finished his drink, swilling freezing vodka round his gums and swallowing hard. A few moments later, there were frantic taps at the door. Becky stood there in a bikini top, shorts, and sandals. She had her hair up with sunglasses perched high on her head. Bell breathed in her aroma, as a pair of sandals clacked past him on the composite floor. They were briskly flicked off with a masterful action, hitting the wall in exactly the same place. Becky then launched herself backwards on to the bed, grabbing a pillow in the process.

'I didn't recognise you with your clothes on,' teased Bell.

'A girl can only take so little.'

She sat up without warning, putting her arms around his neck. The kisses started lightly on the lips, then longer and harder.

'Tom, where have you been? I've been out looking for you!'

'Dodging that boyfriend of yours, of course!'

Becky sniffed.

'What's that smell?'

'Let's just say I've had a few medical issues to sort out.'

She looked at him quizzically.

'It's not what you think,' said Bell, laughing.

'A friend of mine's in hospital. A and E, nothing too serious. Drink?'

Becky relaxed visibly and purloined the other pillow. He returned with some opened bottles and squeezed up next to her. Her hand stroked his cheek gently.

'I really wanted to see you again, Tom. How about coming on the Club25 booze cruise tomorrow? It'll be fun!'

She crushed the life out of her cigarette, leaving a long stub, chiming her bottle against his.

'It goes right down the west coast, stopping at some of Ibiza's best beaches. Lunch is included.'

She handed Bell the leaflet.

'Okay, count me in, but don't get me into trouble with laughing boy.'

Becky was ecstatic, putting her arms round Bell's neck again.

'That's wonderful, Tommy!'

'But that's not all you wanted to tell me, is it?'

'No.'

Her eyes were nervous and defensive, unable to conceal the tension she felt, which was unbearable now that she had him back in the flesh. She wanted to go beyond the boundaries of a one night stand, but relive the exciting closeness they had experienced as total strangers. Would it be just a sex-by-the-hour arrangement, or could she get a little closer to him?

Did he even want her?

She sat up properly against the headboard, ditched the sunglasses and shook her hair loose. With the pillows and her bravado puffed up in equal measure, she was ready to ask the burning question.

'Look, are you sure you're pleased to see me?'

'What about action-man?' said Bell, gazing up at those big eyes.

'I'm looking at him.'

9   Playa privado

'Cannibalise a USAF hydrogen bomb?!...b..but I'm a chemist not a physicist!' bleated Helmut Kranz.

'You may need some of these...Krytrons,' replied Ilya Pago.

'Croutons?!' squealed Kranz.

Pago opened a cardboard box, and removed one of the individual Krytrons from its cushioned holder. It looked like a tiny valve from an old-style radio, with thin wire prongs.

'No, not a small piece of spicy fried bread but an atomic trigger device.'

'Atomic trigger?'

'Exactly! This component makes the explosive charges around a hollow sphere of uranium detonate correctly. You should know that, Kranz, you're a bloody scientist!'

Krytrons are manufactured by EG & G of Wellesley, Massachusetts, under strict US Department of Defence controls. America had foiled many attempts by foreign governments to get their hands on these little beauties.

It functions as a tiny switch, able to produce a precise jolt of high-energy electrical current to the detonators in as little as a microsecond. They must be fired simultaneously, so that the correct amount of pressure is exerted to compress the nuclear grapefruit rapidly and evenly. The more Krytrons, the more predictable the blast. Quite simple, really.

The last thing Pago wanted was a fizzle, where the chain reaction didn't engage and you just spread radioactive dust over a small area. He wanted to obliterate Dos Lunas, and abandon the island by the end of the week. He alone would decide the exact moment when the west coast of Ibiza was bathed in the heat of one thousand suns.

The detonation would vaporise El Cartero and anyone else who was sniffing around. It would definitely throw the Alacrán cartel off his scent.

Pago cursed recent events; he needed a clean break. He would start again in a new place, as someone else. He fancied his own private island this time, maybe off the coast of Vietnam or Indonesia. Kranz sweated heavily, looking frightened, fiddling with his lab coat buttons.

'I'm only a chemist, I tell you, I only deal with chemical reactions not nuclear weapons.'

'You'll need to set up these fairy lights in such a way that the fissionable material achieves critical mass and kicks off a chain reaction...six point five megatons worth.'

'I can't do it, I don't know how!'

'The bomb in our possession was designed to be dropped, hence the need to rewire the whole thing and rig up a timer,' continued Pago.

'I am unable to do it, I tell you!'

Ilya leant forward, his black pupils drilling into Kranz's.

'You can do it and you will. Just get on the Internet. I authorise you to engage the services of a hacker from the dark web. Start with the US Naval base servers in New Jersey. You'll need to download circuit diagrams and instructions to rig up the thermonuclear device. It's an American B28 type with a class D warhead. Now fuck off and get clicking.'

Pago felt exhausted and sat back in his chair. He placed a scented marzipan ball into his mouth, and glanced up at the Pizarro oil painting staring down at him. He made a note on a lavender-coloured pad and ran his palm slowly over his bald head. He looked up with a reptilian smile.

'There, Kranz, no need to worry, relax, enjoy the sunshine. When you have completed your task, that is.'

The briefing was over.

Kranz wished he was back in Switzerland poisoning primates with lethal compounds, but not as lethal as uranium 235 and plutonium 239. He feared for his health. He didn't know which scared him more, Pago or nuclear fission. This constituted disturbing mission creep. He was up to his neck in the brown stuff, for sure.

***

Linzi picked at her belly button piercing.

'Jesus, JJ, it still itches!'

'Better that than something else I could think of below the waistline. Did you really shag that creep last night?'

'Sod off, JJ, my head's killing me, and I think I'm going to throw up. The boat leaves in fifteen minutes. Is everyone aboard?'

Linzi swayed with her clipboard, looking queasy.

'Linz, take a swig on that, you'll feel better.'

'Jeez, I hope it's gonna be calm. Where the hell is my sun hat?'

At that moment, Janine turned up, swigging a take-out coffee, hidden behind huge Jackie-O sunglasses. Her white T-shirt proclaimed: '*I have the pussy, so I make the rules*'. JJ and Linzi, standing dutifully on the quayside by the bow of the Alba Nueva, looked at each other.

'Morning, Janine,' they chimed.

The Club25 booze cruise would moor at Cala Bassa first, and then hug the coast down to Cala Comte. The tried and tested formula of excessive drinking, lewd party games, and a lunch consisting of paella, Spanish omelette, and garlic bread. The crew knew they would have to hose the whole boat down afterwards. That's what the plastic covers were for.

Bell took the trouble to develop a rapport with the captain, Carlos Molina, as the boat headed south. Bell had already studied the nautical charts and satellite photographs for this stretch of coastline. Molina would be able to flesh out what Bell had already learned, especially prevailing current patterns.

He was making the assumption that Walters hadn't been tipped overboard or dropped from a plane, for this line of enquiry. It was the substantial properties with private beaches that were in the frame; places big enough to conceal a drug factory.

Bell raised his binoculars, as a large motor yacht came towards them on the starboard side.

'The Valhalla, Señor, one hundred metres in length,' said the captain.

Bell noted the bull-head motif on the snow-white funnel, the three decks, helicopter pad, and gleaming superstructure.

'He owns the Labyrinth Club, Dos Lunas, and an empire of flesh and corruption,' grinned Molina.

Bell had this guy on his list, but had ruled him out on the basis that he was a successful pornographer, not a drug baron.

'Who is that?' asked Bell, convincingly.

The captain bellowed a laugh.

'Rey Porno. Señor Ilya Pago, King Porno himself, of course. He has much money and many, many beautiful women. You have not heard of him?'

Molina took his hands off the wheel for a moment to poke his index finger in and out of his curled finger and thumb. Bell missed the universal gesture, while he turned to focus on the Vallhalla's rear decks, as it passed two hundred metres away.

Bell held the frame of a photographer, dripping in jewellery and wearing an open white shirt. Lighting stands pointed at a tall slim girl with long dark hair, removing her wrap. The girl stretched out, her arms in the air, revealing dark unshaven armpits but a silky smooth pubic area.

Bell's pulse quickened.

A muscular woman with short blonde hair in a yellow bikini stood nearby. She removed her wrap-around shades, and appeared to be giving the instructions. She moved towards the model and caressed her naked buttocks, nuzzling her neck, licking the girl's ear. Business as usual, thought Bell, struggling to hold steady as the bow wave hit.

The girl had lain down on a divan bed. All he could see now were her kneecaps, far apart. Had Stephanie Walters been from the same stable? Was hair in the right places some sort of house rule? A kind of pornographer's hallmark? It was a flimsy, tenuous link, but worth investigating.

In an instant, Anna turned and stared in his direction with feral cat eyes. Bell could sense the malevolence of this woman, who seemed to hold some kind of authority, reaching out to him across the water.

The Alba Nueva rounded the Punta de sa Torre into choppier water. White horses occasionally crested the waves. The Isle de S'Espart could now be seen down to the south west.

'Where does the Valhalla berth, Carlos?' said Bell, as he pulled the binoculars away from his sweating eye sockets.

'Often in Ibiza Town, but more usually offshore by Puig de Molins. There is a long private beach there. Many large estates owned by very rich people.'

'Can we get in close there to take a look?'

'That is not possible, it is too dangerous.'

'Why is that?'

The nervous captain fired an imaginary pistol into his temple.

'Privado, muy peligroso.'

Bell produced a five hundred Euro note. Molina simply shook his head and shrugged.

'I, Carlos Molina, do not have a price.'

Bell produced another of the crisp notes, the ECB holograms dazzling Carlos in the midday sunshine.

'Ok, maybe we have some engine trouble or get lost a little,' smirked Molina, trousering the cash.

'You have good reason to go there. They may forgive a drunken loveboat full of Brits.'

An element of risk, but Bell wanted to assess Pago Corp's reaction to a harmless intrusion.

'I like to mix business and paella.'

Bell checked his own GPS device, as they cleared the headland and came closer in shore. He was well concealed as just another legless pisshead. None of the revellers noticed anything, owing to the fact that they were all making out and knocking back alcohol to the pulsating Bora-Bora beat.

Becky sat with Lee in the canopied stern section of the boat. Lee, the kick-boxing hardnut, gripped her tightly around the waist with one hand, a plastic tumbler of Stella in the other. His muscled arms, defined torso, and thick neck were no strangers to the inside of a gym. Bell could just read the 'Made in Manchester' tattoo on his bronzed shoulder, as he went to take a bite out of Becky's neck. Becky glanced across at Bell with big eyes and a look that said 'get this creep off me, now!' As Bell returned to the bridge, Lee's vengeful eyes burned into his back.

Bell could discern movement just beyond the tree line; three red buoys bobbling in the shallows, and an empty stretch of beach.

Two Kawasaki wave riders and a rib with twin Volvo outboards had been pulled clear of the water on to the golden sand. A sun-bleached sign caught his attention which displayed a welcoming: '*Playa privado, Eintritt verboten*'. He scanned the high cliffs for any sign of life. Molina would hold the Alba Nueva at a slow idle for only a few minutes, and then head back out to the open sea.

Out of nowhere, two fit characters ran down the beach, and expertly launched the rib down greased, oily runners. The starter howled and a cloud of diesel fumes was soon dispersing over the choppy water. The rib turned to head straight for them. Bell now had all the photography and GPS co-ordinates he needed. He would review the satellite shots again later. Molina felt his trouser pocket. Let's hope a thousand euros is going to be worth it.

'Turn away, this is a private beach,' blared the loud hailer, as the heavily armed guys circled repeatedly.

'So sorry, so sorry,' bleated Carlos, emerging from the wheelhouse with his hands raised. One of the guards ran off a few digital photographs and pointed to Molina.

'Alba Nueva, you have been warned, turn away now!' shouted the guard. 'There will not be a next time!'

Bell hid amongst the jeering revellers gawping over the port side, who were blissfully unaware of the danger they were in. A couple of guys were even mooning over the gunwale.

Bell caught sight of two Uzi machine guns, strapped to the front bulkhead of the rib. Both guards were in military fatigues, carrying Glock sidearms in polished holsters, clearly visible under their life jackets. Their fatigue caps, with draped cotton neck protectors and high-end sunglasses, suggested long marches in the desert, far away from any water. They were obviously experienced military personnel, probably special forces: taut, muscular and ready to drop anyone who got in their way.

Carlos turned the Alba Nueva hard out to sea, stepping on the diesel. Any other craft would have been shot up, sunk, whatever, no witnesses. Were it not for a loony booze cruise full of harmless kids, it would have been a different story, for sure.

Rich people went to a lot of trouble to maintain their privacy. But the armed threats he'd witnessed came under the heading of a disproportionate response. Just what he'd been hoping for. Bell had seen enough: Dos Lunas and Rey Porno were now at the top of his list.

Did a shaven pussy and some beach muscle add up to an ecstasy factory? Maybe. It all still hung on Sienna number two, back in San An. Also, according to the tidal data, an object floating in the water here would be carried in the drift up the coast.

Stephanie Walters.

***

Janine took a slug of ice cold Coke, and prepared to bury her dirty mouth back over the guy's glans, glistening with her saliva.

JJ and Linzi were frantically working the other two volunteers who were on their backs, in a line with hers. Linzi still wanted to throw up, the rum and sangria were curdling into a noxious glob in her gut which could explode at any moment. She also had a sore throat.

The first to get one of these blokes to climax would be the winner. This improvised sex show was now expected of them. Digital video cameras were recording the act of gross indecency, which would appear in the British press the following week. Janine knew she would win again; she had a secret weapon: a pierced tongue, and she had only become a rep to get laid.

Give head and take head.

Alcohol or no alcohol, she would be first to suck all the hot, sticky love piss out of this guy, come hell or high water. The seminal fluid exploded in her mouth. She pursed her lips and promptly sprayed it back in a fine jet on to the guy's stomach, to a frenzied roar from the crowd. JJ and Linzi immediately gave up, leaving the other two dummies half hard and playful, pulling up their shorts, but not before Linzi had vomited all over her sated five-minute lover. Linzi lay there gasping and retching, wiping her face feverishly with her pussy T-shirt.

'Get me some water for fuck's sake,' she bawled.

All good, clean holiday fun, thought Bell, whose mind was now focused on the reach of the Pago business empire.

The Alba Nueva witnessed the sunset, as it moored up for the night back at San Antonio.

Bell was starving, ready to pass out. In all the excitement, he'd only managed a few scraps of garlic bread.

He walked away from the quayside, and saw the golden 'O' revolving on a tall metal mast in the distance.

O'Learys was a fully automated fast food joint.

Always natural and fresh - twenty-four seven.

No shop front, just a line of ten ATMs, each with a vending chute. Robots in an unmanned kitchen somewhere behind the wall prepared the meals, the last word in fast food automation. Uniform-sized food disks were retrieved from storage, prepared, and put together with extras, in accordance with the customer's order. The custom assembly would fit snugly into its hinged dough casing, get wrapped, add a drink plus fries, and be despatched.

Siempre natural y fresco - veinte cuatro siete.

Bell traced over the keypad and trackerball, checking out the screen menu. He punched the satisfying elliptical keys quickly: tandoori chicken, avocado and salsa on panini plus a can of melon iced tea. The machine sucked in a twenty Euro note, and spewed out some shrapnel plus a receipt.

As he waited, a young drunk in a Hawaiian shirt fumbled hopelessly with the keypad, six vending slots away.

He'd been propositioning unresponsive groups of girls in skimpy outfits, heading for the pre-club bars. He should have kept his fingers on the keypad, instead of trying to locate the perineum of a tall sassy blonde in high heels and loose fitting hot pants.

Big mistake.

Bell watched, as seconds later, the guy was surrounded, but he was so wasted he hadn't noticed, and the first punch went in on the side of his head. More blows and kicks poured in from all sides and he crumpled to the deck. He was so inebriated, all he could manage was to curl up instinctively, like a foetus, to protect himself.

It had taken just one minute. If they continued to work him over at this rate, he would be dead in two. A flash of cold steel. They were going to finish it with three or four fatal stabs into his vital organs, and make a run for it.

Bell acted quickly.

He pulled a Taser X26 gun from his bag and took aim at the knifeman, who was within range.

'Policía!' screamed Bell, as the compressed nitrogen exploded, firing two small probes, attached to the gun by conductive wires. The miniature barbs hit their mark, easily penetrating the guy's blue football shirt. An electrical pulse instantly paralysed the knifeman's peripheral nervous system. It caused him to drop the knife and turn into a screaming, frozen puppet.

The attack stopped immediately. The other three guys dragged their groaning mate away, tearing the mini fishhooks out of his skin in the process. In seconds, they had melted into the night. It was an impressive display of teamwork under fire. Bell helped the bleeding guy to his feet.

'Thanks, pal, I owe ya,' he groaned, in a hoarse American accent.

Just then the other Marines arrived, crowding round and keeping Donnie Olsen on his feet. Donnie had picked up some superficial scratches and grazes, and maybe some broken ribs, but he'd live. His face was beginning to swell.

'Put the blade away Richie, he's one of us,' gasped Donnie.

Zack relaxed. The glint of cold steel disappeared swiftly under his American football shirt.

'Motherfuckers!'

'I told you those guys were trouble. They were sore as hell with you, Donnie. You should never have messed with their chicks.'

'Where can we go for a good time?' asked Brad. 'Somewhere where you don't have to fight over them with the locals.'

'Seems like we're going to have to pay for it tonight,' lamented Zack, looking downbeat.

'I might just have the right thing for you guys. First, let's get a bag of ice for Donnie,' smiled Bell.

'A titty joint?' inquired Zack.

'Tracy Island, in Figuretes,' said Bell.

'Hey man, we'll drive.'

10 Tracy island

The doors on the Humvee M998 slammed shut, and Brad fired the six and a half litre AM General diesel engine. All six of them were squeezed into the available cab space. As he pulled away from the kerb, he took the wing off a brand new Audi A4.

'We're just off the USS Indianapolis,' smirked Brad, unconcerned at the sound of splintering metal.

'Collateral damage?' spluttered Bell, forcing chicken and avocado down as quickly as possible.

'Let's just say Baghdad gives you a different perspective.'

These guys were old enough to have their legs blown off in Iraq, but too young to buy a case of Bud in their local store. Brad ground the engine up through the gears, as they picked up speed. They were headed for San Rafel, in the middle of the island, and then on to the capital, Ibiza Town.

'Meet the guys, Zack, Richie, Ben, and goddam Donnie who you thankfully saved from a severe beating. We're all with the 3rd US Marine battalion, except Richie who flies.'

'AH64s,' added Richie.

'I'm so pissed we weren't there to whip those guys' asses,' grizzled Zack, shaking his head with regret.

'We're just grunts used to dodging frags and car bombs, but Richie is a mean air jockey, bustin' caps from the sky, man.'

'The AH64 Apache ground attack helicopter is a sweet mother with a thirty-millimetre M230...'

'Knock it off, Richie for fuck's sake...this is I&I remember, what's your name, buddy?'

'Tom, Thomas Bell. I'm just here on holiday and a little business. You guys on the island for a while?'

'Not a whole lot, just enough to recover for our next tour. We have to undergo a six week psychiatric programme on the USS Indy...the rest of the time we can come out to play.'

'Well, you certainly came to the right place.'

'Sheesh! You limeys certainly know how to party. Hey, does Britain own this island?'

The Humvee settled into a deep, hoary rumble, intimidating all the other traffic on the road. Brad broke the silence.

'So, you say the Spanish own this place, huh? I knew college wasn't for me! Joined the Marines instead, like some dumb shithead, didn't I? On my first day at Camp Pendleton, the bus pulls up to the reception area, and this mean looking mother in a Smokey Bear hat gets on board and starts screaming 'Get off this bus you fucking assholes!' Then, we're standing in our underwear to attention by our bare metal racks, and the same drill instructor hollers to this guy to my right:

'You queer for me, boy? You wanna suck my cock?'

'Nossir!'

'You don't have the hots for me, boy?'

'Yessir, I mean, nossir!'

'You calling me a cocksucker? I'm hard for you, boy!'

Then, the instructor punched him so hard in the stomach, he dropped to the deck like a bag of shit, scraping at the ground like a crushed roach.'

While Brad rambled, Zack closed his eyes and visualised his pimped 1967 Chevelle Malibu, parked in its garage back in Jacksonville. Brad took his eyes off the road and looked at Bell, raising his eyebrows stoically.

'Then it got tougher. They took my hair and took my mind. When I finished AIT, I was sent to Iraq. I've completed four tours, and now they won't let me go back. It's what I signed up for! I wanted it and I got it! I love this shit! They sent me for analysis when I told them all I wanted to do was kill. They said I'd built up multiple layers of mental scar tissue.'

Brad laughed and looked at Bell again with the soulless eyes of a great white.

'I just keep taking the pills and tell the army shrinks whatever they wanna hear.'

'Brad's a pussycat, really,' soothed Zack.

'Someone mention pussy? Can't you get this crate to go any faster?' pleaded Richie.

They rolled past Amnesia and the lights of Ibiza Town got closer, the mound of the Dalt Vila, the old town, framed in the reinforced ballistic windscreen.

'Say, that was a pretty neat phoney policeman trick back there...so where exactly are you taking us?' inquired Zack.

'You won't be disappointed,' said Bell.

They parked up and Donnie swiped the locks of the camouflaged Humvee, which looked to be brand spanking new. Brad could read Bell's thoughts.

'Three weeks in Fallujah and it won't look like this anymore.'

'You limeys sure as hell coulda provided a vacant parking lot for this fuckin' MRAP lite!' screamed Zack, emerging from the greenery.

They'd created a space near the Lidl supermercado, on some wasteland densely covered with tall rushes. A Pacha hoarding advertised a pair of giant rosy lips sucking on ripe cherries. Carrer Navarra, Figueretas, was just a short distance from the sea. The six of them stood outside Tracy Island, neon breasts pulsing steadily over the entrance. A thick purple carpet stretched out into the gutter, and a Japanese doorman stared at them warily. Donnie showed Zack the time.

'Say, it's only early man, we're too fucking early....,' fretted Zack.

'Not if you want sloppy seconds,' replied Bell, knowingly.

The Marines howled with laughter as they smacked high fives, a little more post-traumatic stress leaching from their subconscious. You wouldn't know it but they all had PTSD, post traumatic stress disorder. Time for some more therapy.

They inched around a new stretch limousine parked outside with a small 'T1' logo exquisitely painted on the front doors. Bell showed Kenzo, the doorman, his VIP card, who nodded and opened the black lacquered door into tottydom.

Subdued lighting, a bar area, a leggy blond halfway through her pole-dancing act. She draped herself around the pole, wearing skin-tight black latex and fishnets. As the deafening music halted for a few beats, she gave them a sex kitten pout then swung upside down with inverted splits, revealing a hairline thong. They took a couple of tables, ordered the obligatory champagne, and company arrived. G-strings and mini-skirts snuck in next to them.

Tracy Island was a well-known Mediterranean hotspot: a stylish bordello offering lap dancing and all the extras. A wide range of customers were willing to pay high prices for exceptional service. Tracy Island could count the rich, the famous, the chic, and the powerful as its clients.

The air-hostess-style house uniform, in several variations, was inspired by a popular TV puppet series, and maybe a poisonous pop video. Light blue and yellow livery; high heels or pale blue boots. Silk sashes and a nicely styled 'International Relief' logo depicting a clenched palm. It had all been dreamed up by Tracy herself who had designated the company yacht as Thunderbird Two, and the Learjet parked in a private hangar at Ibiza airport as Thunderbird Three.

It gave the whole operation an efficient corporate 'look and feel', like a leading airline, and the clients loved it. It wasn't long before franchised operations had opened in New York, Tokyo, London, and Berlin with merchandising following close behind. In time, the brand became so stylish and recognisable, it had almost completely abstracted what they were really selling: a good hard shag.

'Hey, I wanna beer!' shouted Donnie, impatiently.

Sitting still wasn't going to entertain these guys for long. The four Marines and Richie, the pilot officer, and Bell now found themselves relaxing in a quiet plush lounge, away from the pole dancing and disco numbers, feeling pleasantly mellow. The girls entered the room in strict Indian file, smiling at the six new customers.

'Shouldn't they have number tags?'

'Ben, we're not in Manila right now. These are sophisticated ladies…ladies of the night,' said Zack.

Ovidie and Richie's eyes met. Ovidie was a twenty-three-year-old French girl with a degree in philosophy. She had jet black hair in a bob, matching her clothing and eyeliner. She was tall and sleek with shapely legs, wide eyes, and prominent red lips. Unable to get a sensible job in her native Paris, she had gradually drifted into the sex industry.

First, she had been a mistress catering to the cinq à sept and le vice Anglais. Then she had found herself abandoned, followed by a rapid descent to street level: The Pigalle, St Denis, Rue d'Amsterdam.

A short vacance in Ibiza had led to her breaking away from urban pornophilia, and finding work at Tracy Island where her confidence had returned.

Richie's eyes were even wider than Ovidie's. He felt a sudden whoosh of hot air from an RPG, as this girl sat down next to him on the two-seater sofa, with glasses of champagne. She too was smitten by this bone-headed young guy with sky blue eyes and a welcoming grin.

The others were making their own choices. Soft music, softer lighting, a little pre-combat chat, and more expensive grape juice before the main battle upstairs. A Ukrainian blonde approached the still unattached Bell and leant forward gracefully.

'Madame will see you now. Room 69.'

Donnie, within earshot and still a little nervous of the vivacious, attractive girl sitting next to him, shouted out…

'Woo! Hey guys, you hear that? Room 69 for the limey!'

'Donnie, old chap, you're in room 88: two fat ladies!'

More laughter from the troops; they were having a ball. The dry arid taste of tension and fear, the waiting, the unknown invisible enemy which came and took their young lives and limbs, and then just melted back into the desert wastes seemed a million miles away.

'Hey Tommy, do they take dollars?' inquired Brad.

'They'll take anything,' said Bell.

Bell took the lift to the second floor. The same purple carpet, subdued wall lighting, and flock wallpaper which lined the long corridor, gave a feeling of hush which muted the rhythmical couplings as he passed each numbered door. He could have been upstairs at the Silver Dollar saloon, in Kansas City in 1880, ready to hang up his spurs and his Colt 45 for the night.

Bell let himself into a dimly lit, but spacious, boudoir and shut the door.

'I'll be ready in a minute,' came the voice from the dressing room.

'Fix yourself a drink.'

Bell poured a glass from the open bottle of vintage Louis Roederer Cristal.

All of a sudden he was sick of champagne.

Tracy entered wearing a bustier, stockings, suspenders, and short leather boots, a black ribbon tied around her neck. She regularly treated herself to a new set of lingerie from La Perla.

Tracy was no supermodel, but she was curiously attractive. She had a great body, memorable features, and long dark hair…she also worked as an informant for MIX. What an asset. It was a long time since she was pulling pints in the Railway Pub in Pitsea.

'So what took you?'

'Just some American Marines I picked up along the way.'

'We'll be paying you commission next, and we're flat on our backs as it is, what with half the US sixth fleet anchored off San An. Where's your drink?'

'I'm tired of champagne!'

Tracy turned and bent inside the well-stocked minibar, which looked to contain more than just alcoholic drinks, and produced two bottles of Stella Artois.

'Get this down you, then!'

Tracy sat down next to him on the king-size bed, suspenders straining.

'How do I look?'

'Something revealing would be nice.'

Tracy crossed her legs and took a long swig.

'And of course, just when we get busy, three of the girls are off with thrush and Marlene, one of our best dancers, has developed an allergy to the nickel content in the pole. She's a pole dancer for God's sake! I've even had to take a few shifts myself.'

'How did you get into all this?'

'I started doing tricks when I was young, and I don't mean the Magic Circle. I learned about sex from an early age. There was nothing else to do in Pitsea except heavy petting and getting F grades. They taught you all about sex in class but not how much I'd want it.

I left England and set up Tracy Island here in Figuretes with financial help from a wealthy client who had, how shall we say, unusual requirements. He died trying to do it on his own, and the huge loan he'd given me kind of evaporated. So it's all mine now! We've got girls from Eastern Europe, Russia and the UK. So what if they're not all beautiful? At least they're available. I've had to issue the girls with kneepads since the US fleet dropped anchor. That's my story. Did you like Thunderbird One out front? I owe all my success to enjoying sex.'

Tracy had sat on something solid which was hiding under the bed covers. She pulled out a purple vibrator, and smiled ruefully at Bell.

'Thunderbird Six?' said Bell.

The other guys had all gone upstairs.

Richie and Ovidie had fallen for each other, of course, and had got lost in conversation, gazing into each other's eyes. She pressed her Givenchy red lips against Richie's, and whispered into his ear.

'Time to go upstairs.'

'I want to make love to you.'

'Je sais. Baise moi, maintenant!'

They were getting up, when Anatoly Kadic came up from behind, and grabbed her left arm. The menacing hulk of Marcel stood close by. Marcel had been expelled from the French Foreign Legion for murder, and made the Incredible Hulk look like a seven stone weakling.

'Ovidie, my dear, where are you going?' asked Kadic.

'Can't you see I'm busy?' came the terse reply.

'I thought you loved me. What are you thinking of, performing with this young puppy instead of me? Regulars take priority, surely?'

'Anatoly, not tonight,' pleaded Ovidie.

'You're mine remember, surely you prefer a real man to this little boy?'

Richie froze, incandescent with rage, and tried to stand but was held down by the giant Marcel. He couldn't believe that the guys weren't here to help him. He was powerless to do anything. Anatoly pulled Ovidie away from the sofa.

'I'm a US Marine not a little boy,' he spat.

Anatoly laughed.

'Marines are pussies. Go home to mama, it's past your bedtime.'

Marcel had to physically restrain Richie, as Anatoly marched Ovidie, in a painful armlock, across the room to the door. She struggled violently, crying, her eyeliner running down her cheeks.

'I'll wait for you,' bleated Richie.

'Will there be anything worth waiting for?' said Anatoly with a cruel, sadistic grin.

***

Bell stood up from the bed and drained the Stella.

'Another one?'

Bell nodded.

'What do you know about Ilya Pago?'

'Some of our prettier girls left to work for him. Strange, none of them ever pay us a visit or keep in touch. The money must be that much better, I guess.'

Bell visualised the body of Stephanie lying on the cold slab, her chipped magenta nail polish, and matted hair, indicating fragments of her tragic story.

'Could there be a hidden ecstasy factory up there at Dos Lunas, do you think?'

Tracy fell back and stretched out on to the bed, puffing up scatter cushions behind her head. She took a cigarette from the bedside table, and gazed up at the ceiling, thoughtfully.

'Look, he's just a specialist pornographer. Magazines, websites, owns a yacht and a nightclub, nothing unusual, just earning a crust like the rest of us. Why would he bother anyway?'

'Does the name Stephanie Walters mean anything?'

Tracy sat up and took the photograph from Bell.

She studied it carefully.

'No, not one of ours...I did go to a party there once, though.'

'You're saying you've actually been up there?!'

'Sure...a slave and master party, as I recall. The place was knee deep in laudanum, leather and lubrication. Pago certainly knows how to make it go off with a bang.'

Bell was now on the bed with her, looking into her clear hazel eyes, fine mascara clinging perfectly to her long eyelashes. She moistened her lips, and adjusted her position slightly, looking up at him.

'Well?'

'Did you see anything, anything at all, which was out of the ordinary?'

'No…nothing.'

'Positive?'

Tracy cast her mind back through the alcohol and drug-fuelled haze of that evening and laughed. She jolted at the sudden recollection.

'A funny little fellow! I was standing near the lift, and a stunted rodent of a man, in a doctor's white coat, emerged. He was wearing glasses like the bottom of beer bottles. Wrong party I thought. Then he turned tail, shot back into the lift, and was punching the buttons like a nutter. Wrong floor I thought.'

'Wrong floor? Hmm…I wonder,' mused Bell.

'So, what turns you on?'

'Everything.'

She reached down lazily and released the spring-loaded undercarriage of her corset.

'Fancy a freebie?'

***

Tracy's gecko-phone buzzed impatiently, the green handset glowing bright with every ring. Gecko telephone handsets were a must-have White Island accessory this year. She was off the bed in seconds, listening to the grim news.

'Get dressed quickly, we've got trouble, and they've made a run for it!'

Tracy was out of the door with Bell close behind.

'A hooker always keeps her shoes on,' she said laconically, as they split up on the back stairs.

Kenzo had been no match for Marcel and Kadic. Martial arts training had failed to protect him from twelve inches of razor sharp steel entering his rib cage. He lay dying on the ground gasping, coughing up blood. He clenched Bell's arm with his strong oriental hand, and pointed at the Yakuza tattoo on it with his other hand.

'Pa....Pa...Paloma...Az....Azul!'

'The blue dove. A blue dove tattoo?'

'Hai! Hai!' blurted Kenzo, fading fast.

Bell pointed to the door and Kenzo nodded.

'Ki them!'

Bell left Kenzo dying, red mixing with purple.

He burst out into the street in time to see an Isuzu four wheel drive burning rubber left out of Carrer Navarra. He looked around in frustration, no bloody wheels! The killers were getting away.

Bell noticed a Ramon's Pizza delivery bike, its dirty exhaust puttering by the kerb. The boxman must be busy somewhere with warm Margheritas. Bell ran over, tightened his backpack, and leapt on to the 250cc motorbike. He twisted the gas and took off after them. There was only one way back to Dos Lunas.

He could catch them.

The 4WD had taken a second left out on to the Avinguda d'Espanya, making for the roundabout. It then hared up the Sant Josep road, the PM-803 heading west, leaving Figueretas and the mutilated body of Ovidie behind. Bell chased at speed, and after four kilometres had caught up just after Can Bonet.

He was now two cars behind them. Marcel's huge silhouette, in the driver's seat, was hard to miss. Bell glanced to the left in the direction of the salt flats and the airport, clearing his eyes for a moment. The Yamaha and three deep pan pizzas were hanging in there.

***

Tracy stood over the body of Ovidie, her corpse tied to the four corners of the bed in a star shape. Her mouth had been gagged, her dark eyes staring up at the ceiling. What sick animal could have done this? she thought, almost retching, scanning over the carefully made cuts and incisions.

Donnie and the others held Richie back in the corridor, as he screamed her name repeatedly, clawing to get free to see her. Tracy shut the door of the room behind her, and looked at the struggling Marines and the weeping faces of her girls, all bunched together in the corridor.

'Dial 092 and 061,' she said, punching the wall.

***

Bell kept the vehicle in his sights. Lines of two-tone bollards, demarking no-entry grids, flashed past periodically along the long straights and wide sweeping curves. Signs down to Sa Caleta and Es Cubells.

After keeping position for over ten kilometres, the road curved to the left and up a gradient into Sant Josep past a Cepsa filling station, shops, and restaurants. Then out the other side, leaving the little town behind and back to open road.

The Isuzu took a sudden fork left at speed off the 803, which would have gone all the way north, back up to San Antonio. There was no other traffic on these minor roads which all led to the west coast eventually.

Bell hung well back and killed the lights. Stone walls, scrub, olive trees, and multiple signs to beaches whistled past. He just had to bide his time.

He prayed that the guys wouldn't hear the sound of the tortured Yamaha engine yinging along behind them. It had been so much happier doing local pizza drops. The engine could seize at any moment. Without warning, the Isuzu slowed and turned right off the track into a crescent shaped main gate lay-by.

Dos Lunas.

11 Dos Lunas

Bell parked the Yamaha well into the trees. He watched Marcel, the legionnaire, emerge from the dusty Isuzu and press his eye up to the iris scanner embedded in the stone wall.

Bell observed the mauve light escaping from the sophisticated entry pad, and lay low just off the road. His quarry returned to the idling jeep, as the stainless-steel gate retreated into its emplacement on smooth, polished runners.

Marcel looked around, training his Glock pistol into the darkness, listening intently. Nothing seemed to have spooked him.

Marcel glanced casually up at a CCTV camera above him, then turned, holstering his handgun, and jumped back in the vehicle to disappear at speed up the gravel driveway to the finca.

Bell saw his chance.

The security camera had turned on its high metal pole to follow the 4WD.

Big mistake.

The gate was closing now, the guide-wheels scraping across the entrance. Bell ran flat out towards the closing gap, and flung himself through as it clanged shut.

Time to check out the main house.

Looking back, he could see high tensile wires, held by insulators running along the top of the sixteen-foot high walls. Over six thousand volts, if he wasn't mistaken.

Judging by what had happened at Tracy Island, if he was caught prowling in the finca compound it would mean torture

. How to get back past that electrified fence? Not sure ᴜᴘ ɪs stage.

The perfume of oleanders and roses hit him as he got closer. He skirted around the side of the house to the rear seaward side, past ornate ponds decorated with abstract stone sculptures. The architecture changed from traditional Ibicencan stone and whitewashed walls to modern glass, steel, and a vast infinity pool.

3:00am.

The house was a blaze of light.

Bell sneaked up and deployed the Marine Emporium biobots out of sight, at the base of a potted orange tree, and retired back to his observation point. Stay concealed. Bell would see his little insect pets make their entrance, and then he'd be off.

Presently, a fierce looking woman, with short platinum blond hair and wide hips, opened the glass security door. This was what Bell had been waiting for.

He recognised her immediately.

Anna's eyes stared out into the blackness.

It seemed to Bell that she had seen him.

Impossible.

She was dressed in camouflage pants, held up with a military belt, and a tight-fitting green singlet which revealed her hardened, ripped physique.

She lit a cigarette, took an exquisitely long drag and exhaled into the night air, rubbing her crotch as she did so.

Bell's biobots, a Manduca moth and two spitting cockroaches took the opportunity to fly or crawl unnoticed into the building, while she stood there daydreaming.

Now I have eyes, thought Bell.

Anna thought she'd go back to using the little blonde one with the cute, upturned nose and delicious arse. The brunette she'd had earlier had come too quickly. She drew again on her Marlboro Light, then stubbed it out against a low granite wall, and went back inside. The thick tinted glass closed tightly shut behind her.

The cyborg trio represented US military ingenuity at its finest. Developed by DARPA, biobots were real insects with micromechanical and electrical systems implanted directly into their nervous systems.

This unnatural intervention would be carried out during the early stages of development of the pupa, before metamorphosis into an adult. This cyborg approach to microsurveillance systems meant mother nature provided the capability to crawl, scuttle, fly, and hide anywhere, for free. Biobots could replenish their energy by simply eating biscuit crumbs…no batteries! The choice of modular micro components offered static images, sound pickup, air quality analysis, and even ionising radiation monitoring.

Bell carefully placed the powerful relay transmitter out of sight in a natural cleft of one of the ornamental almond trees. Every thirty minutes it would transmit a biobot data pulse via satellite to the CIA in Houston, Texas. Bell would then simply download all the data to his laptop.

Now, let's get the hell out of here.

Anatoly Kadic completed the pass in night vision image intensifier mode, and switched to infrared. The cameras ran their pre-programmed sweep of the complex again.

He lazed back in his chair and puffed on a Fortuna, one of Dario's. They were a bit stale but he wasn't worried. He thought back to the fun he'd just had at Tracy Island, and started laughing, then stopped dead. Camera seventeen, by the main gate, had picked up a thermal trace in the bushes opposite.

Kadic sat up quickly and zoomed in on the heat source, using the joystick. They were on heightened alert with this Cartero thing. Kadic put it on maximum magnification, and ordered the guards down to the front of Dos Lunas to investigate. A few minutes later, they had retrieved the battered motorbike. Kadic tried a segment of the quattro stagioni pizza, which was still warm. He pulled the lid off a clear plastic cup, with a tight-fitting lid, which was full of fluid.

'What's this?' asked Kadic.

'Some kinda dip,' replied the guard.

Kadic dunked a garlic bread slice into the congealed glitch and took a bite.

'We gotta catch this bastard...it must be El Cartero.'

The motorbike had given Kadic a brilliant idea.

'Check the plate and search the grounds, someone's got in. Marcel, were we followed?'

Bell was contemplating his exit strategy, when a magnesium flare shot high and white into the night sky. It descended slowly on a parachute which illuminated the finca grounds with ominous shadows. The alarms were sounded for a second time in several weeks.

'Shit!'

Then the sound of dogs released from their pound.

Dobermans for sure. Forget the Yamaha, they had probably found it already. Bell was already running for the beach, sprinting like buggery.

They mustn't catch him.

In one way, exit by another.

Bell made it to the first of the rustic windmills, but had unknowingly triggered the invisible beam covering sector H.

It had been a long day and he'd dropped his guard. He was tired. Too much sun and a little alcohol. Waste of time dwelling on it.

Bell left the ordered rows of olive trees behind, and dashed over the stony red dust into the scrubby pine forest. He calculated that he had a five minute lead, but not over the dogs. The beach he'd observed from the booze cruise was his only chance.

Just as Stephanie had done, Bell was heading straight for the cliff edge.

As Bell emerged from the last of the trees, he stopped dead and hit the dirt. Two quad bikes hurtled up the ramp from the beach, headlights on full beam, swinging hard left and back up to the finca. He glanced out to sea. The Valhalla was back at anchor, moored some five hundred metres offshore.

The bikes had unwittingly stopped him from running off the edge of the cliff, and landing on the rocks below. The main house alarm wailed on and the dogs were getting closer. He ran down the ramp to the beach.

He would have to swim for it.

No time to ponder the idea.

He caught sight of Pago's jet bike, tethered to one of the buoys. Was the key in it? Was if fuelled up?

He waded in, fumbled at the handle bars, felt for the coiled flex, unhooked the Kawasaki from its mooring and clawed himself up. Where Ilya Pago's corpulent buttocks had been earlier, Bell's smaller pair now gripped the sculpted seat. He turned the key, pressed the starter, and the engine kicked into life. He wasted no time twisting the throttle back, holding on with all his strength.

He was now doing over twenty knots out to sea, well astern of the Valhalla. Its navigation lights acted as a welcome beacon and reference point in the darkness.

He could discern groups of fishing boats further up the coast. After a good run, he brought the bike down to a burbling idle, and the craft sank back down into the water. He looked back towards the shore and could make out the rib with searchlights heading off in the wrong direction. They would be back. His pursuers had not expected him to head straight out to sea, but to flee along the coast.

Very soon they would realise what had happened.

The Valhalla was his only option.

He stripped down to his Calvin Kleins, stuffing his clothes under the plastic seat. He would lash the plastic key flex around the throttle. It was going to be difficult. He set off again and managed to jam the twist handle, which would maintain the craft at a low speed. This would send the Waverider on a long and final disappearance into the Mediterranean shipping lanes.

He rolled off and the bike picked up more speed without his weight.

Now for some efficient crawl. Clean powerful strokes which would haul him quickly through the water towards the stern of the Valhalla. Then hitch a lift.

We can do this.

The lights of the Valhalla gradually got closer.

He was now thirty metres from the stern. In their haste to prepare for departure, and get the ship completely refuelled in Ibiza Town, the transom ladder had fortuitously been left down in the water.

Bell heard the heavy anchor chains being raised. The Valhalla was preparing for immediate departure, and he still had some distance to cover! The twin diesels burst into life, sending an exhaust shockwave through the water. Soon, the screws would be turning and Bell would be left helpless, floating too far from the shore, exhausted.

Bell made a decision to break into super-fast crawl, four strokes, turn and breathe, four strokes, turn and breathe. He veered out to the starboard side, pulling his way through the water at full stretch.

The Captain double-checked the course to Ibiza Town, via Es Vedra, Cap Llentrisca and Playa den Bossa. The first mate stood ready. The anchors were stowed now, the Valhalla floating free in the gentle tide.

Ten metres from a beautiful chromium rung.

Bell powered his arms at maximum work-rate, clawing hard through the water.

Five metres now.

'Slow ahead,' ordered the captain.

Two metres.

The white gunwale beckoned him. He focused on the bottom rung and lunged up out of the water, as the screws of the Valhalla finally engaged.

Now he was being dragged along in boiling white water. He hung on and hauled his aching arms, one by one, up the ladder and on to the fun deck. He snuck out of sight behind some dinghy hulls and an inflatable sausage, heaving from the exertion.

Next stop...Ibiza Town.

Bell shivered at the back of the Valhalla, the cool evening breeze sapping his body of heat, but he was glad of it. Soon they were heading east, past Cap Llentrisca, Punta de Poirroig and Playa den Bossa. Bell left his hiding place and made his way up to the helipad.

He noted the characteristic rotor tips under the tarp, but there was no more to be seen in the darkness. It seemed to be a type of military helicopter, with tell-tale bulges straining under the straps. Before he could investigate further, he heard footsteps.

Presently, the Valhalla entered Ibiza Town harbour. They were now doing only around three knots, and the crew would soon be putting out the fenders.

He slipped back over the edge into the wash, and was quickly clear of the bubbling white water. He was left floating in the darkness with a bit more swimming to do.

04:30 now, possibly.

There were still multitudes of revellers on the quayside, queuing to get into El Divino. Bell swam towards a group of fishing boats, moored up and unloading their night's catches. He was glad to be using his muscles again, and finally managed to get close to the planked pontoon. The water was oily and full of fish guts. He clung on to a vertical wooden pile, suckered with slimy brown sea anemones and other gruesome fouling.

The giant hand of a fisherman, who must have been in his seventies, leant over and hauled him bodily up on to the boardwalk. Bell lay there gasping but elated.

'Muchas gracias,' murmured Bell.

The trawlerman trailed the hose-pipe over, and re-lit the cigarette glued to his bottom lip. Without warning he sprayed Bell from head to toe with freezing fresh water.

'Agua sucia!'

'Thanks,' said Bell, through his blue lips, dropping back into English.

'Ah, ingles...dirty water,' replied the trawlerman.

'Do you have any spare clothes? Ropa?'

The rough cotton shirt and dungarees felt wonderful against his skin. Bell downed a welcome glass of Spanish brandy, as he sat in the fishermen's all-night cafeteria.

Silvio smiled across at him.

Un extraño turista ingles!

05:15.

The sun was already lightening the sky in the east. There were only a few hours before he would find out whether the quacks at the Galeno clinic had pulled it off. Had they been able to breathe some life into sleeping beauty?

12 Baal

Wednesday, 3rd August.

It was late afternoon and the sun's heat was easing, shadows lengthening, holidaymakers leaving the beaches. The consultant had extended Sienna Hutton's observation period, to be absolutely certain.

'You can see her now,' said the duty doctor.

Bell had been fully briefed and held the release papers. He entered the room to see Sienna sat upright in bed, flicking through a copy of Hola! Magazine. The pale blue ID tag was still attached to her wrist. A Spanish TV gameshow jabbered annoyingly in the background as she read. Her hair had been washed and her eyes looked clear and alert. Her empty handbag had been placed next to her freshly laundered clothes. He'd discover what she remembered, if anything, in due course. The medical team really had done a great job pulling her through.

The sun streamed oranges and reds through the blinds as he approached the bed. She threw Hola! down and killed the TV with the remote.

'Yes?!' asked Sienna, pertly.

'I'm not a doctor,' grinned Bell.

'I can see that,' she replied, looking him up and down.

'Well, I might have been a consultant in toxicology,' he replied, gamely.

'So, who are you and where is my sister?'

'Sister?'

'Amber, where is she?'

Bell drew up a chair. He was delighted at her sharp responses, but perplexed by this new development.

'I'm sorry, we don't know anything about your sister.'

'She's not here, then?'

'When did you last see Amber?' said Bell, gently.

Sienna's mind tried to focus, struggling to rationalise events.

'Last night,…she must be at our villa, wondering where the hell I've got to.'

'Slow down, Sienna, you've been quite ill, that's why you're here.'

'Okay, so I was out on the lash last night.'

'You lost your money and your mobile.'

No matter how hard she tried, she could remember nothing, only a vague recollection of arriving at the airport. The rest was a dark void.

'I must have passed out. Amber won't know I'm here, and she's no way to get hold of me.'

Bell drew the chair closer, speaking softly.

'Today is Wednesday. You've been in a coma for seven days. You were spotted collapsed amongst the rushes in one of San Antonio's storm drains. It was only the skill of the doctors that enabled you to recover.'

'Seven days?' she gulped, incredulously.

'You had a cocktail of alcohol, ecstasy and GHB in your bloodstream. They say that the storm water puddle you almost drowned in kept your body temperature down and saved you.'

Sienna stared blankly through Bell into the middle distance.

'A whole week?…I need to get back to see her, like, right now!'

She leant forward, weeping and shaking her head.

'Steady, you've been through enough already. The local police will find her if need be, this is an island remember,' comforted Bell, although he suspected that they would have little luck.

'You haven't answered my other question.'

'My name is Thomas Bell. I've been authorised by the British Consulate to look after you.'

'Like a child minder?'

'Exactly.'

'Just drop me back at our villa in S'Argamassa. My dear sister will be pleased to do all the nursemaiding. Everything'll be fine.'

'We'll see.'

***

The electronic fob, luckily still attached to a zip-pull, got them through the gates of Villa Cereza. Sienna leapt from the vehicle and retrieved a spare set of keys from the flowerbed. The heavy deadlocks of the Moorish-style front door responded easily, and she dashed into the hallway frantically looking for signs of life.

Nothing.

The lounge was exactly as they had left it on their first night. She walked over to the hastily opened pink Samsonites, and pulled at one of the LGW-IBZ baggage tags pensively. Outside, Sienna stood by the edge of the pool, calling Amber's name in vain, then collapsed, sobbing, on to one of the canopied daybeds.

Bell brought in the bags, his equipment, and Sienna's medication, and locked up behind him. He rested his palm gently on Sienna's shoulder

'I will file a missing persons report,' he said.

Looking around, Bell couldn't help noticing what a fabulously secluded villa this was, with superb views overlooking Santa Eularia bay. During the day, the sea would shimmer as speedboats and jet skis buzzed around in the distance, like angry wasps. On the topmost floor, an observation pod offered even more spectacular views, using a huge brass telescope.

He'd parked his Seat Cupra in the triple underground car park, which was accessed via a lazy concrete curve, at the right of the building.

He re-focused his mind on the need to check the progress of his biobots. He would use the study to set everything up. First, the satellite link.

Satisfied that his control centre was now fully operational, he headed outside to check on the patient.

Still curled up tight, she hadn't moved a muscle.

'Let me fix you a drink. How does garlic prawns in chilli sauce and a salad sound?'

Sienna looked up and wiped the tears away, struggling to smile.

'Please, tell me this isn't happening! It's all a terrible dream isn't it?'

'You've got to be strong, Sienna, your sister would want that.'

'So, gourmet cooking as well as baby sitting?'

'The clinic have asked me to make sure you take fluids and eat well. Oh, and your pills, of course.'

This time, she managed a smile and hugged him.

'Say, does the British Consulate provide this service for everyone who's had a bad hangover?'

'We'll talk about that after dinner.'

Gambas al ajillo.

Bell set about making his favourite spicy Catalan sauce, thickened with ground Marcona almonds, chilli, olive oil, and garlic.

The tiger prawns sizzled on the griddle by the pool, as he drank a large glass of dry white wine. Sienna nursed a still mineral water, not budging from the day bed, keeping her eyes shut and savouring the delicious smell.

He had also prepared some Russian salad to go with the exquisite jamon serrano, made with potatoes, vegetables and mayonnaise sauce. As they were hanging around at the back of the fridge doing nothing, he'd added shaved gruyère, escarole lettuce and walnuts.

Bell served up the Romesco sauce, and they dipped the hot prawns. The intense flavour was offset by popping cherry tomatoes which burst freezing juice into their mouths.

After a long silence across the teak table, Bell freshened his glass, and switched his attention to incoming satellite transmissions. He glanced at his watch with excitement. It prompted Sienna to say something at last.

'Time for me to know who you really are, Mr Bell. I know you're not a doctor and I don't think you're from the British Consulate, either. You don't look like a form filler to me.'

He laughed and threw a group of plastic evidence bags on to the table. Each contained a separate Blue Dove packet of either crack cocaine or ecstasy.

'Know anything about these?'

Sienna sat up, fingered her way through them, and shrugged.

'Only the vitamin E looks familiar.'

'Both types were found on a girl called Stephanie Walters.'

'So?'

Bell dropped the 'No penicillin' bracelet on to the table.

Sienna gasped.

'Where did you get that? Stephanie Walters?!'

Bell nodded.

'My bag…it was stolen last year.'

'Here on the island, yeah?'

'My favourite Gucci handbag. Passport, money, everything.'

'That would explain a lot.'

'So, what does Stephanie have to say about that?'

'She doesn't…she's dead.'

Sienna gasped again. Bell leaned forward.

'Stephanie had been using your passport. Anyone with an unhealthy interest in her may still have an…interest in you.'

Sienna's eyes narrowed with alarm, calculating the implications.

'…in something she did?'

'It's highly probable that you and Amber had been specifically targeted. You got away, your sister didn't.'

'For what exactly?'

'You're both the right type: young, beautiful, and blonde. But there's more to it than that.'

'They think that they killed her or me, and now they're still after me? Is that it?'

'Yes.'

'How did she die?'

'A broken neck. She was found washed up, semi-naked, on the beach at Cala Comte.'

'I know the place.'

Sienna's eyes remained fixed on the sealed evidence packets. She spoke slowly and deliberately now.

'So, identifying them could lead to some sort of drug gang which took Amber, if she's still alive.'

Bell had the last jigsaw piece ready for her,

'…And the gang, as you put it, manufacture Paloma Azul ecstasy somewhere here on the island, a factory the EDEA have been hunting for some considerable length of time.'

'Why are you telling me all this?'

'We may not have much time. You are the key to the puzzle.'

'You're using me as bait, aren't you?'

Bell grinned and drew a Beretta from his waistband.

''Fraid so. You're stuck with me, but I'm here to protect you. I'm sure you want to see your kid sister again.'

'With all my heart,' Sienna replied, softly.

A steely resolve had come over her, out of the blue.

'The important thing is that your memory returns, even flashbacks might help. Tomorrow, you'll come with me to Cala Comte, and we'll get up to San Antonio after sunset.'

Bell produced flyers for Club M, Ramba, and the Esclavo bar, which he'd found in the kitchen.

'We'll be trawling these bars to see if you remember anything. It'll trigger something, hopefully.'

Sienna detected the subtle hint that he found her attractive, and threw her head back, laughing.

'Sex on the beach!'

Sienna caught the misty half-memory of a line of Blue Lagoons on a bar-top. She jolted and the mirage was gone. Bell knew that was enough for one day, and she knocked her three pills back in one.

'Time for bed, doctor's orders,' said Bell.

Safe in her room, she curled up under the cool sheets and stroked her teddy bear's button ear. Moments later she was fast asleep.

Bell had the link connected, and the data streamed down to his laptop from the CIA satellite, somewhere above the Balearics.

The biobots had had time for a good nose around Dos Lunas; enough to map the complex in three dimensions. It seemed to comprise three floors, one of which was underground.

The entire property was the fusion of old finca building in traditional Ibicencan stone, whitewash, and wooden beams, with a large modern construction added to the seaward side. It provided a vast amount of accommodation.

Bell labelled each feature using the software, which would print the press-outs necessary to construct a detailed 3D cardboard model. He noted that located directly underneath the panelled office on the ground floor, there was what looked like a fully equipped torture chamber. Bell decided that it must be just another realistic film set.

An intense sweep of the whole complex had revealed nothing out of the ordinary. There was no MDMA factory to be seen. Mr Pago was clean and he could go. Nothing to report. Bell sat back disappointed. So that was that, and it had looked so promising. He would have to keep looking.

Sienna's eyes flickered with rapid eye movement, as her dream intensified. She and Amber now stood together at a bar, drinking Black Russians out of pint glasses. The barman kept refilling them from a hosepipe.

Now lost in a dense fog, she could hear Amber calling her somewhere in the distance.

A bull creature appeared before her. It had muscular limbs with dirty talons which tried to grab her. She screamed, turned and started running. She tripped and fell forwards awkwardly, landing hard face down. She lay there completely winded, but was still conscious. The creature was now astride her, pinning her back, smothering her. It exhaled foul breath, dripping globules of saliva into her eyes from its bared teeth. She could only stare up into its soulless eyes, waiting for it to bite…

Bell was still deep in thought when he heard the scream. Seconds later, he burst into her bedroom. Sienna lay under the sheets sobbing and sweating.

'It was going to eat me! Please don't leave me alone.'

'You woke up from a bad dream.'

'But I can't wake up from it!'

Bell held her gently in his arms, stroking her hair and soothing her. She settled after a while, and Bell went off to lock the place down for the night. He returned to find her sitting upright in bed with her knees drawn up, hugging the sheet close to her throat. She had cleaned her teeth and rinsed her face, in a bid to shake off the night terrors.

'I'll kip down here,' said Bell, pointing to the sofa bed up by the far wall.

Sienna shook her head with a broad smile.

'Oh no you won't! Come over here so you can protect and comfort me.'

Bell was certainly not going to complain.

'Yes, m'lady,' he grinned.

Sienna rolled over into a foetal position, and Bell snuck in behind her, likewise. He folded his right forearm over her stomach and she took it with hers, holding him tight. He flared his nostrils for a second or two, drawing in the sensuous smell of her, as they both drifted off into delicious sleep together.

With good reason, he would delay filing the missing persons report till first thing in the morning.

***

The following day, Pago sat quietly in his office. He stared up at the oil painting of Jesuit priests, in crimson robes, burning unbelievers at the stake. The zealots clutched crucifixes and rosary beads, woven tightly into their white-knuckled fists, as they observed the cruel spectacle.

Pago allowed his thoughts to drift. If he could rectify his mistakes then all would be pure again, washed clean, absolved.

The Valhalla was now fully refuelled, and the process of loading the laboratory equipment would commence shortly. The operation had to be completed by Friday. The last ever production run of Paloma Azul would also be loaded up into the vessel's hold.

He would have to wait a few days until he was snuggled up in the lapis lazuli lounge, in the heart of the Valhalla, heading westwards out of the Mediterranean.

So, El Cartero was already here on the island.

He studied the grainy photographs again carefully. The cartel assassin had been casing the joint that night, and had evaded Dos Lunas security with ease. Definitely someone to be reckoned with.

A single bullet or a slow, painful death?

Pago's arsehole puckered involuntarily. It seemed to him that he was breathing too quickly.

The Alacrán cartel wanted to set an example.

He would cover his tracks in a cleansing fireball, and if El Cartero went up with it, so much the better.

Pago contemplated plastic surgery for a moment, but he could not countenance going under the knife.

Kadic entered the office, placed three documents on Pago's desk, and sat down.

Sienna Hutton's passport.

An airline immigration report.

A D17 missing persons report.

While Pago carefully studied them, Kadic considered the fact that he was sitting on top of a trap door, concealed by an expensive rug. As he waited, he subconsciously braced himself for an accidental stamp on the red foot pedal, hidden beneath the desk.

Pago popped a powdery chocolate ball into his mouth, licking and smacking his pale thin lips as he did so. Anatoly hated that noise. He especially loathed the sucking and licking of the tips of Pago's swollen, moistened fingers. It took all his strength to stop himself flying over the desk to slice Pago's head clean off with a sharp blade.

'At least we have Amber Sutton,' said Pago presently, looking up with a slight reproach, for allowing Sienna to slip through the net.

Kadic nodded, fully aware of his master's hatred of failure or incompetence. Pago continued.

'So this girl escapes on 17th of July, stealing some items from my office in the process. She is presumed dead but no body is found. She then flies back into Ibiza a week later with her sister. Armed with excellent intelligence, we then attempt to abduct both girls in the Labyrinth Club, but fail to do so due to the untimely meltdown of the ventilation system. How unfortunate.'

Pago allowed his succinct summary of events to coast into an uncomfortable silence, which Kadic broke gently with some additional detail.

'She flew back into Ibiza with Easyjet, on the morning of Wednesday 27th July.'

'Fortunately for us, the girl informs the Police of her sister's disappearance, providing us with the address of her villa in S'Argamassa. Does she have some sort of connection with the security services?'

Kadic lit another Samsun. He held the pungent smoke deep in his lungs for a moment, and then exhaled up towards the ceiling vents.

'I don't think so. She's no professional but it still doesn't make sense. We have to assume that she has shown what she took from your office to someone in authority. If that's the case, the EDEA probably know about it.'

'We're not to waste any more time on this. You are to kill her immediately. Any bright ideas?'

Kadic knew he would be asked this question, and was ready with an answer.

'Let's cause an international incident; the Spanish are increasingly fed up with the US military presence on the island. Being a member of NATO has come with some unfortunate obligations. Let's give the chopper a spin.'

'Approved. El Cartero, what have we got?'

'Matching the mugshots against the entire Police database has revealed nothing. Maybe he arrived by sea.'

'Not enough time. Unless he was already on the island.'

'Unlikely. He arrived in the last few days and got straight to work. Just one bullet, he'll be their top man.'

Pago picked up another chocolate ball from the box, and plopped it into his mouth.

'Yes, in the centre of my forehead,' slurped Pago, who pressed the point of his index finger in the right place, leaving a brown cocoa mark on his white, greasy skin.

'He may be a clever and resourceful assassin, but he only has three days to get to me. Keep looking. If you can catch him alive, do so. I need to know how far the cartel is prepared to go to punish me.'

'Dos Lunas is on constant red alert,' replied Kadic.

Pago nodded appreciatively, slugging down some apricot juice, and spilling a little on to the desk. He scuffed the drips away with annoyance, pointing at Kadic manically.

'Get me Kranz.'

Kadic stood up and opened the double doors. The ordeal was over. So was his cushy life on this island. So was his existence on this planet, if he was left standing anywhere near that frightening atomic device when it blew.

Now it was Kranz's turn to sit above the hidden trap door, in blissful ignorance, nervously fingering the radiation badge on his lapel.

'So you've got the bloody thing working, then?'

'Yes, it was quite easy really, after accessing some very helpful web resources.'

'You'll have to set yourself up as a thermonuclear device repair man,' teased Pago.

Kranz failed to laugh. He wanted to get out of here.

'Now the timer, I hope you've installed a large red LCD, one that counts back to zero, just like in the movies.'

'Exactly as you specified, Herr Pago.'

'And it's rigged to explode spontaneously if anyone tampers with it?…and I get to start the countdown?'

'Yes, Herr Pago.'

'And you say I'll get a yield of around six point five megatons?'

'Yes, Herr Pago, the equivalent of six and a half million tons of TNT, which should flatten the entire west coast of Ibiza. There will be nothing left to indicate that Dos Lunas ever existed.'

'Well, don't you just love it!'

Kranz didn't quite understand Pago's last outburst. He was waved to leave the room, but he sat glued to his chair, driven to ask a burning question.

'Er...just one thing…'

'Yes, what is it Kranz?' Pago's expression had hardened at the breach of protocol, and the poor chemist cringed inwardly.

'Where will I be when the bomb actually goes off?'

Pago thought for a second, pressing his tongue against his lower lip, flicking the chocolate box lid with his fingers.

'You will stay here to ensure that the bomb detonates, of course, you know very well it is your loyal duty.'

Kranz's face whitened with terror, his mouth open, realising that he would never see Switzerland, cuckoo clock houses, and fine chocolate ever again. Another painful, teasing silence.

'Only joking, Kranz, what do you think I am, a barbarian? Where's your sense of humour?'

Kranz was now a nervous wreck.

Pago got serious again.

'You are my chief chemist and therefore you will be sitting with me on the Valhalla, as it sails for Gibraltar at full speed.'

'Thank you, Mr Pago, thank you, thank you,' stammered Kranz.

He left the room but still with a nagging doubt at the back of his mind. You could never be totally sure with a madman. Pago looked up at the oil painting again, the medieval fire burning fiercely, dealing with the problem.

Everything would be alright.

Despite his damaged adrenal gland, he ordered a large gin and tonic, and looked forward to a thorough, deep-tissue massage on the terrace. The explosion would take any remaining evidence, nosy investigators, and cartel hitmen with it. He would disappear without trace and the trail would go cold.

How wonderful.

***

Carlos Salazar, the head of el cártel Alacrán, the scorpion cartel, studied a single photograph placed in the centre of his desk. The puggy, white, bloated features of the latest person to try their luck with El puño de hierro stared back at him.

Ilya Pago.

He removed his gold-rimmed spectacles for a moment, and looked wearily out over the Durango countryside, towards the mountains. He spared a thought for his adopted son, Dario Hernandez, who had perished in unknown circumstances, far from home. Salazar turned back to look at El Cartero who was sitting patiently opposite him.

Despite the pressure of controlling the Alacrán narcorporation, he had taken time out of his busy schedule. The 'Bella Fortuna', carrying six tonnes of cocaine worth three hundred million euros, had just been intercepted off Gran Canaria. He was having a bad week.

It wasn't the loss of two million dollars, the breakdown of a new venture, or the unfortunate death of someone close to him that really mattered.

It was the insult. The insult, the lack of respect, and the indication of weakness which would act like the scent of blood in the water.

He was therefore prepared to commit an inordinate amount of resource to resolve this. No one could be allowed to cross the Alacrán cartel and prevail. It was not really a decision, it was merely a question of survival and operational logistics.

'Our memory is long and our vengeance is total,' said Salazar, finally.

'Si,' replied El Cartero.

'You have your orders.'

13 **Cala Comte**

Day 4 - Thursday 4th August.

Bell emerged from his slumber and stretched his arm out across a cold, empty space.

Female proximity alert!

His mind raced as he leaped from the bed, down the stairs, and out to the pool.

Sienna looked up at him casually from her day bed. The sun was already beating down on the canvas parasol, as she lay there in her mint-blue swimming cozzy.

'Coffee, tea or me?' she giggled.

Bell involuntarily tensed his stomach muscles and slumped down next to her, still wrapped in the bedsheet.

'You're such a tease,' he grinned, delighted.

'Last one to get wet makes breakfast!'

In an instant, she threw down her Gucci sunglasses and dived in. Bell deliberately let go of the sheet, as he stood provocatively in his birthday suit, trying to look cheated.

'Mmm...nice!' screamed Sienna, panting and treading water.

'Permission to come alongside,' said Bell cheekily, feet apart, hands on hips.

Sienna threw her head back, laughing, and sank below the water. Bell dived in, catching her playfully by the foot. She screamed again and went under with a gulp. He brought her back to the surface, with an arm firmly around her waist, the other anchored over the concrete edging, just above the line of pool mosaics.

They were pressed firmly together, legs entwined. She held him close, with one arm around his neck, getting her breath back, enabling Bell to gaze deeply into her eyes. Her lips closed in on his, only to veer off at the last moment to lick his prickly, dark stubble. Her fingers gently brushed the recent wound on his left temple, then tenderly traced over his moist, parted lips.

'Tea, then?' said Bell.

'Skinny latte, if you don't mind.'

Sienna raised an eyebrow, released her grip of Bell's taut scrotum, and slid a knee up between his legs. He had no choice but to push off from the side.

'Okay, okay, skinny latte it is!'

***

The crew of the Valhalla removed the tethered tarpaulins. Twenty minutes later the twin-engine chopper was fully prepped. The Apache AH64D helicopter took off from the back of the main deck in a vortex of kerosene fumes, leaving the painted 'H' in a white circle far below.

The stolen machine, courtesy of the US Army and the American taxpayer, still displayed its Afghanistan theatre markings. It had barely seen any action in Helmand province, but the Apache would still be put to good use in the private sector.

The most lethal and deployable multi-mission helicopter in the world was armed with eight Hellfire air to surface missiles. The two-man crew checked the operational status of the thirty millimetre M230 Gatling gun, and they headed further out to sea for some routine test firing.

***

Bell and Sienna drove in silence.

Earlier, he had spent time in the underground car park checking his Seat Cupra over. All systems were operational and armament fully enabled. His communications equipment and Sienna's suitcase were now squeezed in on the back seats. One bay along, a vehicle stood all alone under a tailor-made cover. Out of idle curiosity, Bell walked across and peeled the fabric back. A silver Ferrari Dino 246GT, on Swiss plates.

Maybe when all this is over.

The missing persons report had been filed online; it may not take long before they would see some action. Chances were that it would be unsafe to return to Villa Cereza.

He guessed that the people interested in Sienna would have a mole at police headquarters or a hack into their computer system, or both. It was a positive development; it would flush them out into the open and he would be ready.

They continued their journey west through open country to Sant Josep, oblivious to a black speck in the sky tailing them with ease.

The popular beach of Cala Comte was already well parked up with vehicles. Bell deliberately squeezed the car between one of the clumps of tall bushes on the edge of the wild sand dunes, which extended southwards. The land at the rear of the car was clear, and fell away into a grassy ditch.

In the baking heat, they walked to the edge of the sandstone lip, which overlooked the narrow strip of fine golden sand and out to sea.

Bell noted the small beach promontory where Stephanie's body had been found.

'This is my favourite beach...that's Sa Conillera,' said Sienna, pointing to the sloping, barren island just offshore.

'I'm on special guard duty today, remember?'

'A quick dip for me, then we'll have a drink. I'm meant to be on holiday, remember?'

'Mmm, okay,' replied Bell.

He watched her dive into the gin clear water.

Sienna's mind had subconsciously decided to unhinge itself from the recent overload of events. A break in the tension might assist in the process of recovering her memory, otherwise her head might burst.

Bell felt the Beretta under his clothing and kept a sharp lookout through his mirrored wrap-arounds.

He noticed a dark shape in the clear, azure sky coming up from the south. At the speed it was going, it rapidly grew into an instantly recognisable shape.

Probably on routine patrol from USS Indianapolis. The rapid whap-whap-whap of the rotor blades came and went, and Bell didn't give it any extra thought.

He had turned his attention back to Sienna who was emerging from the foamy surf, her bikini clinging tightly to her smooth skin. He imagined what it would be like to hold her in his arms again, and make love to her this time.

The Apache crewman had taken accurate facial shots of El Cartero, right down to the individual whiskers of stubble on his face.

Soaking wet, Sienna had run to the freshwater showers at the back of the Sunset Ashram bar. She had quickly emerged fully dressed in a cool, white linen dress, her blond hair pulled back into a neat bun. She pushed her pink Gucci sunglasses stylishly up over her head, looking refreshed and happy.

'Haven't you got the drinks yet? I can still taste the seawater!'

Bell got on it and they ended up in a booth-style seat looking out to sea, spearing olives with cocktail sticks from an earthenware dish. Sienna ordered another beer for Bell and switched from water to Pepsi. When the order came, she checked her watch, and took another three tablets just as the clinic had specified.

'I feel so much better. Do you think they're watching us at this very moment?'

'They'll make their move, sooner or later.'

'I'm hungry. I know a great place for lunch. It's a pleasant walk along the edge of the dunes. Yeah, so like, they ruined Cala Comte when they replaced the stony track with a tarmac road, and added a bloody bus stop. Now everyone can get here!'

Bell nodded at her observation with a dreamy look, happy to listen to her carefree gabbling all day long.

'Let's do it.'

'Say, how did you get hurt?'

'I was saving a girl from being mugged…on a train as it happens…then, I got mugged myself.'

'And now you're meant to be looking after me? I hope you've sharpened up a bit since then!' she laughed.

A sudden change of mood.

'Do you really think I'll ever see my sister again?'

'You're on their wanted list. As soon as the balloon goes up, we'll know about it. There is hope.'

She came closer to him, brushing the hair out of his eyes then kissed him softly on the lips.

'Let's go and eat,' she said, excitedly.

They were now a good distance along the deserted coastal path which marked the edge of the expanse of unspoilt dunes.

The sea view was breathtaking. All that light and space. It was also a notorious location for those seeking casual sex. Occasionally a head would bob up in the distance.

Bell felt the earthy vibration of a helicopter, as it buzzed abnormally low overhead.

He had taken his eye off the ball. The abrupt realisation that something very bad was about to happen hit him in the pit of his stomach.

He could smell the burnt aviation fuel from the downdraft as it shot past. He looked up and saw it commence a banking turn to starboard. In a split second, he registered that they were the target.

It was coming back, perhaps a strafing run firing twelve hundred rounds per minute from the cannon mounted under its nose. Bell knew that the gun would be equipped with a ten degree pivot, which meant it would track from side to side five degrees off centre.

In military training films, if the chopper passed over an area the size of an American football field, it would hit a wild racoon on the loose anywhere in the kill box.

Every time.

They had maybe forty seconds to take cover.

Bell noticed a small concrete weather station nearby which was almost totally concealed in a dune hollow. He grabbed Sienna's hand and heaved her over the lip just as shells pocked the sand behind them.

There was no doubt now.

It was some sort of meteorological station with solar panels and roof-mounted probes. It had been constructed out of high-grade concrete, to the same standard as a defensive pillbox.

Bell peered over the lip as the Apache finished its second pass. It had committed to a very sharp turn to port, the note produced by the twin engines changing as they took the strain. He could just make out the USAF markings.

They were now tucked in tight, like meerkats in a burrow, on the leeward side. Bell dug out his Samsung and tapped the classified phone app. The noise of the approaching Apache increased along with the continuous deep belch sound of the cannon. As the gunship passed again overhead, they were sprayed with chunks of concrete, but were safe from a direct hit or a ricochet.

He now had control of the Avenger air defence system, cleverly installed in the boot of his car. As his finger traced over the screen, the boot lid opened automatically, and two Stinger missile pods popped up on hydraulics, pointing skyward.

Let's see how those guys handle a fire-and-forget surface-to-air missile. Hey, assholes, now you're gonna kiss my butt!

Another starboard turn took place in the distance. Better get locked on and fire before they unleash some other type of ordnance. Napalm? Better be quick!

Two mini, FIM-92M, ground-to-air Stingers whooshed out of their pods. Had you been standing in the car park, it would have been enough to make you drop your underwear and your picnic box.

The projectiles gained height rapidly and closed in on their target. He'd have given his left arm to see the reaction in the cockpit.

The Apache banked again, awkwardly this time, registering the threat, violently twisting this way and that. Both missiles stayed doggedly locked on to the Apache's exhaust plume.

The helicopter raced off at full speed, heading south. It was like a cat dancing on hot coals, bobbing and bucking, dispensing chaff and hot flares to shake off the Stingers.

Bell and Sienna returned to the car park as quickly as they could. A lucky escape.

On the way, they came across three naked men on a large pink inflatable bed, shaking with fear and smothered in baby oil. Like serious cuddling. They clung on to each other, arms and legs intertwined, staring at Bell and Sienna as they yomped past. Bell guessed that it wouldn't be long before they were at it again.

Thirsty and exhausted, Bell gunned the Seat through the dusty bleached back roads till he rejoined the main PM-803. He drove sedately now, not wanting to attract any attention. Sienna was still in shock, curled up in the passenger seat, gazing into space.

It was unlikely to have been an attack by a crew flying rogue from the deck of the USS Indeanapolis. Yet it might be reported in the newspapers as such. He thought back to the rotor tips, partly obscured by tarps, that he had seen that night on the Valhalla. I wonder.

The incident was probably not going to help Sienna's memory loss. Unfortunately, they couldn't return to her villa with its familiar surroundings, where she could feel safe. So, plan B: a tardy lunch, somewhere else.

***

It was late afternoon at Nico Beach, an expensive beach club on Cala Jondal, west of Sa Caleta.

You could count thirty bottles and six Cristal magnums of champagne beside one poolside mattress alone. Very little had been drunk. It had been sprayed, litre upon litre of vintage champagne, like cat piss, over stunning east European hookers in killer heels and tiny bikinis.

Nico Beach owned a private bay of pure white sand, reserved exclusively for the beautiful people. It was backed by a pristine pine forest, where massage therapists worked under the trees. The emphasis was on simple chic minimalism for the super rich.

Flotillas of yachts with fluttering pennants, and sizeable motor yachts, brought them ashore for an extended cocktail hour, straight from a long lunch at Club Nakoya or Puffino's.

Many had spent the day moored off the unspoilt island of Formentera, to the south, simply swimming and having sex, waiting for dusk.

Exclusive club members ran amok around the pool, attempting to dunk one another to the hubbub of squeals, popping corks, and breaking glass. The pool now had a milky surface film of sun tan lotion and champers.

Funky house music percolated out to the expanse of potted palms and teak day loungers with crisp cotton covers. Rappers, models, chic fashionistas, and pop idols rubbed shoulders with bankers and wealthy industrialists. Afford it?…just think how much it costs to refuel that fucking yacht parked out there!

In the final analysis, you can only eat three meals a day. When you have unlimited wealth, there are only two things that really matter: youth and beauty.

The two hitmen had eaten, and they now sat back to enjoy their strong Colombian coffees.

Nico Beach was an ideal place to talk business.

Julio de la Concepcion Silvestre, also known as El Cartero, sat with his associate, Enrique 'Manos' Pimienta.

Julio was a tall, slim Mexican, with sinewy muscles concealed beneath his lightweight suit. He had keen, cold, dark eyes which missed nothing. He had the cunning and patience of a wolf. Julio had spent a decade enforcing the will of the Alacrán cartel, encouraging people to change their minds, or to wish that they never had.

He was a professional assassin who had joined the Mexican army as a teenager. He became a highly trained marksman and commando, taking part in black operations, having received specialist training at the military School of the Americas in the United States. He spent the latter part of his illustrious military career as a member of the army's elite Airborne Special Forces Group (GAFE), apprehending drug cartel members. Motto: *'Not even death can stop us. If death takes us by surprise, it is more than welcome'.*

Seeking higher rewards, he had switched sides, and left to join Los Zetas, a group of former special forces troops who acted as paramilitary enforcers for the drug lords.

Both men were weary and irritable after the long flight from Mexico City via Madrid to Ibiza, despite flying business class.

Julio had wanted to get an immediate feel for the White Island. The island where Ilya Pago would draw his last breath.

He studied the high resolution satellite photographs carefully, using a magnifying glass from time to time, consulting the map, then reverting back to the aerial shots.

Finally, he studied the mugshots of Pago, Kadic, and a number of other known associates, and handed the complete dossier over to Manos.

Julio leant forward and stripped the cellophane off a pack of Marlboros, coughing as he did so, and offered one to Manos.

He, as expected, shook his head with a knowing smile, and expelled a Mustang from its crush-proof box.

'We'll make the hit on either Friday or Saturday evening.'

Manos nodded sagely.

'There'll be the usual bodyguards; nothing we can't handle.'

A conga of drunken bankers, interwoven with Ukrainian and Moldavian hookers, wended its way through the day beds to shrieks and whoops, getting nearer and nearer. The music seemed to be louder as well.

Manos was becoming increasingly agitated. He would rather have been back in Mexico City, drinking pulque in his favourite cantina bar, 'La Pirata', in the Escandón neighbourhood. He always sat with his back to the wall, watching the door. Mexico City was a tough place to live, but an easy place to die.

The tail of the conga swept close by them, and caught Manos clumsily on the shoulder, causing him to spill his coffee. Manos struck like a cobra, and forced the man's left arm up his back, while expertly squeezing his carotid artery. Back home in a dark alleyway, he might just as easily have punctured the man's skin with two fingers, and compressed his aorta shut. But not here.

The banker would simply collapse on to a lounger with an epileptic seizure and lose consciousness inside one minute. People would look on and assume that it was just another Champagne Charlie who'd overdone it a bit.

Manos returned to his seat and calmly lit another Mustang, beckoning the waiter.

Manos had been sprung from the notorious El Cefereso prison in Mexico to join Julio for this mission. An unmarked helicopter brazenly landing in the exercise yard, leaving three guards and two inmates dead.

He had arm tattoos, just hidden by his long-sleeved shirt, a thick neck, eyes like slits, puffy cheeks, and a very heavy build. Manos had a history of explosive violence from a young child. It caused his mother to direct her son into training to be a free wrestler, or luchador, in order to dissipate his surfeit of energy.

Manos had excelled in this field, building his strength, and mastering the rapid sequences of complex submission holds demanded by lucha libre. He'd had a good run in the ring, developing new and exciting aerial manoeuvres, which delighted the screaming crowds. Eventually, a series of injuries had caused him to hang up his mask forever, and become an underworld enforcer.

He was now struggling to open a couple of chocolate wafer biscuits, in difficult to open wrappers.

'Bastardos perezosos!' blurted Manos, exhaling a dense plume of tobacco.

'Any thoughts?'

'Si! What kind of island is this?' he grinned.

'Get used to it. This is a European playground.'

'Anything you say, chief.'

'Dario and Diego were murdered. We must expect trouble.'

Julio passed the map over, which showed San Josep and the fan of vein-like tracks which all led down to the coast.

'Guns?' said Manos.

'MAC-10s with suppressors, Berettas, a variety of grenades, machetes, and plenty of ammunition. Also some Glock FM-78 field knives, if we want to use them.'

Manos cheered at the thought of a razor-sharp machete strapped to his waistband, an invaluable tool for hacking through the jungle or close quarter combat. He recollected how he had cut a startled Federale vertically from his shoulder straight down to his pelvis.

'So we just park the Telefónica van wherever we like, and nobody asks any questions?'

'Exactly. We'll have tools, ladders, the full telephone engineer thing…and Telefónica overalls. Hope you can get into yours!' chuckled Julio.

'As long as I don't have to shin up a telegraph pole.'

'Remember Salazar wants Pago's head and hands to be sent back home in a refrigerated box.'

'Will I get to arrange that?'

'Only if Pago will let you!'

'We have also been instructed to recover a briefcase containing two million dollars. So, while you are cutting up the squealing fat pig with your blade, you may want to ask him where the money is.'

'I will do the hands first.'

14 The Labyrinth

Day 4 - Thursday 4th August: – late afternoon.
Bell's Seat Cupra approached the outskirts of San An on the C-731, the Avinguda de Portmany, and entered a long colonnade of mature trees at the northern end of the main artery which connects Ibiza Town to San Antonio.

A large hoarding tempted them with the Fiesta del Agua. The black Mercedes C-class with tinted windows, which had shadowed them since the Amnesia club, was keeping it tight on their tail. There was no chance of telling who was inside, but Bell guessed at least two armed hoodlums.

First the Apache, now this. The genie was out of the bottle.

Bell sensed that the Merc wasn't bothering to be discreet anymore. He assumed that, at a chosen moment very soon, goons would jump out, surround them, and unleash a hail of bullets.

The egg roundabout was now only three hundred metres ahead. They were entering the epicentre of San An, a crush of high-rise hotels, bars, restaurants, and mini-marts. Lines of beach-goers, carrying debris from a day in the sun, mooched home along the pink pavement tiles.

The traffic was starting to slow. No question of being boxed in. If it came to it, he'd floor it and play chicken with the oncoming traffic.

Fifty metres. Come on, come on, keep pulling out!

He glanced across at Sienna, with a grim smile.

'Better hang on.'

Bell burst on to the roundabout and took the third exit, gunning it up Carrer de Ramón y Cajal. He looked in the mirror to see the Merc pushing out, denting a taxi, and powering after him, now with two vehicles separating them. Bell sped through a heavily built-up area of grimy shopfronts, offices, and apartment blocks. It was imperative to lose them in the vast maze of tiny streets, that helpfully all looked the same.

As Bell reached the next roundabout, he exited at speed into Carrer de la Soledat, but the Mercedes was hanging in there. The Seat accelerated hard up the gradient, as Bell formulated a difficult-to-follow escape route.

Whoever was driving knew what they was doing. The two taxis had annoyingly both turned off, sensing yet another drug turf-war chase. The Merc was now at liberty to close the gap. If they got within range, the shooting would commence.

Bell swung violently left at the cross junction into Carrer de València, then another left, speeding down Carrer Cervantes in the direction he'd just come.

A switch on the dash released a couple of smoke grenades behind them. The street instantly filled with dense plumes of phosphorous pentoxide, as the canisters rolled into the gutter. The curtain of white smog was corralled by the five story apartments either side.

Then a right into Carrer Bartomeu Vincent Ramón, heading downhill back to the port. They quickly emerged into a small square, past startled drinkers, and were out the other side in seconds.

Nothing in the rear view mirror, so next right after the Ship Inn. Still nothing tailing them. Looking good. But wait! The Merc had been held up at the previous intersection, outranked by an 'Aves Chico' delivery lorry, which crawled past the bonnet of the C-class, in first gear.

'Lucky, lucky,' whispered Bell.

The Seat hung a left at the Carrer de L'Estrella T-junction. Within seconds, a final left at the Eroski supermarket took them into Carrer Vara de Rey.

The steel garage shutter further along the street, had just finished opening. The instant the car was over the threshold, a microswitch dropped the shutter like a stone. Bell killed the engine, and burst from the car. He was just in time to see the Merc cruise past on the external CCTV monitors.

Then, the Merc started to back up slowly.

Bell switched on the audio.

Men in black got out and stood there with ear pieces, dark glasses, and walkie-talkies. Then, a second identical Mercedes turned up which blocked the road off at the junction with Carrer del Mar. Bell intently scanned the whole scene, split into multiple HD camera segments, eager for any identification clues.

Up and down the street, broken phrases garbled in French and Italian.

'Où?'

'Disparu!'

'Là?'

'Come un fantasma!'

They were checking all the shopfronts carefully.

The CIA safe house had previously been a sherry store. Its dilapidated frontage and buckled ironwork cleverly concealed what was inside. The only possible giveaway was the sophisticated entry keypad by the front door, which had attracted the attention of one of the goons.

Bell found himself staring into the eyeball of Marcel, the 4x4 driver he'd chased back to Dos Lunas that night. Marcel studied the device carefully, while Bell obtained high definition facial images. Bell could have easily triggered the explosive charge which would have burst Marcel's head open like a ripe watermelon. Might have given the game away, though.

Shame.

A few minutes later, the Mercs disappeared and Bell relaxed back into his executive chair, totally exhausted.

On cue, Sienna parked a chilled beer on the desk and ran her hand through his hair.

'So this is where you live?'

'It's a safe house, so no need to be afraid now.'

'You make me feel safe, Tom. Thanks for driving!'

'We may need to stay here for a while.'

'Just you and me? Without you I'd be terrified.'

'Until I've organised a few things.'

'Hmm...I think I need to lie down.'

'Try the next floor. I'll be up shortly.'

The place was a bit gloomy, but fully kitted out with everything you would need to run a covert operation. It was cleverly located in a grubby backstreet next to tired apartments, a rundown supermarket, and an electricity sub-station.

Its arched ceilings dripped with calcite, and it still smelled of musty oak barrels and distilled liquor. Bell surmised that the hooch had been dripping on to the terracotta flags long before the invention of package holidays. An era when only schooners, under full sail, would visit Ibiza, a sleepy, almost forgotten Spanish possession.

As far as Bell was concerned, he now had his ducks lined up in a row.

He had all the indicators and evidence which threaded a link all the way from Marcel's eyeball back to the contents of Stephanie Walter's denim jacket.

To top it off, Pinky the cockroach had managed to transmit some corroborative data, just before going offline. The biobot had somehow got down to the lower levels of Dos Lunas, and had finally detected the existence of a fully operational drug factory.

Images and air analysis.

Pill stamping machines, chemicals, and packaging lines, plus grainy shots of production personnel in white bunny suits.

Irrefutable.

Bell guessed that Pinky had scuttled into the lift after a technician, collected the data, but had come to a sticky end courtesy of a size twelve army boot.

No matter.

It would all go into his report, which he would transmit to MIX that evening.

He fixed himself another beer from the chiller, and settled back to think it all through.

They'd only managed a couple of bocadillos and a coffee earlier, having missed out on a proper lunch. He'd order a takeaway for later on. Sitting in full view in the middle of a restaurant was now completely out of the question.

London would liaise with the Spanish authorities and Interpol. A raid at Dos Lunas would require a large number of heavily armed police, and possibly special forces. Bell didn't expect Pago's men to give up without a fight. Hopefully all the girls being held against their will would be liberated unharmed, and that should include Amber Hutton.

He just had to sit tight with Sienna for now.

It would take time to obtain authorisation and assemble police combat units. A large number of arrests, including Pago, would be the perfect outcome to his first mission.

He realised that he had to nip back to his hotel room to pick up his encryptor. It was a calculated risk, especially with Sienna in tow, but it had to be done.

Shouldn't be a problem.

As he got to the top of the stairs, he could hear the rush of water from the bathroom and the steady howl of the extractor unit.

Bell lay out on the bed she had chosen, still warm and fragrant from her.

The shower door opened, steam spewing forth, Sienna's nymph-like form just visible through the condensation. A hand emerged waving a tube of body exfoliator.

'Scrub my back, will you?'

Bell stripped off in an instant and snapped the cabinet door shut.

'It says to apply and rub briskly, then stand under stone cold water for two minutes.'

He wondered whether his winter training in Norway had prepared him for this task.

'I'll do all of you,' grinned Bell, as he squeezed the coconut paste on to the exfoliating glove.

'They say French women get perkier bodies for it.'

'Ready for the cold?'

They clung to each for an eternity in the freezing deluge, as it rinsed the aromatic scrub away.

Bell was pleasurably drenched in life-giving warmth, as she twisted the dial back.

'There's something I can do for you,' said Sienna.

'Yeah? Does it come in a tube?'

'Turn around.'

The command was accompanied by a playful slap on the arse, which he wasn't complaining about.

He could feel her silky hands on his muscular back and shoulders, as the massage began. She moved expertly over him with her fingers. Bell noticed her hands getting lower and lower to just above his buttocks, and he felt his control slipping away. Her hand came around and clasped his erect member, expertly easing back his foreskin, and stroking his exquisitely tensioned frenulum.

'Let's do something else,' she said, breathlessly.

'Like, not getting wet?'

He turned to face her, and kissed her passionately in the lukewarm downpour, his erection pressed up against her abdomen.

'It's a big thing...the very first time,' she gasped.

'Let's get out of here.'

Sienna lay naked with her wet blond hair on the pillow, mouth slightly open, her large blue eyes upon him. Bell approached the edge of the bed, his penis standing firmly to attention, as he knelt into the mattress.

Then he was beside her.

They caressed each other's intimate parts, and kissed with feverish, uncontrolled passion. He made sure that she came first, sensing when she was close, then delaying and building the power of her orgasm till she exploded.

He placed the pillow under her behind, and entered her with long, deliberate strokes.

Before he came, he withdrew and lay on his back, whereupon Sienna placed her head on his stomach to fellate him to a slow, agonising climax.

Sienna eventually leaned over and retrieved the much-needed tissue box. Upon her return from the bathroom, she adjusted the aircon, and rolled back exhausted, snuggling up to him.

'Promise you'll look after me, Tom,' she said softly, stroking his chest.

'I promise. Synchronised orgasms next time!'

She impressed her lips upon his.

'Every time from now on, Mr Tom! Come on! What is this?'

'We'll keep trying till we've mastered it!'

'Why don't we take the ferry to Valencia, and drive the Ferrari all the way back to Calais?'

'I'd like that...but only when all my chickens are in the pot.'

***

Early evening.

They had wolfed down a takeaway. Bell returned his attention to the matter in hand.

'We have to go out. I have to retrieve something.'

'And a drink as well? I know I'm in your safe hands.'

'Only if it's quick. No dawdling.'

'Stick in the mud!'

'You'll be in disguise.'

Sienna stood in front of him as he made the inspection. Long black wig and chilli-red lipstick.

'You'll do.'

'Yessir!'

'I'm your holiday fling, remember?'

She was staggeringly beautiful; he felt like an imposter.

They left the rear of the building into a rubbish-strewn alleyway and emerged into a crowded Carrer de Sant Antoni. Just another young couple out for an evening stroll.

Bell held her arm tight as they walked, staying vigilant, acutely aware of his Beretta 92F, tucked into his waistband. They would soon be at the Hotel Palmyra. As they approached, the Esclavo bar gradually came into view.

'There! That bar, Amber and I were in there!'

Against his better judgement, in they went.

'We started in here, I remember it now.'

One drink later, they were back outside when she drew her hands to her face in horror.

'The head of the Bull! There it is the...the Labyrinth Club! We have to go in there!'

'Sienna, we can't! We have to go.'

'But Amber will be in there waiting for me!'

Bell held her back. She started to cry, and people began to stop and stare. Now she was screaming, lashing out at him and desperately pulling to get free.

The Esclavo Bar had been the initial trigger. Her memory was flooding back, causing an emotional overload. It seemed to Bell that she had been transported back to that evening, a week or so earlier. For her, Amber really was in the nightclub.

'Andy and Dino!' she screamed.

She broke loose and legged it to the busy main road. A rare gap in the traffic enabled her to run straight across, just as Bell nearly caught her up. After he'd finally got after her again, he could see just ahead that the pair of tough bouncers, in constricted tuxedos, had simply waved her straight in. Normally there would have been a long queue, but not this early in the evening.

He was forced to hide his semi-automatic in a dark alleyway, before reappearing around the corner.

More delay.

Finally, he made it to the club door, and had to pay an exorbitant one hundred and fifty Euro entry fee. After a walk through the X-ray machine, and a rigorous frisking, he raced off inside to search the rabbit warren of sparsely lit chill-out areas and bars.

The Labyrinth club attracted the world's glitterati, hell-bent on a decadent night out. Bell admired the décor and nocturnal goings-on, as he struggled to carry out a controlled sweep of the place.

Walls adorned with bulls, unicorns, naked succubi fornicating with serpents, and lecherous gargoyles. Go-go girls glistening in baby oil, gyrating on podiums amidst the noise, ribbons of smoke, and laser beams. Punters puffing waterpipes laced with LSD, while knocking back vodka shots and mojitos. Everyone rocking to the deafening beat, staring upwards at giant video screens and glitter balls in a trance-like state.

What's not to like?

She was nowhere to be seen.

Meanwhile, Sienna was perched on a tall bar stool, nursing a Long Island Iced Tea. The barman left his post for a moment to deposit pretzels and marinated olives on the low tables nearby. Amber would be back from the Ladies any minute, so she ordered another one. She had her 'what-took-yous' lined up ready, just like her potent cocktails. Andy and Dino must have gone off somewhere. Men!

She decided to sit down on the giant pair-of-lips sofa, and pick at the snacks while she was waiting.

'I'll bring your drink over, love,' said the barman.

Sienna put her glass down and reached for a black olive with a cocktail stick. The motorised sofa smoothly rolled in on itself and she was gone.

Bell turned the corner just in time to see a barman clearing away a half-drunk Long Island Iced Tea from one of the tables.

He'd scoured the place. Where the hell was she?

He helped himself to a black olive, as he considered what to do next.

Of course, it had to be the Ladies. Nowhere else left.

Or had she done a runner?

Bell approached the Ladies queue and targeted a blonde wearing a see-through top and black hot pants. Her hair had been put up to emphasise the faux diamond earrings she was wearing.

'I'm looking for a girl,' said Bell.

'So, you're not fussy,' the girl replied, tartly.

'A girl with long dark hair.'

'I'll be just as much fun. Try me. But, let me have a wee first.'

'I'll be back.'

Bell ran into the Gents, which was curiously empty.

He stood at the wall of urinals, thinking fast, pissing slowly, staring at an explicit ad for a pack of three Climaxa, fully lubricated.

Soddit! I swore I'd never lose sight of her! Now what? Back to the Ladies, I guess.

Cubicle two, behind him, opened a fraction.

Someone not having a shit or snorting a line.

The nose of a tranquilizer gun became just visible, as the door inched slightly wider.

Bell instantly sensed danger.

He felt a slight prickle, as a subconscious warning indicator, deep inside his brain, changed to red.

His right hand automatically went for his waistband.

Hell!

As he started to turn, a burst of compressed gas shot a dart into the centre of his back. The flying syringe, full of barbiturate, took immediate effect. Bell collapsed on to the grubby toilet floor, in a paralysing torpor.

As the drug tightened its grip, he could smell the sticky film of urine pressed next to his face. His head lay under the weeping U-bend of trap three, with a large military boot pressed against his cheek. His muscle control and consciousness were fading fast.

'Just a quiet drink…'

A final thought, then blackness.

'We're not to kill him,' said Marcel.

15 One thousand cuts

5 th August - 3.00am Friday.
The room was arranged for torture.

The white ceramic tiles covering the walls were spattered in blood. The concrete floor revealed gory teeth, and fingernails which should have been swept into the corners. There was a rack for breaking feet, a bar for hanging a man upside down, rows of manacles, straps, and batons. There were also pliers for extracting teeth, syringes with used needles, smelling salts, a medical drip, and resuscitative equipment.

Dario Hernandez had so enjoyed his manicure.

Thomas Bell lay strapped in the dentist's chair, his body naked, except for his faithful Calvin Kleins. He came round slowly, his head thumping like it had been hit by a wrecking ball. There were fresh marks on his arm where it had been lovingly swabbed with alcohol, and they had injected adrenaline.

He was acutely aware that his hands were clasped over armrests with flexible steel bands, with one across his forehead, drawn tightly back to the padded headrest. The restraints extended down to his torso, thighs, calves, and feet, like tourniquets. He was held rigid like a taxidermy specimen. As he was unable to move his head, he was forced to stare dead-ahead at the poster of a giant, black-and-white spiral.

A plastic ball gag was held in his mouth by a leather strap. Bell could run his tongue over the teeth marks left by earlier patients. The difficulty in breathing forced Bell to snort double-time through his snotted-up nose. The only parts of his body that he could move were his eyes, which stung from the bright light, and were dry and crusted up like car battery terminals.

Bell guessed that he was at Dos Lunas. He had lost any sense of time, having no idea how long he'd been unconscious. He sensed that he must be somewhere under the main finca, the first basement level. Of course! The dungeon he'd thought was simply a film set.

Where was Sienna now? Was she still alive?

The moment Sienna had entered the Labyrinth Club, the game was up.

'Remove the gag,' ordered Anatoly Kadic.

Marcel stepped forward and undid the leather buckle. Bell closed his teeth back together, and felt the dry roof of his mouth with a furry tongue. His jaw muscles ached. There were no gaps in his pearly whites, that was something positive, at least. Kadic spoke again.

'Water? Maybe a little for our friend, Señor El Cartero, so we can hear our little bird sing his song.'

Marcel and Kadic, unseen shapes outside of his field of vision, broke into juvenile laughter.

'Where is my girlfriend?' rasped Bell.

Kadic immediately slapped Bell hard across the face, a bit harder and it would have shattered his cheekbone.

'We ask the questions.'

Marcel then punched him lazily in the stomach, with a skilful blow just below the solar plexus. Bell was unable to recoil and double up. His eyes bulged with the pain, fixed on the queasy swirls rotating on the wall opposite which seemed to be sucking him down into a whirlpool.

'You will no doubt be familiar with the techniques you will be subjected to today,' said Kadic.

'I prefer to use physical pain rather than truth compounds, like scopolamine. Drugs should be restricted to recreational use, don't you think?'

Kadic grinned at Bell, while scratching his own arm, which was peppered with tiny scabs in the vicinity of the elbow joint. It had been a while since he'd reduced a human being to a gibbering, bloody pulp, pleading for mercy. He was going to enjoy this.

A moan from a female, close by, broke the short silence. Bell instinctively tried to turn to his left. He guessed it was Sienna. She was still alive.

'Yes, your girlfriend. Pretty little thing isn't she? I will be using her...later on.

Bell thought of Ovidie back at Tracy Island, and what these two goons had done to her. He visualised her pathetic, mutilated corpse, covered in blood and cuts.

Bell's body tensed in a shudder of anger and frustration. He suppressed the urge to cry out, choosing instead to harness his energy on getting out of this predicament.

He knew that he'd have to work the mistaken identity ploy, to start with. Stick with his legend at all costs.

Kadic helped himself to a Kool Ultramint from Sienna's bag, and clenched the filter tip tightly between his nicotine-stained teeth. The room was already dense with Turkish cigarette smoke. A Bic lighter, embossed with a gold lizard, flared, and was thrown randomly on to an unseen surface. Kadic took a long, delectable drag, walked over, and exhaled a spearmint-flavoured cloud into Bell's face. He held the glowing, radiating tip close to the patient's right eye for an unbearable moment.

Another deep inhale.

'Of course, I prefer the strong tobacco in Turkish cigarettes; menthol is nice, but it's a bit girly. Women's handbags are so revealing don't you think?'

The question lay unanswered, as the echoing sound of approaching flip-flops filled the corridor. Kadic stood upright, as Pago entered the room wearing a billowing toga with deep purple Tyrian stripes. Thankfully, it easily hid the sweating rolls of puffy, white flesh concealed underneath.

Tonight, he was the Emperor Tiberius at a lavish themed party hosted at Dos Lunas. The honoured celebrity guests and hangers-on were blissfully unaware of the brutality being meted out on the next floor down. They were focused on enjoying the high. Cocaine, champagne, and ecstasy, followed by getting your leg over.

Pago removed the gold wreath from around his head, and placed it next to a row of scopolamine phials.

Time to get down to business.

Bell mulled over everything he'd been taught about withstanding torture, and hoped he'd got it.

Pago stared at Bell like he was a captured butterfly, and moved in close, breathing alcohol and garlic over him. He held an Aztec sacrificial knife, its handle carved into the shape of an eagle warrior. Bell could discern the ultra-sharp edges of the blade, made so long ago from obsidian volcanic glass. It could cut human flesh cleanly straight down to the bone.

'So, you are the angel of death?'

Pago adjusted his robes and contentedly rubbed one of his nipple rings.

'What is your name?'

With the gag temporarily removed, the angel was able to answer.

'Thomas Bell.'

Pago thought for a moment, his mood darkening. He did not wish to neglect his guests for long. The variety of narcotic substances provided by their host would, however, go a long way to mitigate any lack of social protocol.

'What is your name?' Pago repeated.

'Look, I'm just an accountant here on holiday for the week. There must be some mistake,' Bell bluffed.

Pago took some time to digest the answer, as Kadic and Marcel stood nearby like brooding sentinels.

'You are El Cartero, are you not?'

'No, I'm just a holidaymaker. You've got the wrong person. Please let me go. I've done nothing!'

Bell played the frightened innocent, caught up in this horror by an unfortunate case of mistaken identity.

'Why are you with Sienna Hutton?'

'I picked her up in a bar. I don't know anything.'

'Ah! A holiday romance! So nice to know that true love is not dead, but you soon will be, my friend, if you fail to answer me correctly. Which bar?'

Pago pulled up a stool, and lowered his generous buttocks down on to it. He looked very amused, steepling his chubby fingers together and bringing them up to his lips. He pondered for a moment, carefully adjusting the thong straining under his toga.

'The girl!' barked Pago.

Sienna had been strapped down using the same barbaric arrangement, right next to Bell. Marcel took a grip of Sienna's face, and tilted a large mirror so that Bell could gaze into her eyes.

'Tom!' she whimpered.

'Anatoly is fond of giving pedicures. He would have made a talented chiropodist. To him, the ripping out of the nail by the root is graceful artistry.'

Kadic stood ready with a set of thirty-inch bolt cutters. Anna suddenly entered the room, in a stylish Marie Antoinette outfit, its highlight being an elegantly ruffed miniskirt. She surveyed the captives, unmoved. Kadic delved into Sienna's handbag, and handed her passport to Anna who studied it carefully, glancing up a couple of times at the girl strapped in the second dentist's chair.

'This is a different girl, yet the passport we already have matches the girl lying here.'

Anna produced a second passport, and handed them both to Kadic.

'Both passports belong to this person: Sienna Hutton.'

'The girl who was made to work here, and we knew as Sienna Hutton, must have stolen it,' deduced Kadic.

'That's right,' blurted Sienna, speaking for the first time.

They all ignored her.

Bell sensed a chance that they might be allowed to go, unharmed.

'...which means that we've picked up the wrong girl.'

Pago smiled and turned to Bell.

'The facts would appear to corroborate your story. I am therefore duty-bound to release you both immediately, with a full apology.'

Pago let the words hang in the air, like the stale tobacco smoke floating in undulating layers. Before Bell could make a speech about kidnapping and false imprisonment, Pago beat him to it.

'Were it not for one minor detail.'

Kadic handed Pago a brown manila envelope.

'This is a series of photographs of you on our private beach, taken at around 3:15 a.m. two days ago. I do not believe you are who you claim to be.'

'Start with the girl.'

Kadic selected metal shears and heavy-duty pliers from his tool box, both gummed up with dried blood. Marcel twisted Sienna's left foot into position. She screamed as Kadic inspected the row of shiny polished nails, perfectly trimmed, shell-like, like a baby's.

'So finely trimmed, I can't get a grip. Shall I cut the toes open?' asked Kadic.

Pago had the answer.

'No. Let's try amputating each toe, one by one.'

'Okay, I'll talk! Torture me not the girl.'

'How wonderful! Before you reveal all, there's just one little thing we have to do.'

With little warning, Kadic plier-gripped the nail of each of Bell's big toes in turn, and ripped the nails right out. Bell let out excruciated howls as the crude surgery was performed.

'I-I-I am El Cartero!'

'That's better. You came to Ibiza to assassinate me, didn't you?' cooed Pago.

'Y-yes!'

'Do you know Dario Hernandez?'

'No...no...I'm just a hired assassin,' gasped Bell, as his brain raced to compute a stream of coherent, logical answers that would buy more time.

'How were you to kill me?'

Bell considered that a simple bullet to the back of the head was too clean and easy. He wanted this creep to be troubled with nightmares.

'I was to slit your throat from ear to ear, sever your head, and FedEx it back to Bogotá in a refrigerated box. I've been paid half in advance.'

'How much was the contract?'

Bell feigned convincing agony, as his poor toes bled on to the tiled floor. What the hell was the going rate?

'Two hundred thousand dollars.'

Pago nodded and subconsciously rubbed his neck.

'Back to Bogotá, not Mexico City? I am confused. I am also confused as to how you came to meet Sienna Hutton. In a bar, you said.'

'I picked her up in Bar M. She was hanging around, looking for a casual fuck.' said Bell, hoping that the candid response would throw them off track.

Pago knew that Bell was lying. It didn't stack up. Despite his grotesque figure and looks, he had a powerful, logical brain that could process complex information quickly.

'Who are you, really?' asked Pago.

Pago nodded, and Sienna's foot was held for a second time. In a few moments her little pinkie toe would be on the deck. Bell couldn't let it happen.

'I'm from Europol. My name is Thomas Bell.'

'So, you're just a bloody copper then!' laughed Pago.

'We got a lead when Sienna Hutton, also known as Stephanie Walters, was washed up on Cala Comte beach with your new product line in her pocket. The EDEA are coordinating the operation to find your factory. It's as simple as that.'

'Well, well, the bird sings. It is true that I am to ecstasy what Willy Wonka is to chocolate. It is, however, also true to say that I have fallen out of bed with a certain Mexican drug cartel. As a consequence, we have been anticipating a visit from an assassin, dubbed El Cartero, the postman. It has made me a little nervous.'

Pago ran his tongue over his top lip and tweaked his right nipple ring. It was always the right one that itched.

'Pornography is just so mainstream now. When I first started, it was all black and white photography, brown paper bags, and tons of imagination. Now everyone's selling gynaecological textbooks and the bottom's dropped out of the market. There's absolutely nothing out there that hasn't been done. Free web porn has killed the business. Just log on and jerk off. Still got to do something for a living, haven't we?'

Pago rose from the stool, and was handed a razor-sharp, Japanese fugu knife. Its purpose was to slice away the face, beak, and poisonous tetrodotoxin guts of the deadly puffer fish while it was still alive, gagging for breath. A little vivisection did produce some exquisite sashimi, though. Pago stroked the polished bamboo handle and sat down again, changing the subject.

'Mr Bell, the rocket launcher concealed in the boot of your car is an amusing toy, supplied by the Americans, I suppose. You certainly gave my pilot a fright.'

Kadic handed Pago a glass jar, which he held in front of Bell's face. Bell could make out the crushed remains of the Manduca moth biobot.

'One of yours? The CIA, no doubt,' mused Pago, checking his Rolex.

'Time to rejoin the party, eh? Mr Bell, you are a professional who knows very well that his life is over. Death by one thousand cuts. It is a hideous way to perish. Even a puffer fish feels great pain, but the torment that you will suffer at the hands of my torturers will be beyond human imagination.'

Sienna was released from her bindings, frog-marched away under guard, and the room was quickly vacated.

Bell was now alone, still bound in the dentist's chair.

While they partied, he would be saying his prayers. In an hour or so, they would be back to turn him into chicken strips.

***

Kadic secretly questioned the wisdom of not vivisecting this EDEA agent right away. Operatives like Bell should be under close guard at all times. He should have hobbled him with the iron bar. Too late now. Lamentably, the elusive El Cartero was still unaccounted for.

Or was he?

Bell seemed to have a Russian doll's worth of legends at his disposal. The EDEA back-story was ingeniously plausible but probably a switch-sell. He would advise his boss accordingly, and prove it after the gaiety was over. How many shreds of human flesh in a plastic bucket would it take? He would just have to tough it out upstairs, with a glass of champagne, for an hour or two.

***

Bell coolly assessed his situation and tested all the bonds. His toes hurt like hell and the blood loss worried him. He tried to lever his whole torso up from the seat to wrench the backrest out of its socket, but to no avail. There was virtually no slack in his bindings.

He did notice that the right-hand armrest had a slight amount of give. It was the only thing to go on.

He imagined it was mounted on a steel prong and anchored into place. He vigorously tested the play again. Sure enough there was a little more give in it.

Bell rocked his arm back and forth, then forcefully snapped the armrest forward again. It skidded another couple of clicks. He was really aching now, joints and sinews jarred with each colossal effort. He took a deliberate rest of two minutes, and focused on the undoubted outcome that it would snap clean off next time. He visualised it clearly in his mind.

Time to say a prayer.

Bell inhaled a deep lungful of air and exploded all his chi into the armrest, just as Danny Wilson had taught him. This time, the armrest catapulted off the steel prong.

He quickly unbuckled his head, left arm, and legs. Bell's spirit soared as he looked around the room for anything useful. The Japanese fugu knife was just lying there. Now it was in the back of his CKs.

Lucky, lucky.

He glanced up at the ceiling, and noted the trap-doors which connected to Pago's office on the floor above.

He was just about to run for it, when he spotted a slim metal briefcase pushed up against the wall. It was surprisingly heavy but he decided to take it.

He opened the door a couple of inches and the alarm sounded, just as it had done on Monday night.

Bell could hear guards running down distant staircases to muster points, and the corridor pulsed with blinding strobe units. He guessed that no one would use the lifts during emergencies, so he sprinted down the corridor and stabbed the call button.

Up or down?

Bell plumped for down. Level B4, the lift doors opened and he ran to the MDMA factory entrance, dead-ahead.

Technicians, in protective suits, were still filing out through the airlock to attend roll call on one of the upper levels.

He darted into the empty locker-room.

It smelt of contamination, sweat, and talcum powder. He quickly pulled on a discarded singlet, overalls, trainer socks, white rubber boots, and a dinky laboratory cap. From now on he wouldn't be dripping blood with every step. The fugu knife fitted snugly in one of the smock pockets.

The lab get-up would stop him freezing to death, at least. There were some sweets, a screwdriver, and a ten euro note in another pocket. Sort of useful.

He emerged back into an empty corridor. The plan was to hide in the depths of the factory until the emergency was over, and then make an escape. The radiation exposure badge, clipped to his lapel, gave him an inkling of what he might find in there.

He made it through the airlock, and could feel the sudden change in temperature, caused by icy-clean air pouring down from the overhead vents. The artificial ceiling was low, but the place was massive and went off in all directions. As he headed deeper into the factory he passed various production and storage facilities, and then a series of individual laboratories. Each was fronted by thick, clear glass and a lockable, airtight door.

One, in particular, caught his attention, its spotlights blazing brightly in the gloom.

Bell peered through the vacuumed, triple-ply window, and digested what was laid out before him. A red LED display was mounted upon a large cigar-shaped object. The static line read '24:00:00 06:08 SATURDAY'.

Underneath, he saw what must be the time now: '04:51:14 05:08 FRIDAY'…and counting. Tenths of a second whistled past in a crimson blur.

Monitoring equipment on castors trailed wires into the front end of the pointed metal tube. At its base were battered and misshapen tail fins. He knew immediately what he was looking at. The decal on the nose-cone simply read 'USAF'.

Better get the serial numbers for later.

If there was going to be a later.

16 The eyes of Anubis

5th August – 4:55am Friday.

The workbench was strewn with printouts and flow diagrams. A large map of Ibiza hung on the wall. Dos Lunas was pinpointed as the epicentre of a series of concentric rings, which radiated outwards. Someone had shaded the inner rings in red crayon, and scribbled the expression '6.5 m/t' in big letters.

Bell deduced that it meant a yield of 6.5 megatons, to be produced by the thermonuclear device which was standing right next to him. It looked like the missile had been specially rigged to detonate while in a stationary, prone position. That feat had required incredible expertise.

A Geiger counter clucked sporadically nearby, registering alpha and gamma particles emitted from Kranz's stash of the radionuclide Radium 226. The detector measured the pulses erratically in millisieverts, indicated by a twitching hairline needle.

The B28 RI hydrogen bomb straddled a specially-made wooden trestle, on directional wheel-bogies. Its nose-cone had been partly removed to gain access to the naughty bits. Dozens of coloured wires, identified by paper tags, led into the open front panel, and out to separate control monitors and power units. Anti-tampering circuitry had to be assumed. Close up, the casing was battered, scratched, and corroded. It had suffered extensive oxidisation, testament to the month it had spent lying on the seabed, which hadn't done it any favours.

Bell was acutely aware that by being in this room he was probably being irradiated. It looked as though the whole set-up had been cobbled together in a hurry, but by someone who really knew their stuff. It would explode on cue in forty-three hours' time with no further human involvement.

A laser dot traced the back wall for a split second. He was not alone.

Armed guards had entered the factory to conduct a systematic search. Bell ducked down, and crept out of the lab into the open. Keeping low, he headed for the outer factory wall to buy some time. The annoying squeak of his rubber boots was thankfully masked by the noise of the air conditioning. But not for long. The beneficial fog of sound sadly fell silent, and now you could hear an ecstasy tablet drop.

A loud hailer sang out.

'Mister Bell, please come out with your hands up.'

The guards, well experienced in urban house-to-house combat, fanned out. Luckily, the factory was just so much bigger than the upper levels; no one would ever have guessed. Pago had taken advantage of the vast maze of Phoenician catacombs lying undiscovered under Dos Lunas. He'd hollowed out great sections of it to build his secret factory complex.

It was an act of criminal genius.

Bell's toes still hurt like hell, almost as bad as his stomach. Was it the blows he'd sustained earlier or just aching hunger? The last thing he'd eaten was a king prawn, dipped in Romesco sauce, a long time ago. The toes rubbed nastily inside his sweaty rubber booties, which he guessed were filling up with gooey, blood plasma.

The goons were well trained, cleverly closing the trap. Bell was now at the back wall, with nowhere to go. It was a bitch being unable to get the gun case open. Bell visualised a MAC-10 with suppressor lying idle inside.

If he got any chance to fight, it would have to be hand-to-hand combat and the taste of Japanese cold steel.

Now he could see traces of the original catacomb workings and the steel struts designed to shore up the ancient excavations. No place to hide. He found himself standing next to a steel door like you'd find in a submarine bulkhead.

He ignored the no-entry symbol and levered it open. They were almost upon him now, carmine dots of laser light criss-crossing every surface in the poor light. Bell worked out that there were three of them. They uttered no sound and moved like phantoms.

The clang of Dario's case on the door lip advertised his precise location. He heard running in his direction. He had to act quickly. Peppery dust arrested his nostrils, as he slammed the heavy door behind him. A low-wattage bulb illuminated a row of powerful torches on a recharger stand. Also on offer were laminated catacomb maps, but no balls of string.

Bell grabbed one of each and raced off into the unknown. After twenty yards, the tunnel divided into two. He was already being followed, and had no chance to navigate using the vague diagram sketched out on the card.

Bell took the left-hand tunnel and kept running. The arched ceilings ran in a straight line and, occasionally, he glimpsed sequences of strange symbols carved into the passing rock. Bright light was following him, and it was getting closer. He could hear the determined foot falls pounding behind him, and the odd bullet shot from a hand gun which pocked the ancient walls in vain.

Another fork. Bell took a right and ran faster, but they were still on his tail. He was breathing hard now, hampered by the case, but he was unwilling to discard it. He kept the torch facing dead ahead, desperate to widen the gap. He sensed that only one goon remained on his tail, who continued to fire hopeful shots.

Bell was surprised to run into a clearing, like a circular chamber, which had five tunnels running off it. The exits were equally spaced and triangles of skulls rose from the dusty floor against the available wall space up to chest height. Rows of femurs hung down from the centre of the ceiling on copper wires, like tubular bells.

No time to hang around to marvel at the ghoulish spectacle. This was an opportunity. In a flash, he ran into the third exit to the left, and stopped dead after twenty yards with his torch extinguished. Just as he did so, he sensed that someone had entered the chamber. Bell distinctly heard the word 'Jesus!' uttered in horrified surprise.

Surely now this guy would give up and turn back? Bell waited in the darkness, hanging on to the slightest sound, his mouth bone-dry with tension. He prayed that Pago's man would call it a day and fuck off.

Unfortunately, the goon donned his night vision goggles, and correctly identified Bell's exit choice. No need for running now, stealthy footfall and a technological advantage. Bell ducked and bolted as the laser dot illuminated his shoulder. More tiresome bends and curves deeper and deeper into the uncharted catacombs. Although he was near to exhaustion, he just had to keep going, refusing to give up.

You could get lost down here.

The rough-hewn tunnels all at once became larger, and Bell noticed a change in the gradient. The rock walls gave way to huge, geometrically-cut slabs of granite and carefully-fitted cladding. A stone archway appeared, constructed of a massive stone lintel and interlocking verticals. He hared up some steps, almost retching with the exertion, and came face-to-face with a pink, granite pedestal supporting a model sailing boat with exquisite, miniature figurines.

Bell sank down behind it, as another bullet whizzed past and then another exploded the priceless maritime antiquity into pieces. The metallic clatter of magazine-changing was audible nearby, forcing Bell to break cover and climb even more stairs at the end of the passageway.

A large temple opened out in front of him, and he gingerly negotiated a narrow walkway, with a deep pit each side, towards an altar. Next to it stood a massive incense burning vessel and a dark statue, on a plinth, of a wild dog-type creature. He glimpsed a mural inlaid with gold leaf, depicting a procession of three Egyptian boats. The boat in the middle was the largest, carrying the pharaoh.

There was a flicker of light behind him and yet another bullet whistled past. Bell killed the torch. The footsteps were getting closer and they entered the room, just as Bell took cover behind the plinth. The goon stopped at the threshold and sprayed the room with a full magazine of AK47 rounds, shattering valuable artefacts into smithereens, and desecrating walls covered in ancient hieroglyphs.

Then silence.

Bell had the fugu knife ready and kept absolutely still. His overalls made a scriffling noise, even if he moved just a fraction.

'Here's Johnny,' the guard taunted, in a husky voice.

Bell remained silent, curled up tight, clutching an earthenware dish he'd found.

'Where are you, my pretty?'

Bell had only one viable idea: lob the dish across the room in the darkness, blind the guy's night goggles with the halogen torch, rush him, and plunge the fugu knife in up to the hilt.

Could work.

The dish arced its way through space, as Bell raced across the stone floor ready to drive the bamboo handle home. The goon had easily regained his composure from the pathetic ruse, had been completely untroubled by the torch light, and now had his semi-automatic levelled at Bell's gut.

It had been a last desperate effort.

He was five strides short of nailing this tenacious goon, who was going to use Bell's nipples for target practice.

It was all over.

The goon maintained a steady aim, produced a cigarette, and started to laugh.

'You're a slippery bastard!' he rasped, stamping the floor with his combat boot.

In an instant, the black basalt stone before the plinth gave way, and the goon disappeared in a cloud of dust. Bell warily crawled round the edge on all fours and recovered his torch. The Egyptian mantrap was a cleverly tapered shaft, five metres in depth. The goon had landed on cruel barbs, anchored into the base, and his body hung there motionless, like a broken bird. The night goggles were still switched on, almost torn off his head.

Bell leaned over the edge. He had been killed instantly, one spike protruding a clear foot out of his rib cage. Bell shone the light over the body which revealed a powerful torch, handgun, an AK47, and some other useful stuff which was tantalisingly close. If he could retrieve this kit, including the night goggles, he could work his way back to the factory.

In the meantime, Pago would assume that Bell and one of his men had been lost in the tunnels. But what if they had welded the door shut, or booby trapped it, or were at this very minute releasing nerve gas into the catacombs to make sure that he was definitely finished? The bomb would settle it one way or the other.

Bell brushed the speculation aside.

He studied the stones carefully. The ones his pursuer had stepped upon were not stone slabs at all: they had been deviously constructed with a lattice of wooden strips and papyrus, and some kind of lime plaster mixed with soot, to mimic all the other blocks. Ingenious. Bell carefully checked every other slab nearby. Best to avoid any other Punji sticks that had been waiting millennia to get their man.

Bell moved up a level, through another stone portico, into a chamber containing a statue of Anubis. A granite table was laid out with canopic jars, unguents, implements, and pages of hieroglyphic text. There were dozens of exquisite gold charms ready for binding inside the folds of muslin, as the mummy was prepared. An inscription, indecipherable to Bell, proclaimed: *'He who removes my treasures shall meet death'.*

An embalming room, no doubt about it. Definitely all the paraphernalia needed to get someone off to the afterlife.

Looked like they hadn't got round to doing it. A hooked rod made out of bronze and a flint knife caught Bell's attention.

So, an underground Egyptian temple. The Phoenicians were known to have colonised Ibiza in the early days, but the Egyptians? Wasn't the western Med a bit of a hike from the Nile Delta?

Bell checked the power level on his torch which registered eighty percent depletion. He quickly needed a length of rope, so decided to sacrifice the top half of his lab smock to make strips, cutting it quickly with the fugu knife. The fabric was tough and would do the job well. It just had to be long enough to reach the dead goon. Add a hook and it would be a bit like playing on the lucky-dip machine at the end of the pier.

Bell frantically plaited the strips. The light was now losing its intensity and he needed to hurry. Armed with a good five metres of home-made rope, he knotted the embalmer's rod to the end.

Time to go fishing.

He raced back into the smaller chamber, and managed to stub his toe in the process. Soddit! He screamed out as he let the line down over the edge, the hook twirling annoyingly. The beam of his failing torch illuminated the suspended corpse. He aimed for the woven loop of the goon's torch first, the hook now dangling just a few inches above it.

Locked on!

A sharp yank should unclip it from the guy's utility belt, and up we come. As Bell struggled to hold position, the torch power indicator entered the red zone. Without further warning, the white light turned orange and faded to nothing.

Pitch darkness. Hold your nerve.

He pulled firmly on the line but it wasn't happening right. He tried to memorise the exact position of each lucky-dip object. If only he could get the torch.

Concentrate…careful now.

A firm tug and reel it in.

Yank!

But the tension had gone, and he heard the metal implement clang sickeningly at the bottom of the shaft.

Bell gulped back the despair. Those items could have saved him! He turned away from the pit and felt his way back to the embalming room, where the gun case and the knife were waiting for him.

He shivered in the darkness, partly from fear and partly because he now had only a thin singlet to cover his torso. The cold sweat from his fruitless efforts accentuated the creepy chill enveloping him. He felt a little relief to touch the gun case and his trusty knife again, like meeting up with two old friends.

Bell considered what to do next. He knew that there were about forty-two hours before the bomb detonated, and he would be taken with it if he stayed here. The proximity of the nuclear blast would probably bring down the roof of this undiscovered tomb. Without a source of light, he was never going to find his way back. He hugged his precious items for comfort.

The events of the past week whistled past: Sienna, Tracy, the Marines, Becky, then Judy, London, England. He would never see any of them ever again.

Bell thought of his own cherished dreams and aspirations. A crisp October morning in Sussex, where he would visit his own tract of prime woodland, shafts of sunlight piercing the trees. Cutting logs with a chainsaw, his Landrover parked nearby, and his two dogs rooting through the damp carpet of fallen leaves. Then a drive to a local pub for a pie and a pint, the open fire going in the blackened hearth, surrounded by re-pointed brickwork.

Bell smiled to himself ruefully. It was not to be. He was now marooned on Someday Isle. Thomas Bell MIA. Missing in action on his first mission.

The gulp of panic came up from his gut like cold sick. The dawning realisation that he would suffer a chilly and lonely death. He would never see the sun rise again. Game over.

He edged back up towards the polished, black marble statue, and in a sitting position drew up his knees. Anubis, the god of death watched over him, its eyes, fashioned from rock crystal, looked out into an eternal night, as black as pitchblende. He had to keep delirium at bay, along with thoughts of hunger and dehydration, if there was to be any hope.

A big if.

Bell fought to get a grip of his mental processes. He clasped his hands tightly over his face, holding back the urge to leap up from his resting place to scream for help. Bell drew strength from his MIX training. He controlled his breathing, calmed his mind, and systematically revisited everything he had been taught.

Bell analysed the possible outcomes. One: he would simply die here from either starvation or the explosion. Two: he would find his way back to the factory by complete fluke, groping in the darkness. He would then escape or be shot on sight. Three: he cracked the combination of the gun case and, if it contained ammunition, he would shoot his brains out. Bell mulled over whether he would put the gun up to the roof of his mouth or to his temple. It might be the last decision he ever made.

Four: There was another way out of here.

Bell considered the most optimistic option, number four.

He needed vision, light and warmth.

He needed fire.

Hadn't he seen braziers mounted on all the walls? He guessed that they still contained inflammable bitumen. There were plenty of wooden objects lying around, and maybe some viable tree resin.

Of course! The flint knife he had seen earlier. Striking it with the steel fugu knife he should be able to create a tantalising shower of sparks.

Producing an ember was one thing, he needed some tinder which would burn easily. His own hair perhaps? He had been well trained to make fire with a bootlace bow and some pieces of wood. No problem. Making it happen here in total darkness was too much.

It was hopeless.

He sagged to the ground in despair.

The silence and the dark were akin to a sensory deprivation chamber in which his mind was starting to play tricks on him. He thought he'd heard something scurry across the polished marble floor and stop. Was it an echo or a giant scarab beetle? Bell jolted and shuddered, cradling the smooth bamboo handle of the fugu knife against his chilled body for comfort. A number of deep strikes to his own abdomen would still mean a slow, excruciating end.

How about his wrists, instead? Wasn't that better done in a hot bath, with a tumbler of vodka and a handful of paracetamols?

He made a tough decision. Option three.

A bullet to the roof of his mouth would be quick and painless.

He hauled the flight case up on to his knees and got to work on the locks.

17 Hey, sister

Anna pushed Sienna into the dimly lit room and slammed the metal door shut. Two single beds were pressed up against opposing walls. A stainless-steel pan and basin occupied one of the corners of a bare, supermax-type prison cell. A familiar whimpering, like a lonely, unhappy child crying, was muffled by one of the duvets.

'Sis?'

Sienna's heart jumped, as she pulled back the cover to reveal her baby sister curled up in a ball.

'Amby, it's me!'

Sienna bent down and hugged her.

Amber sat up on the edge of the bed with a jolt and hung her head in despair.

'Oh, no! Not you as well!'

Sienna sank down next to her with her arm around her, cradling her head, wiping her tears.

'Tell me what happened.'

'Knowing that you and the police were out there looking for me gave me hope.'

'You're alive and we're together again. That's all that matters.'

'You don't understand what we've fallen into.'

'Don't worry, we'll get out of here.'

'I wish I could believe that. Our lives are over.'

Sienna stared into Amber's dark, sunken eyes, mascara running, her spirit broken. Her hair had been cropped and dyed a pure platinum blonde. She was dressed in just pants and a T-shirt.

'It's pretty basic in here.'

'Get used to it.'

Sienna stroked her arm, their heads pressed together, as Amber told her story in matter-of-fact monotone.

'We're not allowed anything in our rooms. We get dressed, go to makeup, and do our next shift.'

'Next shift?'

'Fraid so.'

'Your hair's very short.'

'We have to wear different wigs.'

Amber walked casually over to the tiny washbasin to clean her teeth and apply moisturiser.

'Don't they ever let you out of here to see the light of day and get some exercise?'

'There's a full lockdown on at the moment,' replied Amber.

'Of course, the alarms!...'

'All the filming and live sessions, done on the next floor down, go out over the web. Play-acted sex scenes for on-line subscribers. Girl-on-girl action. Bondage. Asphyxiophilia. That bitch Anna controls the whole thing.'

'At least you're alive.'

'If you can call it that.'

'What happened in the Labyrinth?'

Amber glanced at the cheap clock on the wall, and scuffed away her tears.

'I don't remember. You got away?'

'It's a long story.'

Sienna immediately had a vision of Tom, when she had first set eyes upon him in the clinic. She recounted how she'd been in a coma for six days and had been lucky to come out of it. Then the revelations about her stolen handbag, and the mix-up over her identity with another girl whom the bad guys were trying to trace and kill. The helicopter gunship, a car chase, and holing up in a creepy safe-house. All the while being protected by this wonderful guy from the embassy who was some sort of secret service agent.

'…then I seemed to be back in the Labyrinth waiting for you.'

'Me?'

'You were in the Ladies, I think. Next thing I know, I'm bound and gagged in a smoky room.'

Sienna told what she could remember. How she had screamed while Tom had been trussed in a chair right next to her. Then a sharp needle, being dragged away, and leaving him there.

'Maybe he's escaped?'

'I wouldn't count on it, sis. All the men who turn up here are tortured and killed pretty quickly.'

'Please don't say that.'

'We're on our own, kid.'

'There must be a way out.'

'Yeah, and I have to go soon.'

'There must be…'

'Anna is the boss, remember that.'

'Anything that could be used as a weapon?'

'You mean like this?'

Amber produced a nail file and a plastic butter knife.

'Hmm, so there are other girls kept along this corridor like us?'

'Yes. Before I arrived, two of them tried to escape.'

Sienna looked around the room, tapping the walls. No electrical wall sockets. Solid concrete floor.

'So, how did they get out?'

'They didn't live long enough to tell. Security was tightened, unfortunately for us.'

'What about that?'

Sienna looked up at the light well, a square chimney shaft which allowed some natural light to filter down from above.

'No chance, you'd need to be a spider monkey and there's a locked glass lid at the top.'

The door was opened abruptly and Amber was gone. Anatoly Kadic entered the room.

'You! Come with me,' he said, sharply.

She would have to do whatever it took to get through this. Was Tom still alive or had he been murdered hours ago?

They were now in the guards' quarters. Kadic led her into what looked like a cheap motel room, with a lounge area and a bathroom.

'Shower first. I like my pussy fresh,' he ordered.

Sienna unhinged her mind from what was happening. She was now somebody else. After showering quickly and leaving the water running, she tested the bolted windows. It was curiously uplifting to see bright sunshine streaming in. She lifted the toilet cistern lid quietly, looking for any sharp metal parts.

Nothing.

Kadic hammered the door.

'Enough!' he screamed.

Sienna walked into the bedroom, combing her wet hair. The place was full of pungent cigarette smoke and bursts of laughter from the TV. She threw the towel down on to the carpet, and stood naked before him. Kadic lay on the bed in his boxer shorts, his hair still in a ponytail, smoking yet another

Samsun. A thick gold chain nestled in a dense covering of chest hair with the consistency of wire wool. He zapped the remote and looked Sienna's alluring body up and down.

He smiled at her, secretly pleased that he hadn't cut all her toes off. It was comforting that her boyfriend was now sealed in the catacombs, with piles of grinning skulls for company. It was his sacred duty to take over where lover boy had left off.

Sienna saw that there was no gun in the polished leather holster hanging on the wooden bedpost. Shame. No chance of blowing the brains out of this hairy ape while he was drilling her. Kadic had noticed her furtive glance and nodded towards the door.

'One of my men is always outside. He won't mind, he'll get his turn later.'

Kadic got up and kicked his underwear away, revealing an equally hairy back. He hurriedly stubbed out the cigarette in a cheap foil ashtray. This girl was exceptionally pretty, with perfect skin. Good hunting. One of the perks of the job. He normally liked to wind a silk scarf tight around their necks, especially the ugly ones, but Anna would never forgive him. Anna wanted this girl for herself later on, and would more than likely drive an ice pick into the back of his neck if he interfered with her pleasure.

Girls will be girls.

Kadic twisted alongside her on the bed, breathing a mixture of fags, garlic, and coffee into her face. There was a hint of Spanish brandy in there somewhere, too.

'You love me, so you want to kiss me.'

Sienna's spirit now looked down upon her from the ceiling, watching herself caress this man's face, and kiss him eagerly. She thought of Tom, and packaged away the tenderness that they had enjoyed into a secret place, so that no one could touch it. She kept faith that he was still alive.

Now sitting astride her, Kadic squeezed her nipples and looked into her lovely face. Sienna's eyes opened wider than ever and looked up into his. She thought how nice her molester's eyes would look, with spikes driven in, all the way.

As Kadic screwed the girl, he mulled over the last tedious briefing session he'd had with Pago. Bell would die somewhere in those revolting tombs; a slow and lonely death. He was still not sure whether Bell was El Cartero, or an agent from the EDEA or whatever. Now he would never know.

All the important laboratory kit, including Pago's works of art, would be stowed on the Valhalla, in accordance with the departure timetable.

Pago had used the word 'we' throughout the session. The implication was that he, Anatoly Kadic, would still be on the payroll when all this shit was over. He was not so certain. The Apache was scheduled to evac him at 23:40 hours, a mere twenty minutes before the nuclear detonation. A bit tight. Very tempting to save a load of aviation fuel, and leave him marooned at Dos Lunas as the chain reaction kicked off.

Maybe an alternative disappearing act might be more reassuring: piss off early under his own steam.

One of the rigid-hulled inflatables with a full tank.

Run down to the beach, swim out, and fire it up.

After a one-hundred-kilometre dash, at full throttle, across to the Spanish mainland, a relaxing train journey back to Eastern Europe.

Like it.

He'd better get hold of the spare key.

18 **Money to burn**

5th August – 4:30am Friday.

Turning the combination tumblers with his thumb had steadied his nerves. The repetitive task provided Bell with a weird kind of solace in the darkness. His stomach stabbed with acid pains, all his muscles ached and his toes were still stinging.

He was running on empty.

Soon it would all be over and nothing would hurt any more. There were over seven hundred combinations on each side of the metal case, which he'd balanced across his knees. The case that Dario Hernandez had brought all the way from Mexico City.

He had started with the rightmost wheel, click one to nine. Then the second wheel, eventually the third wheel. It could take at least forty minutes each side to complete. He tried the latch after each incremental combination, visualising the numbers spinning round like a one-armed bandit. After twenty-five minutes, the left-hand latch opened.

Bell's spirit lifted a little.

Success would be a double-edged sword. The final, irreversible decision to pull the trigger on himself. He switched to the remaining latch with renewed energy. As well as everything else, his bum now hurt from sitting on the hard floor. He stood up for a moment to restore the circulation.

He got straight back to it. Despite feeling so fatigued, he had to ensure that he turned the tumblers accurately, otherwise he might skip that vital matching combination. Another fifteen minutes and the latch finally clacked open with a satisfying smack against the aluminium casing. Bell felt a sense of achievement; a small consolation prize.

He took a deep breath and pushed the lid open, expecting to trace the outline of a semi-automatic. Instead of gunmetal, all he could feel were flat plastic packets. He tore one open, smelling the new currency notes. If they were high denominations, at least he would die rich! He felt the first note carefully, like a blind man. No gun, no bullets, no quick method of dispatching himself.

Just piles of paper.

The solution hit him.

Flint plus fish knife plus paper currency equals fire. Bell folded the C-notes into zigzag, concertina shapes, and built a crumpled heap, ready. He started hacking at his hair with the razor-sharp flint knife, then scraped off some of his own pubic hair, for good measure. What the hell! He needed as much tinder as possible. Now he was all set. Bell made shooting stars by repeatedly striking the fugu knife against the flint.

Hack, hack, hack with the knife, producing a stream of sparks, blowing on to the mound. A red glow eventually appeared. Bell blew and blew, the smell of his burning human hair flooding his nostrils. He kept blowing until he was quite light-headed.

Bingo!

A burst of flame appeared. He placed the burning ball on to the stone floor and added more and more bank notes, as the flames grew in strength. In the flickering light, the hieroglyphs of racing chariots and warriors seemed to animate on the walls. Portraits of the US president Benjamin Franklin looked up at him momentarily and melted away.

He had quite an inferno on his hands, but it wouldn't last long. Tinder immediately required. He walked briskly through to the throne chamber. Any priceless artefact, that looked vaguely combustible, was scooped up. Sandals, combs, spoons, models of Nile barges, and painted figurines. He smashed up the pharaoh's wig box, an ornate stool, and a board game called 'sent', and ran back with armfuls of kindling to grow the flames into a roaring bonfire. After a couple of trips, he had a nice stockpile of wood.

It was an act of archaeological vandalism that was lamentable, but necessary. A journey to the kingdom of Osiris would have to keep. They could weigh his heart some other day. Bell knew it was important to get the fire temperature up, so that he could ignite the bitumen in the wall torches.

Once those guys were lit, they would last for hours and light up the whole place. As the embers were now glowing red hot, he placed four of the torches in the fire to get them started. Although the air was now filling with smoke, Bell could work out the size of the throne room, and identify various side rooms. Soon the whole temple was illuminated by lines of torches, secured in their wall sockets, the bitumen burning steadily.

It looked like someone had left in a hurry. No burial had taken place because the lid was still off the blue-basalt sarcophagus. It was empty. That would explain why there was so much stuff lying around. Even papyrus scrolls from the book of the dead were just strewn haphazardly around on the stone floor. Where was the dead pharaoh?

Over twenty corpses were piled high in one of the antechambers. They were fully dressed and the skulls had clearly been smashed open. Whatever had happened here would remain a mystery.

It was truly exhilarating to marvel at fire and light, with eyes he had thought would never see again. Three torches blazed brightly in the embalming room. In the main temple, there were two massive thrones and a decorative frieze going right around the room, in beautifully painted sections. Bell took a seat and surveyed all before him.

The backrest was decorated with a heavily gilded eye of Ra, the visible sun, giver of vitalising light and warmth. In front of him was a black marble table. He had placed the lead-lined flight case upon it, next to his trusty fugu knife and the screwdriver. The bag of sweets was long gone.

He estimated the time to be approaching noon on Friday 5th August.

Was there another way out of here?

There were apparent exits in all directions. Bell tried the first one and came to a dead end within ten metres. Then the next one, blocked by yet another pile of corpses, went nowhere. The bitumen would not last forever, and he would eventually be plunged into darkness again. He'd been dealt a lucky break and needed to capitalise upon it.

His search had drawn a blank. All he could do was sit on the throne and think. If he could find another brass hook, he might try the lucky-dip again. Scaling down the shaft was a non-starter, like falling headfirst down a dry well.

It was very smoky now; the pungent smog of burnt wood and tar was affecting his lungs. It reminded him how thirsty he was. He returned from the embalming room, empty-handed. All he'd been able to do was fill his pockets with gold charms. Not a hooked implement in sight. Bollocks!

Bell sat back on the throne again, taking in the images of Ra, Osiris, and the representations of the firmament. He couldn't do this forever.

The polished black marble statue of Anubis stared back at him. Were those blazing pupils, which flickered in the light of the torches, mocking his efforts? The god of embalming and burial, half man, half jackal, held him in its gaze, as he lay slumped there, racking his brains for a solution.

His eyes opened after a period of deliberation. He gradually noticed that there was a disturbance in the horizontal folds of acrid fumes. The location was diagonally across the room.

Behind a statue standing sentinel by a pillar, the smoke was being sucked clean away. He traced his way carefully round the smooth stone with his palm, then squeezed through a vertical slit in the block-work, armed with a burning torch. After a few narrow steps, he illuminated what looked like a long passageway with a rising incline. The smoke was floating steadily up the tunnel! A vent on the surface was creating a draught, or so he hoped.

He returned to the throne and collected his things. He'd calculated that the case contained well over a million dollars in one-hundred-dollar bills. He'd burned two hundred thousand dollars of it. In time, the firebrands would go out one by one, to plunge this place back into darkness for the rest of eternity, unless Pago's bomb was detonated. He double-checked that he still had the scrap of paper with the USAF serial numbers on it. Bell shivered, as if enveloped by a malevolent presence.

It was time to go.

Laden with his possessions and three spare torches, he commenced a hopeful walk into the unknown. He trudged for a long while down the passageway, rising a single step every now and again. The flames from the braziers traced the ceiling, as his plastic booties scuffed painfully along the ancient stone slabs. He sensed that he was nearing the surface, but couldn't be sure. Presently, the stones became rougher and smaller, and the passageway came to an abrupt halt.

Shit! It was a dead end!

Bell felt a pang of alarm until he looked up. He had not needed to use the other two torches, so he wedged one in the rock and lit another, with one to spare.

The sheer, vertical shaft offered a tantalising pinprick of light, high above. Oval foot-and-hand holds, carved into the limestone at regular intervals, indicated what to do next.

Bell prepared for the ascent.

He used his faithful piece of home-made rope to strap the metal case to his back. As he climbed, he permitted himself the occasional upward glance. The light source gradually got bigger as the tarry smoke rose up with him. He sneezed and had to hang on tight. Don't lose your grip! He dared a downward glance at the firebrands still burning, a long way below. He just had to hold his nerve all the way up.

A few more steps and Bell became gradually aware that he could hear music, if he wasn't mistaken. It was 'Stairway to Heaven' being played live, but not by Led Zeppelin. It occurred to him that he might actually be dead, and was being spirited aloft to the kingdom of Osiris, after all.

As he reached the top, the space got a lot smaller and narrower. Tree roots had begun to appear. It was akin to potholing, where ideally you needed baby-oil to squeeze successfully through. Bracing himself, he unhitched the metal case from his back, and pushed it ahead through the jagged aperture.

With a few new scratches, Bell crawled out over the edge into sweet, fresh air and the heat of the day. He collapsed on to his back in a dappled glade, behind what looked like an old wooden summerhouse. He rested for a moment as arrows of sunlight pierced his eyes. He had made it. 'Stairway to Heaven' was still playing; it was a good cover version.

'If there's a bustle in your hedgerow,

don't be alarmed now,

it's just a spring clean for the May queen'

Bell came out into the open, eyes blinded but operational enough to see two burly security guards racing towards him. The music was quite loud now. Bell had stumbled into lush gardens, full of wedding guests, and there was a huge white marquee. A helicopter buzzed overhead. The combination lock numbers had been committed to memory. As the guards approached, he spun the rotating dials of Dario's money box. This wasn't the right place to slit their throats, or spill their guts with his beloved fugu knife. He'd just have to blag his way out of this one.

'Look, he's got a camera case! We'll have that for a start!'

'Who are you? Hello magazine or OK!?'

'I'm an archaeologist. I was working in the Phoenician catacombs, and I got lost.'

The security men howled with laughter.

'Prove it!'

'I've lost all my equipment, I'm afraid,' smiled Bell.

'So, Hola! magazine. You'll have to come with us and hand over all your film.'

Bell stood his ground, bedraggled in his ripped, plastic shorts, with his Calvin Kleins showing through. He doggedly held on to Dario's metal case, refusing to comply.

Their move.

The first security guy came at Bell to relieve him of the camera case. Bell side-stepped as the bouncer tried to lay a punch on him. Bell easily twisted the guy's wrist and kneed him hard in the face, crushing his nose. The guy squealed, and fell to the ground clutching the bleeding damage.

'Your call,' said Bell, stepping back.

The other bouncer was about to attack, but Bell was ready for him, primed to strike like a Durango scorpion. These security guys were both overweight and out of condition. They were more accustomed to manhandling disturbances on a dance floor. The second guy realised that the San Miguels he'd drunk earlier had shaved valuable milliseconds off his reaction time. This guy had skills. It would dictate an outcome where his balls would end up lodged in his mouth. He hung back and swallowed his pride...not his testicles.

The one-sided combat spectacle had swiftly drawn a crowd, armed with champagne glasses. Bell was now surrounded by a semi-circle of curious guests, who were taking care to maintain a safe distance.

Johnny Lazzara, the lead guitarist of Para Noya, stepped forward, his new bride, a vision in white, hanging on to his arm. The music had stopped mid guitar-riff. All the guys from the tour support band, Aerothon, who had been playing the Led Zep numbers, came over as well, to check out the action.

'You gate-crashed my wedding, pal,' said Johnny, with measured authority.

'I'm an archaeologist, see...'

Bell remembered the magic charms and baubles he'd stuffed into his pockets. He produced a handful of gold ankhs and amulets. Lazzara homed in on the most exquisite piece, made from eastern desert gold. Intricate craftsmanship always drew his attention. He recognised priceless Egyptian artefacts when he saw them. He was very astute with his money, royalties and investments; unlike the lead singer, Michael Kroll, whose reputation for excess was legendary.

'I've discovered a tomb back there, underground.'

Johnny glanced up at the helicopter.

'So, you're Indiana Jones, not a pap?'

'Yeah, an Egyptian tomb. I came out through an air shaft, hidden behind your summerhouse.'

Bell had convincingly made his case.

'Everybody's trying to get pictures of my wedding. Meet the wife!'

Bell took a good look at Mrs Lazzara. A doe-eyed blonde smiling at him excitedly. He held on to the metal case and stood there resolutely, showing off his bruised and battered body, awaiting judgement.

Johnny smiled at Bell.

'Ok, I believe you. So long as you stay to celebrate our sacred union. You look like you could use a drink. May I keep this?'

'All yours,' said Bell.

'Hey, someone get this thirsty guy a glass! You can clean yourself up inside and then join the reception. BJ will look after you and get you some fresh clothes. I'm Johnny Lazzara, by the way.'

As if Bell didn't know.

He held out his hand and Bell shook it.

'Bell. Thomas Bell.'

'He's cool,' said Lazzara, turning to the remaining security guard.

A silver tray with glasses was pushed though the throng and Bell took a champagne flute. After hours without water, it was the last thing he needed, but it was still fluid. They walked into the marquee where he was presented with chilled canapés. Tiger prawns laced with caviar.

Just can't get away from them.

Big Jackie, a buxom redhead and Para Noya gofer, came over and took Bell by the arm. She started gabbling immediately.

'Nice to meet you. The way you handled that arsehole. Wow! I'm impressed! He's been hitting on me all day. You'd think we groupies have no standards. Love your hair by the way, kinda punk apocalypse!'

Bell glanced down at BJ's long black fingernails and then into her star-struck eyes, made up with black eyeliner.

'Yeah, he did need a slap.'

They headed into the main building.

'Here's a spare ID pass, help yourself to the buffet. I'll give you a blow job later if you like, but do have a shower first,' she giggled.

'My real name is Mandy but I still give good head.'

Mandy admired Bell's lean, muscled physique. She was determined to live up to her nickname and give this cool guy the best one ever.

'Mandy, I need a first aid kit and some water. See these?'

'Ugh, how did you do that?!'

'Never mind, I just hope the nails will grow back.'

'The best shower-room is on the top floor. You'll find a medicine cabinet on the wall. There are no clothes as such, just help yourself to the band wardrobe. This villa has been rented by the record company for the week, so do whatever you like. Enjoy!'

Bell made his way along the landing and tried a couple of doors. The third room revealed Danny Borrell, Para Noya's sybaritic drummer, with a couple of babes on a king-size bed. They were all naked, in various states of penetration. Two video cameras on separate tripods were recording all the action.

Bell couldn't help noticing that one of the young ladies had a lubricated hand inserted well past the entrance to the other girl's vagina. They were all so stoned, that they'd barely noticed that someone had burst in. Bell had recognised Borrell instantly, the madman on percussion. Bell pressed the door shut and left them to it.

He progressed further down the corridor, and saw a door with a hastily made label marked 'wardrobe'. Bell was presented with rack upon rack of stage costumes for Para Noya's 'Blowout' world tour.

They were obviously using this villa as the base for their final tour performance, that night, at Ibiza Rocks, in San Antonio. All they had was leather, spandex, chiffon, ripped T-shirts, and impractical footwear. Bell grabbed the likeliest looking gear in its bar-coded plastic covers, and headed off for a much-needed shower. A cover version of Champagne Supernova was now drifting up from the gardens.

Bell stripped off the remains of his boffin trousers and got the water flowing. He stood in the steaming glass shower cabinet washing off all the grime and discomfort. The jets of hot water drilled into his body, as they rinsed off the copious lather of passion fruit shower gel. He luxuriated in a cascade of revitalising pleasure for a further five minutes, then got out. His toes still stung like hell, and he dried them carefully with a fluffy towel. Plasters and antiseptic cream, looted from the extensive medicine cabinet would have to suffice. He then relaxed for a moment with a cool drink, and knocked back a couple of Co-codamols, for good measure.

There was what Bell expected to be an unwelcome knock at the door. Far from it.

'Room service!'

BJ walked in and handed him another glass of champagne. She locked the bathroom door behind her, and had her top off in a trice. A sucker-mouthed river lamprey was on the loose.

'What, here?'

The rest of her kit followed in short order.

***

Bell got dressed into an absurd, sequinned stage outfit, and was about to head downstairs to the party when he heard a desperate, agonising wail coming from further down the passageway. It was followed by something being smashed hard against a wall. He trotted down to the very end of the corridor and burst open the locked door.

Michael Kroll, the lead singer of Para Noya, was sitting on the edge of a four-poster bed, with a length of rubber pipe wound tightly around his left arm. He held a hypodermic, filled with brown fluid, ready to inject, after a frantic hunt for a suitable vein. Bell stared into Kroll's tearful, bloodshot eyes.

The Para Noya frontman was about to commit suicide. The screaming fans would not get to see Kroll's blond hair, majestic lips, and taut, muscled body strutting across the stage ever again. He would perish in a flash of white light, in this white Ibizan heat. Despite the state he was in, Michael still managed to look startled.

On the low glass table in front of him, Bell could see a dozen ampoules of smack, two neat lines of coke, a razor blade, blister packs of Paloma Azul, a lighter, a bent spoon, and a tall glass of whisky. Further to Kroll's left, away from the immediate matter in hand, lay a Beretta, a box of tissues, a tin of Red Bull, and an open bottle of Jameson's. Bell assessed that Kroll had definitely assembled the necessary kit to complete the job.

'I thought I'd fuckin' locked it!' growled Kroll.

Kroll positioned his cigarette on the edge of the glass, without disturbing the lines of la blanca, and clumsily picked up the Beretta. He flicked the safety off easily enough and pointed the firearm at Bell's head.

'Leeme alone! Who the fuck are you, anyway?!'

19 **Para Noya**

5 th August, Friday.
'I'm a curious gatecrasher,' smiled Bell.

'Leeme alone and getouta here!' screamed Kroll, still waving the Beretta menacingly. Kroll's eyes glazed over listlessly, losing all concentration.

Bell was next to him in a flash, and smacked him hard across the face, sending the hypodermic needle full of heroin flying across the room.

'If you're doing what I think you're doing, you're not doing it!'

Kroll bellowed, and tried to run away on all fours, but Bell kicked the rock star expertly in the gut. He curled up like a mewling foetus. Bell pinned Kroll's left arm back into a half nelson, forcing his head back by gripping his extensive mane of corkscrew hair. Kroll squealed with an unmistakable falsetto. Bell held him tight and shouted directly into his ear.

'You're not topping yourself, you got that?! I've invested too much in your fucking music, okay?!'

Bell released him in a heap. Kroll's face lay buried in the carpet, sobbing and coughing. Bell fixed them both a glass of water, using the tall toothbrush tumblers from the bathroom, and sat down against the wall next to him.

A few minutes later, Kroll pulled himself upright, panting and clutching his stomach. Bell stared into his streaming eyes, centred by jet-black, dilated pupils. Kroll attempted to wipe the trails of snot leaking from his nose with his right hand. He stank of booze, sweat, and unhappiness. He ran both hands through his blond locks, and glared venomously at Bell.

'Who the fuck are you?!'

'You're a sorry piece of shit. Looks like I saved some column inches.'

Kroll lunged forward to punch Bell in the face. Bell elegantly avoided the childlike effort, as Kroll's knuckles grazed the wall. Bell gripped the throat which had sung on one hundred million Para Noya albums. First, 'Panphobia', then the incredible 'Inde Sexualis', closely followed by 'Nex Astrum'.

Bell now held a pair of bulging eyes close to his. Foul dog-breath struggled up from those famous lungs, past the voice box that he was trying his hardest not to crush with his immensely powerful grip.

'Try that again, Michael and it'll really hurt next time. I do this for a living.'

He released his grip and Kroll fell back clutching his throat, rubbing his Adam's apple.

'…Bu…but who are you?'

'Let's pretend that I'm your guardian angel. I'm in a hurry, but we can talk for a while. My name's Thomas Bell.'

Kroll settled next to him without any further coercion. He was dressed in stained, white-linen trousers and a tight-fitting black T-shirt. He stared dead ahead at the balcony doors, while twisting a ring on his little finger which depicted a serpent swallowing its own tail. Bell rose from his seated position, and looked down at Para Noya's frontman. Kroll simply gazed vacantly into space, his mouth slightly open. It was a sad sight.

Bell turned and pointed back at him.

'Don't move, okay?'

But Michael Kroll wasn't going anywhere. The events of the last ten minutes had drained him of all of his energy. He sat like an uninhabited husk, paralysed by mental breakdown, a physical manifestation of their first album.

Bell retrieved the syringe full of junk and binned the sharp. He removed the highball tumbler, and bottle, of Jameson's Irish whiskey from the glass table-top, and swilled the contents away in the bathroom sink. Any remaining drugs and implements were scooped up into Signy Ericksen's Balenciaga designer bag.

The pharmacy now bulging out of the expensive holdall was enough to kill a rhinoceros. Bell retrieved the Beretta poking out from underneath the sofa. He flipped the safety back on, and checked the clip, admiring the techno-polymer grip of the brand-new handgun. He noticed a plastic carrying-case nearby, emblazoned with a motif of three arrows inside a circle. Jesus! Kroll had only just got it out of its box!

He opened it. A model 92FS, manufactured by Fabbrica d'Armi Pietro Beretta S.p.a. of Brescia in Italy. He ignored the handbook and put everything back where it belonged, including the silencer. It reminded him to retrieve his own gun, carefully hidden in a squalid alleyway, not far from the Labyrinth Club.

Bell sat down again, firmly pressed up against Kroll's bare shoulder. Only one item on the glass coffee table remained. A gleaming, heavy-duty stainless-steel bolt. Kroll saw Bell looking at it, but he chose not to speak. He knew that Bell knew what it was for. There were just so many ways to end it all.

Kroll had been struggling with his various addictions for some time, and had recently added chronic stomach pains to his list of troubles. He'd been charged with possession of cocaine, and had been banned from several airlines, most notably Cathay Pacific.

There'd been a handful of court cases for assaults and criminal damage, mainly in night clubs or hotels. Salacious tales of yoyo-knickered strumpets performing unusual sex acts. Stories of drug-fuelled threesomes filled the tabloids and the web. Kroll's appetite for sex, cocaine, booze, and sado-masochism, fuelled by Viagra and sex toys was insatiable. He was just as much cock off stage as on it.

Signy, his Danish supermodel girlfriend, had walked out on him six weeks earlier, halfway through the tour. Although she too was completely under the spell of Snow White, she had felt compelled to leave Kroll, in order to save her own career and her lucrative endorsement deals.

It had left Kroll truly isolated, and his nosedive into oblivion had accelerated. He was the brooding, smouldering, tousle-maned, groin-centred rock star rooted in the old school of rock. Surviving on a diet of champagne, cognac, and cheeseburgers. An unhealthy dabbling in the occult completed the picture, which had contributed sinister imagery and jargon to his most recent lyrics.

A recent worldwide newsflash had announced that Kroll had overdosed in Berlin. The papers had printed: 'Para Noya star feared dead', but the reports were exaggerated.

He'd somehow managed to invest part of his massive earnings in an eighteenth century manor house in Suffolk, which he rarely visited. It was used mainly to hold wild parties, and court disaster with late night pool drownings.

For all that, he was the soul and the spirit of Para Noya, capable of writing pulsing rock anthems like 'Satan Serenade'. It was well documented that Kroll could conjure up a hit on the back of an envelope, with the solitary help of a Casio keyboard. Bell could see a new song scribbled out by Kroll on a creased sheet of paper on the floor, entitled 'Jack Mama'. Here he was, pressed up against the man himself.

'I love your first album,' mused Bell.

'Panphobia…yeah,' Kroll replied, pensively.

'I always play it when I've got some serious driving to do.'

Bell thought of his Audi TTS, parked in an aircraft hangar at RAF Mildenhall.

'At twenty-six, I've had everything and everyone. Like they say, I've spent my money on girls, booze and drugs…the rest…'

'You can still party, Michael, but you don't have to commit suicide,' observed Bell, helpfully.

'We didn't touch drugs in the beginning. We used to just drink, fuck chicks, smoke cannabis, and take a few pills. Then, cocaine. It was like rocket fuel, man. My nose immediately knew what it had been put on this planet for. I railed my first coupla lines and I felt like Superman. It was like the best orgasm I'd ever had.'

'So…do something else for kicks.'

Kroll smiled for the first time.

'Like sex? I've screwed in excess of three hundred women. Sex has to be seriously kinky now. Dirty sex with dirty girls, the more the better.'

Kroll leaned over and casually picked up the steel bolt from the coffee table. He turned and stared at Bell.

'When it comes to sex, I've tried almost everything.'

'Yeah, well don't look at me, okay!'

They both broke out laughing, the kind of purgative release that Kroll needed so badly.

'Self-destruction is my way of combating fatigue and the futile joylessness of it all. I have no stop button.'

'Self-destruction is the ultimate self-gratification,' replied Bell.

'Okay, so I hate myself, and I just want to die in my own private Babylon of fame, wealth, and isolation. It's better to go out in a single puff of smoke, than to fade away. Get famous, get rich, and get laid, they told me.'

'But you're only twenty-six, Michael! Some people don't have a choice. Most folks don't have the luxury of knowing when they're going to die.'

'Yeah?'

'You have everything you could possibly desire.'

'So what?'

Kroll groaned suddenly, clutching his stomach in discomfort.

'Milk…quickly…the minibar's full of it!'

Kroll guzzled from the UHT carton and seemed a lot better. He kept another one next to him on standby. It was probably a stomach ulcer, but Bell decided not to go into that.

'You need a doctor. When did you eat last?'

Kroll started to sob again, a sudden mood swing back to the bottom of the pit.

'I can't stand it anymore. The intensity, energy, and creativity have all left me. I can't go on.'

'You're not alone.'

'Really?'

Kroll picked 'Jack Mama' up off the carpet, and petulantly tore the recently penned song into confetti.

Bell thought he would try another tack to hit home his message. It might flick a switch inside that tormented mind, the seed of recovery from the idea that life was totally pointless.

'You only get one chance as a speck of dust in this cosmos; are you sure you want to leave the party so early? It's not too late to stand back from the edge of the abyss.'

'Thanks. No one has ever spoken to me like that before. Maybe I'll think about it.'

Bell couldn't hang around here much longer. He might be able to save Kroll's life for the sake of his music collection, but he had bigger things to sort out.

He thought he could detect a glimmer of the old Michael Kroll, a diamond twinkle in the eyes, revealing the inner core that had made him a success in the first place. The golden aura, the quintessence of super-stardom.

Bell looked at his watch. 6pm.

He had worked out what had to be done, and got to his feet. Kroll looked up at him with a slight hint of sadness that his mentor was about to leave him.

'Thanks for not kicking me in the nuts, by the way. I won't forget what you've done for me.'

Bell was pleasantly surprised to hear Kroll referring to an action sometime in the future.

'A driver will take you back into town.'

'I expect you to be on stage at Ibiza Rocks. Just do it for me…please…I'm one of your greatest fans. I can't stay here and do the rehab thing with you. It's down to you, I'm afraid.'

'You know that I'm still going to kill myself, don't you?' replied Kroll.

After all the passionate and reasoned argument, it was the saddest thing to hear. Just another rock and roll suicide.

'See you in hell, then, if that's the way you want it.'

Bell strode to the door and was gone.

Kroll smashed the wall mirror, and selected a long shard of jagged glass. It glinted bewitchingly in the dying sunlight. He tested it on the cream sofa, slicing easily through the thick, polished hide.

Bell had overlooked the length of rubber hose that Kroll had been using as a tourniquet. Kroll smiled to himself. There were just so many ways to end it all. Kroll rubbed his left forearm and looked for a vein, wrapping the flex round as tightly as possible.

***

Much as Bell would have liked to have spent the rest of the day quaffing champagne and receiving blowjobs, he had things to do...people to kill.

He placed Dario's metal case next to him, as the seven series BMW took off. If he got out of this one, he could add its contents to his personal pension scheme. If someone took it off him, they could add it to theirs.

Bell used the journey time back to the Hotel Palmyra to have a think and fit the suppressor to Kroll's Beretta. He would shoot any of Pago's men on sight now.

***

Room 414. The door was ajar. It had been ransacked, and his luggage, including his encryptor, seemed to be long gone. Bell looked around the room, without touching anything. He peered down to the street through the net curtains. A Mercedes C-Class, with smoked glass, was parked up opposite, against the kerb.

Bell turned back to the doorway.

Becky was standing there, in the same pose she had adopted when standing naked in the bathroom doorway, nursing a Kleenex.

But this time, she had a black eye and other visible facial bruising. She smiled sheepishly and started crying, then ran into Bell's arms. He held her tight, and stroked her hair as she sobbed into his chest, just like a father would do with his teenage daughter. Her face was puffy and swollen, the skin tight. He couldn't help noticing the pathetic attempt to cover up the damage with concealer. Her teeth were all there, and thankfully, her nose hadn't been broken; she'd taken an unpleasant beating, nonetheless. Bell was glad that this plucky little lass, with a nice line in tonguing a guy's frenulum, hadn't come to any real harm.

He resolved to punish whoever had done it.

He wouldn't have long to wait. Becky continued to cling to him, weeping uncontrollably, unable to get the words out. Bell whispered gently into her ear.

'Come on, Becky, I'm here now. It was Lee, wasn't it?'

'He thrashed it out of me.'

Lee and three thugs stepped into the room, one with a baseball bat, the others with what looked like big knives stolen from the hotel kitchens. Becky shuddered and gripped Bell tighter.

He could do without this; he had important things to do.

It was the violent, well-organised crew who'd jumped Donnie Olsen that night outside O'Learys. No mistake. Maybe he could use some extra muscle.

'Well, well, the young lovers. Who are you, the fairy prince?' sneered Lee, eyeing up Bell's camp chiffon and spandex outfit.

'Appearances can be deceptive,' replied Bell.

'Don't hurt him, Lee!' begged Becky.

The four guys laughed and spread out. It was getting crowded in here. Becky broke away and ran to Lee.

'Lee, please don't hurt him!'

Lee threw her off roughly and she crashed to the floor, blubbering. He slammed the door shut, and turned his attention back to the dumb arsehole standing in front of him.

'I thought kickboxing was your thing,' said Bell.

'Not when I have something nice and juicy to carve up,' Lee replied.

'Do we frighten you?' leered Dave.

'You're fuckin' dead, mate!' warned Matt, slapping a baseball bat repeatedly into his palm.

Bell was sure that this thug had used that warning many times before. He could read the '*Made in Manchester*' tattoo on his right upper arm, the flexed muscle tightening the skin and distorting the nicely inked script. Bell was plainly looking like a victim, dressed in purple spandex, a short sequined jacket, and Signy's Balenciaga clutch bag, slung gamely over his shoulder.

'You're gonna bleed, boy. I'm gonna cut you up for porking my bird,' promised Lee in a controlled, menacing tone.

They all tensed themselves ready to rush this loser. Bell backed up towards the balcony doors, giving the impression that he was about to smash through the plate glass, and throw himself over the rail.

'You won't get away mate, unless you can fly. Maybe we'll give you the chance to spread your wings, like you spread Becky's legs.'

Despite their clear superiority in numbers, Lee was starting to feel nervous. This guy wasn't reacting quite right to the imminent prospect of blood and broken bones. People were normally shitting themselves by now, pleading for mercy, but this guy was just standing there, as cool as you like. Bell magically produced Kroll's Beretta, which he had secreted in the copious folds of rock and roll chiffon.

'Wow! A toy gun!' sneered Dave.

They all laughed.

'Go on, shoot then, arsehole!' giggled Matt, relishing the moment.

Bell fired twice into the mirror, which shattered into a million shards, and they all collapsed back against the wall in shock.

'Return my luggage and you'll live. I'm in a rush and I don't give a fuck.'

There was a deathly silence as they looked to Lee for guidance. Bell aimed the gun at Dave's head, Matt twitched and Bell fired again, smoke trailing from the suppressor.

'Try that again...please, and the next one will be between the eyes.'

'The luggage. You have ten seconds.'

'I...it wasn't us, it was some guys in suits, like...like men in black.'

'You're lying.'

Bell stepped closer and fired again, close to Lee's head. The others were mesmerised by the composure of the fairy prince, holding the gun as steady as a rock. They'd been threatening a professional gunman, a trained killer who would pop all four of them in the next minute, if he didn't get his stuff back. This guy must be some kind of gangland enforcer, although he didn't look it.

'I don't know what shit you're into, mate, but we never took your gear, honest!'

Without warning, Bell lashed the Beretta across the side of Lee's head. Lee collapsed to the deck like a bag of spuds. Being the ringleader and Becky's boyfriend came at a price.

'It wasn't us, I tell you!' they all bleated in unison.

'Men in black, you say?' said Bell.

Bell backed off, keeping them well covered, and took a seat near the window.

'Who are you?'

Matt piped up, his voice shaking.

'I...I'm Matt, this is Lee, Steve and Dave. We...we're all from Manchester, and on a two-week break.'

'Uh-huh...staying at this hotel?' asked Bell, casually.

'Yeah.'

'So, you were having a great holiday but wanted some real action, is that it?'

No one answered.

Bell let the silence hang in the air as Lee nursed his battered, bleeding head.

'If I let you live, Lee, you'll need some ice on that.'

'Can we go now?' pleaded Steve, wishing he'd never got involved with this prank.

Bell ignored him, and nodded to himself with a considered smirk. He indicated Dario's flight case which lay in the middle of the double bed, pointing to Matt.

'Open it. There's three thousand dollars for each of you. You're working for me now.'

Matt scrabbled at the plastic packets and counted out the big denominations.

'Each?!'

'Yup, I've got money to burn! Be at this address tonight, 8pm. Don't be late.'

Bell flicked a business card on to the duvet.

'This must be drug money,' said Steve.

'Are we cool or do I shoot you all? A no-show will mean flying back to Manchester in a body bag, but I think you already know that.'

They eyed their new boss nervously.

Bell lowered the aim of the Beretta a little.

'Lee, just one last thing…'

'Yeah?'

Bell strode up and gripped the back of Lee's neck as he forced the silencer into his mouth.

'Don't ever touch Becky again, okay? She's a good girl and gives good head, y'understand?'

'…or you'll…'

'…hunt you down like a dog and kill you…slowly.'

'W...well, if you put it like that,' stammered Lee.

'I do put it like that.'

20 Hi, I'm Candy

The large Mercedes sat tucked up on the dusty kerb. Its black bodywork baked in the intolerable heat of another hot day under a cloudless, azure sky.

Bell emerged through the rotating front door of the hotel, and walked with intent towards the stationary vehicle.

It was time to take the battle back to Pago, to erode his resources, probe his defences, and give the bastard a bloody nose.

Bell was heavily disguised as a bleached surf-dude in a blond wig and cap, orange-mirrored sunglasses, and pastel lip-salve. His long, baggy T-shirt, bordered with palm trees, proclaimed the legend 'Corralejo Club'. The grubby trainers he'd borrowed, which were a bit small, compressed the sticky, painful mess of his big toes. He looked forward to getting them cleaned up properly before they went septic.

What he was about to do may get a coded message to Sienna that he was still alive.

As he crossed the road and walked past the rear of the car, he could hear the engine ticking over. Running the air conditioning, he guessed. There must be at least two goons in there, but he had to be sure they were Pago's. The C-Class looked to be one of the ones which had given chase that night. It was prudent to verify his quarry.

Bell ambled under the 'Bienvenido' sun canopy of the nearby supermercado, through the maze of metal racks of sun cream, sun oil, and beachballs. Brightly coloured lilos and rubber rings, tied on with string, jostled together in the light breeze.

Under the pretence of some relaxing, retail therapy, he kept a close eye on the goonmobile though his wrap-arounds. The hire shop next door had battered scooters and quadbikes out on display, but no customers.

Dead quiet. Ideal.

He abandoned the supermercado, and headed straight for the vending machine. It was conveniently located facing the Merc, about four metres away.

He nonchalantly placed his left elbow on the glass, using its reflection to discreetly monitor any movements. The nearside window dropped about half an inch, as he watched, revealing a pair of Neapolitan eyes which scanned him carefully. A plume of freshly-chilled air and cigarette smoke escaped from the car, as Bell prepared his next move.

Those guys must be bored to death of sitting there, nursing their sweaty bollocks, and wasting their time on fruitless surveillance. Bell turned around slowly, peering over the rim of his shades. He casually flip-flopped his way over to the driver's door. A knuckle-tap on the window made it drop lazily. Acrid cigarette smoke clouded up into Bell's eyes.

'Whadya want, kid?' asked Bartolo.

Bell extracted a crumpled five-Euro note from the waterproof pocket of his Hawaiian shorts. He deliberately held it underneath Bartolo's nose. It looked moist and unappetising, like it had been secreted in his urine-flavoured crotch for a week.

'Say, you gotta coupla euro coins for the machine, man?'

'We got nuthin'! Go run and ask the nice lady in the shop.'

'You sure?' pressed Bell, not moving.

The diversion gave him time to check out the occupants. Bartolo and Dino…if he had known their names. No Sienna held captive on the backseat.

Everything was completely perfect.

'Sure I'm sure, now beat it, kid!' replied Bartolo, irritably.

Dino said nothing, but Bell could see the handle of a Glock pressed tightly against his knee. These guys were jumpy and uncomfortable, having to sit there hour after hour scratching their nuts. Bell decided to turn it up one more click.

'Like, you guys need to surf, feel the majesty of the waves. You're all kinda hung up and angry, man.'

'Just get out of here, you asshole!' blurted Dino.

He'd rather have been back in Naples, cutting twists of heroin, than roasting on this Spanish island. Bartolo had had enough of this cheeky beach-fly, and shut the window. They had been ordered to watch out for Thomas Bell and shoot on sight. Pago had even offered a bounty.

Bell slouched back to the vending machine, like a sloth on Prozac, and pressed his forehead against the glass. Rows of Fanta, Minute Maid, and Coca-Cola stared back at him.

He placed two euros in the slot. F0, A5, B1 and 8E, the first sequence of hexadecimal numbers typed in using the keypad, which ran from zero to nine and from A to F.

'Hi, I'm Candy. What is your command?' trilled the voice generator in a Californian, high-school drawl.

Bell could visualise a blonde cheerleader dancing on the touchline, shaking pom-poms in time with a marching band.

'Please input your parameters.'

Selecting 'EMP' off the credit card guide, he typed in hex codes: 45, 4D, 50, and 0D. Thirty seconds later, the low-inductance capacitor hit max and discharged a high-energy electromagnetic pulse. It made toast of the Merc's electrics, so that all the doors and windows were nicely jammed shut. The goons were now entombed in their hot metal box, unable to shoot through the bullet-proof windows, but not for long.

'Self-destruct. Please confirm.'

He just loved the sound of her voice, shame it had to end this way. What was she doing later? Bell deftly tapped his acknowledgement into the keypad.

'Please specify delay in seconds and confirm,' cooed Candy.

31, 38, 30, and 0D equated to one hundred and eighty seconds. Bell knew that the condenser contained enough C4 military explosive to take out an entire city block.

'Self-destruct sequence initiated.'

Candy's ice-cream soda voice was now joined by a low bipping noise, a polyharmonic tone which was quickening and rising steadily through the octaves. A Coca-Cola rolled obediently down the chute.

'Have a nice day!'

Bell coolly spun the red cap off the plastic bottle, and took a long, unhurried slug of the dark, fizzy liquid. He pulled off his blond wig and peered into the stressed face of Bartolo, who was threatening his Glock in vain.

Dino frantically tried to bust open his own door, making the car shake like hell on its chassis. Bell pouted a lascivious kiss-goodbye to Bartolo and turned to run.

He was now well clear around the corner, his back pressed tightly against a concrete wall, agreeably shielded from the imminent blast-wave. He opened his mouth and pressed his palms hard against his ears.

Kawboom!

The explosion blew the Merc across the road, vaporising its occupants. Obliterated German engineering flew in all directions, leaving a crater of melted tarmac where the car had once been. MIX: One, Pago: Nil.

He dropped into a pharmacy and bought up a stack of bandages, painkillers, and antiseptic gel. He'd have to patch up his big toes again, as best as he could.

It was a bloody nuisance.

Sirens continued to wail in the distance as he arrived back at the safe house. The smell of the sherry casks and musty plasterwork welcomed him.

Time was running out, but he had a plan.

He shaved his head completely. Pago's death squads would be out looking for him everywhere; best to go out now only after dark. He needed to review and document the whole layout of the Dos Lunas complex, the location of the bomb, and work out how to get in there. When the 3D printer had finished its work, he would have a superb scale model of the place. After sending a short, unencrypted emergency signal to London, he retrieved the scrap of paper with the USAF serial numbers, and logged in.

***

The crumpled sheets lay there, just as they had left them. He sat on the edge of the bed with a heavy heart, thinking of her, re-running the movie in his mind.

Scrub my back, will you?

Promise you'll look after me.

He scrunched the fine linen up to his face and breathed in the smell of her. A single strand of her golden hair lay on her pillow. She had gleefully folded it in half, in a fit of giggles, to place it right next to his. Deep in thought, he twisted the precious find around his finger. I did promise. Yeah, synchronised orgasms next time, with a little luck.

There was still a mountain to climb.

In the morning he would order the gut-buster cooked breakfast from the El Pueblo Cafeteria, just down the road. Friday was going to be a long day.

21 Kinoko gumo

The five young Marines eyed up the drinks in the illuminated chiller cabinet.

'The others will be along in a minute,' smiled Bell.

'Others?' said Donnie.

'You got root beer?' asked Ben.

'It's not all carbonated shit, is it?' snarled Zack.

The motley crew sat in the briefing room, assessing a miniature Dos Lunas and its outbuildings. Bell stood by the HD screen, fully prepared.

Semper fidelis. Always faithful. The motto of the US Marine Corps. Beans, bullets and bandages.

'We kill everything, we kill everything we see.'

'A day without blood is a day without sunshine.'

Parris Island's finest - Brad, Richie, Ben, Zack, and Donnie stared back at him with their high-and-tights, relaxing in their loud beachwear. Bell wished he had many more fit killing machines like them. Devil dogs. US Marines capable of marching one hundred kilometres a day, trained in the boondocks in the Philippines. Able to shoot a hole through a dime at a thousand yards.

Reflexively, robotically and accurately.

The end product of operant conditioning: stimulus, response, and reward. A precise mimicry of the act of killing.

'Hey buddy, let's begin or we're off,' threatened Donnie, a chest tattoo proclaiming 'Soldier of Christ' just visible through his unbuttoned shirt.

'Very soon,' promised Bell.

Bell looked at his watch with irritation. Where the fuck were those guys?

Lee and the others were huddled in the doorway, checking the card again. This must be it. They punched in the code and entered the airlock. The outer door slammed automatically behind them.

Bell made the introductions, and everyone settled back for death by PowerPoint, eyeing each other up suspiciously.

A few cautious nods.

'They're not professional soldiers, but they do bring their own brand of destructive violence.'

'So, get rid of them!' hollered Zack.

'Yeah, these guys are pussies, just leave it to us,' echoed Donnie.

'We need all the manpower we can get,' said Bell, defensively.

'Okay, just tell us why we're here. It's a beautiful day outside,' said Brad.

They all stood around the display table, as Bell pointed with a bamboo cane.

'This is Casa Dos Lunas or the House of the Two Moons. A beautiful villa complex set in one hundred and fifty hectares of private and heavily guarded land, way down the coast from here. It even has its own stretch of private beach.'

The 3D simulation, on the big screen, revealed a layout of attractive buildings, pool, helipad, rustic windmills, and outbuildings. Bell lingered on the sinister subterranean levels with the tip of the cane, explaining everything in minute detail.

'The estate runs down to the sea here. Jade Jagger's place is the next villa property along to the north, and here's the slip road from Cala Valletta and the perimeter fence.

'Personnel?' inquired Zack.

'Maybe twenty security men, mainly ex-special forces or the Neapolitan Camorra,' said Bell.

'Uh-huh.'

'Oh, and he owns a private yacht called the Valhalla, which is normally moored just offshore.'

Bell hunted through the slideshow with the remote to produce a shot of Pago's pride and joy.

Donnie instantly recognised Matt, who ignored the obvious glare.

'Hey buddy, do I know you from some place?

'Fucked if I know, mate,' replied Matt, sourly.

'I got it now.'

'You must be mistaken, pal,' grinned Matt, giving Donnie the finger.

'Do that again and I'll gouge out your eyes and skull fuck you!'

'Try it and I'll unscrew your head and shit down your neck, cocksucker!'

Donnie exploded with rage at the double insult, and leapt forward, striking Matt in the face. A scuffle ensued. Donnie had him by the throat now, on the floor, a repeat of the O'Learys incident. Others joined in the fracas, and they all crashed into the table sending Dos Lunas flying.

Bell separated them with a surprise gunshot to the ceiling which showered everyone in ancient lime plaster.

After some harsh words, Bell had them all seated again, with the addition of some grazed faces and bleeding lips. He threw a pile of NATO medical kits into his audience.

'Okay, people, kiss and make up. You're gonna have to shake on it, I'm afraid,' said Bell, impatiently.

Donnie finally stepped forward and held out his hand. Matt stood up reluctantly and faced him, taking the young Marine's grip.

'Donnie Olsen, USMC.'

'Matt Doyle, MCFC.'

Bell immediately handed out plump, shrink-wrapped packs of hundred-dollar bills.

They all stared reverently at the packets, still bound by mustard-coloured bands, just as the US Federal Reserve had issued them.

Bell broke the silence.

'Don't worry, you're going to earn it. Just make sure you get to spend it.'

'Hey, now we can buy as many women as we want!' roared Zack, jubilantly.

'Okay, so much for the nice model I built for you, which took me ages to make. You better fucking concentrate from now on. Save your venom for the mission, okay guys?'

Some unenthusiastic nods.

'As I was saying before you hotheads tried to kill each other. Pago is a big cheese, ostensibly a legitimate businessman.'

They were fidgeting.

Time to talk blood and bullets.

'Our mission is to attack and gain control of this complex by whatever means necessary. Terminate with extreme prejudice.'

Bell was met with a row of eager grins. He now had their full attention.

'We will be presented with some pretty stiff resistance. Expect heavy machine guns, RPGs, trip wires, booby traps, and anti-personnel devices…and that's just for starters. I can assure you they'll do everything they can to stop us.'

'Hey, don't sugar-coat it, man! Give it to us straight!' mocked Zack.

'You are also required to rescue a group of young women, held against their will.'

'Yeah, rescue them from their virginity!'

'Long gone, mate,' replied Bell, drily.

The guys all laughed and took high-fives. Even the Manchester guys were loving it.

'So, what's this Pago guy doing wrong?' inquired Ben, intelligently.

'Yeah, you jealous or something?' said Brad.

'I'm getting to that,' said Bell, pointing the cane directly at him.

'He's operating an underground factory which produces a pure form of MDMA. It rolls out over a million tablets a week under the brand name, Paloma Azul.'

Bell handed out half a dozen packets.

Matt Doyle had a pertinent question ready.

'So what's the hurry? Let the Spanish authorities sort it out.'

'The Unidad de Operaciones Especiales? It has to be done tonight. He's going to make a run for it.'

'Got any guns?'

'We got everything,' replied Bell, confidently.

'Aren't you forgetting something?'

'What?'

'What if we're not doing it?'

'Then take the money and walk away.'

'Just like that!'

'Just like that,' said Bell, stoically.

'You kidding us!'

Silence.

They all considered the unexpected let-out clause.

'Say, isn't all this Mickey Mouse bullshit you've told us classified?'

'Yup,' replied Bell, leaning back, looking relaxed.

'Are you for real, man?'

'If you mean, have I seen it for myself, been caught, tortured, left for dead, and escaped so I can return to slot every single one of those motherfuckers, yeah, sure…I'm for real.'

Stunned faces stared back at him. Bell leaned down, and pulled out an AK47 from underneath the table, then an M16, and an Israeli Uzi.

'Take your pick. Are you guys in or not?'

The Marines pressed their shaven heads together and consulted in whispers. The Manchester lads followed suit.

The Marines had elected Ben as their spokesman.

'It's bullshit, man, you made all this stuff up. Are these real hundred dollar bills or did you print them yourself?'

'Is the mission too hot for you guys?'

'All we can say is, thanks for the drinks and the tall story. If this mission's half as tough as you say it is, we're in!'

Lee stepped forward.

'The holiday ain't that good. Where do we sign?'

'Looks like I made a sale!' laughed Bell, with relief.

'Does this affect my holiday insurance?' asked Steve.

'It comes under dangerous sports, like what you were doing with that blonde last night!' mocked Dave.

The CIA refuge was an Aladdin's cave of Cold War leftovers.

'Grab whatever you want, guys, just make sure you can kill with it,' said Bell.

M16 assault rifles, M72 light anti-tank weapons, M79 grenade launchers, and MAC10 machine pistols. Grenades, body armour, jungle knives, and plastic explosives.

Donnie selected a M60 machine gun. The long black killing tool made him feel complete, fully dressed. A hard heart which kills, we kill everything we see. He checked for kinks in the heavy belt of shiny, golden bullets.

'We're gonna burn someone's ass! Those limey faggots had better shoot straight,' whispered Donnie. The others nodded, rolling their eyes.

Everyone grazed through the candy store, selecting handguns and anything else they thought might be useful. The M4A1 and the Sig Sauer P226 pistol were both popular choices.

The Manchester guys were more used to unarmed combat, carpet knives, and screwdrivers.

Bell would keep it simple.

An AK47, a Beretta, grenades, a commando knife, black combats and Kevlar body armour. The treatment of battle wounds, suture kits, and how to administer morphine to a wounded comrade. He briefed them on their specific role: mopping up and taking prisoners. Face paint? Olive drab, tiger stripe, or choco-chip.

Steve Francis approached Bell with a sheepish, dejected look on his face.

'I'm not sure I can handle a gun.'

'How about a flamethrower?'

Bell selected a unit from one of the wooden racks: a sculpted, ribbed carapace, containing five gallons of lighter fuel, attached to pipes and a nozzle.

'It squirts kerosene jelly, then you fire a stream of white hot sparks which makes it explode see? If you run out of jelly, just fire the sparks. Simple.'

'Nah, it makes me look like a fucking dung beetle.'

'Try this instead, it's like a riot control gun that fires a sort of caramelised dog shit. When it's exposed to air, it expands rapidly, and turns into solidified honeycomb which immobilises your target.'

'So, I get to fire hot, sticky love-piss at people, but no sparks with this one?'

'Yup.'

'I'll take it.'

Dave sauntered over, carrying his Kevlar body armour set.

'Can I have a Gatling gun like Arnold Schwarzenegger, in Predator?'

'You'd need a car battery and the recoil would knock you over,' replied Bell, 'Suggest you stick with the AK47.'

Benzedrine tablets, morphine, laminated maps, and GPS co-ordinates. Bell concluded his checklist. All the kit would be put aboard the three Humvees that the US Navy had kindly provided.

They would have only two and a half hours to complete the mission. Ten hours to kill in the meantime.

Now for the fog of war.

Bell noticed the problem immediately.

'Hey guys, you can't wear those Man City shirts. Camo or black, remember.'

He pointed to the boxes of combat gear, lined up against the damp, flaking wall.

'We'll wear these, thanks,' replied Lee, stubbornly.

'Battledress, if you don't mind.'

'If we're going to fight, we'll fight as Man City.'

'What about away strip?'

'If we have to die, we'll die like this...these colours don't run.'

'Okay, but don't say I didn't warn you.'

***

Judy Madden stared at her iPhone, a nervous fingertip hovering over the dial icon.

The gravitational pull of the nuptial arrangements had been getting her down. Trapped in the accelerating whirlpool of flower arrangements, marquees, and invitations. The noose was tightening. The crushing inevitability of the big day. She didn't love him, she was sure of that now. Her father would go mad. There had to be something seriously wrong if she felt like this.

Marry in haste, repent at leisure. She was overcome with an uncontrollable desire to run.

Her affair with Tom was recalled in exquisite detail, something she had done over and over. The joyous times they had spent together. The way he put his arm around her waist and kissed her neck. She missed him. Bitter regret.

It might not be too late.

She skated over the precious digits of his phone number one final time before delivering the decisive tap.

A foreign dial-tone purred.

***

'Just one last thing,' said Bell.

His mobile rang. Shit!

'Yeah?' he snapped.

'It's Judy.'

'I can't talk right now.'

'I can't live without you.'

'Er…not now.'

'You're with someone else, aren't you?'

'I'll call, okay?'

Bell terminated the call and switched to mute.

Sloppy, setting a bad example like that.

'Sorry...no mobiles.'

They had all risen from their seats, believing that was it.

It had broken his flow, just when he was getting to the money shot!

'Hey guys, what I was really trying to tell you was: Pago's got a device.'

'Yeah, so what are you saying?' asked Lee.

'A hydrogen bomb.'

'Like the ones dropped on Japan?'

'They were only A-bombs.'

'So like, bigger and nastier? Like, 'Game over'?' said Brad.

'It's a type B28RI hydrogen bomb which will yield up to seven megatons. That's one hundred times more powerful than Hiroshima and Nagasaki. It'll vaporise the entire west coast of Ibiza. They'll probably hear the bang in Istanbul, or Tripoli, and definitely Madrid. The US Department of Defense will get to measure it at their place in New Mexico.'

A mushroom cloud appeared on the screen, the final slide of his PowerPoint presentation.

'Where the hell did he get that, for Chissake?!'

'We don't know. It's an US Airforce version, an air-launched tactical nuclear weapon. They've lost loads of ordnance over the years. It's been rewired to explode using a timer, which is set to midnight tonight.'

They let out a collective whistle.

'If the device is detonated, it will create a boiling cloud eighty five thousand feet in height and a crater six miles wide. The blast will suck all the air out of the immediate vicinity, and shine fifty times brighter than the sun. Birds will ignite in mid-air, and buildings will liquefy like wax. The under-pressure left behind will vacuum out human entrails, which will vaporise spontaneously.'

The room fell silent.

'An MDMA factory and now a fucking hydrogen bomb…isn't this place meant to be a holiday island?!' shouted Ben, eventually.

'Not for much longer.'

'You seem to know a lot about this shit,' said Matt.

'Yeah, how come you know all this?'

Bell interrupted them.

'The core of the mission is to deactivate the bomb.'

'You know how to do that?'

'Of course,' lied Bell, smoothly.

'Sounds like very warm lager and factor three thousand to me,' observed Lee, drily.

'If it blows, we'll be able to kiss our candy asses goodbye. Still up for it?'

'Okay, twenty-one fifteen hours. Don't be late! I want to see fighters with hearts of stone emerging from the crypt. No partying, no booze, no women. Keep hydrated and rest. Now go and get a good meal. This will be a dangerous adventure, make no mistake.'

22 Tu culo es mío

Bell stood waiting under the trees next to the Dos Lunas perimeter wall, and studied the menacing, electrified fence. Tensioned wires energised with a lethal voltage, mounted on porcelain insulators. If a connection was cut, grounded, or earthed, an alarm condition and location would be signalled to the control station. An armed response team would attend the fifty metre tamper-zone within minutes. Tricky.

He checked the time again.

They were late.

Bell listened to the persistent hum of the wires carrying the high-tension current. It pulsated like a brooding, nocturnal insect. Somehow, they would have to get over that or blow the front gate.

A gentle sea breeze, laced with the smell of the pines and dry earth, disturbed the evening stillness. A car sound system came and went in the far distance. Nothing to do but wait fretfully with only cicadas and bats for company. He checked his Kevlar body armour for the nth time, and idly broke off some brittle pine-tree resin.

The low rumble of three Humvees creeping down the road would be very welcome.

Nothing.

He felt a twinge of anxiety. It might have been a mistake to dish out all those dollars. His judgement call. For all he knew, the guys were in a bar right now, and he was going to have to take Dos Lunas single-handed.

***

The Marines sat in the Itaca bar, located between the San Antonio beach and the main drag. Departure time was set for eight thirty which would give them an easy thirty-five minute ride to the GPS meeting point. All the kit was stowed in the refuelled M998s, which were parked up nearby. Just chilling out with a fruit juice, or a Coke, and maybe a Benzedrine tablet, exactly as Bell had instructed.

As far as the US Military was concerned, they could have the run of the island, as long as they kept out of trouble. The Marine Corps had more important things to worry about. The Manchester lads, Matt, Lee, Dave, and Steve walked in and took a comfortable banquette, some distance away from their new comrades. The footie was on the overhead projector, and they ordered some soft drinks. A few discreet nods across to the Marines. Best not to attract any unwanted attention. Plenty of opportunity to buddy-up later under fire.

Lee and his pals felt nervous, charged, and alert. Alcohol and drug abstinence had dispersed the daily fog of intoxication. They were now focused and sharp, ready to face the unknown. They were in it together, living in the moment.

The bar was dead. It was too early. They would be long gone before the place was heaving; the ideal watering hole to chill out before the mission kicked off.

'Why don't we take the money and run?' said Matt.

'He'll kill us if that nuke doesn't get us first,' said Lee.

'You really think he'd do that?' asked Dave.

'Yes.'

A group of ten girls, on a hen night, rolled into the bar, screaming and shouting.

They were already drunk.

They had spent the late afternoon preparing for Debs' prenuptial blowout. Shower, after-sun, hair, makeup, nails, and loads of cheap vodka. Get out there early, to troll the bars and score some horny guys.

They swarmed up to the barman, ordering cocktails, vodka, and shots. Becky noticed Lee immediately, chummed up in the corner with his henchmen. They all looked curiously sober. He glowered back at her. There was no love lost now. The bastard. She stared daggers at him, her face starting to hurt again where he had hit her.

Zack eyed up one of the honeys who seemed to be smiling at him. She was wearing a nurse's outfit, white stockings, high heels, a mini skirt, and the headgear. He worshipped any girl in medical get-up like that. He could come in his pants right now. She even had a nurse's fob watch pinned to her left breast. Both bazookas were busting to get out. She could check his pulse any time she liked.

'Hey guys,' whispered Zack, '...are you thinking what I'm thinking?'

The Marines had been monitoring the cock-bait, perched provocatively on their bar stools, since the moment they had walked in.

The bar manager, who knew his business, lowered the lights and put the music on. He retrieved a cardboard box of willy straws from underneath the bar, and poured the next round for the gals. Not to be left out of it, the barman delivered trays of free shots to the guys. Richie looked at his watch.

'Zack, we gotta go in fifteen minutes.'

'Shit!…the hot bitches are coming over, man!'

Debs led her splinter group over to the takeaway testosterone. The others broke off and headed for Manchester.

Footie, beer, and birds. Becky stayed at the bar and drained her
Blue Lagoon. Seeing Lee sitting there had caused her to lose
momentum, and she'd sobered up a bit. She resolved to have a
memorable last night, whatever.

It wouldn't be long before Debs' gang had those guys back in
their rooms to empty both tanks. Sisters of mercy, relieving
them of their burden. The Marines now had a girl each on their
laps. Zack breathed in the heady mixture of alcohol and
perfume, and tried to explain that they had to leave shortly.

'Go? Are you real men or what?! Come on boys, show us
your cocks!'

Donnie shook his head with regret, and explained it to Debs
again. She tossed her head back in surprise, shaking the glitter
balls of her Deely Boppers. She tugged thoughtfully on both of
her plastic, phallus earrings.

'See these? Whatever you've got I want it! Something wrong?
You guys aren't sweet on each other, are you? You can do
anything you like with me,' she winked.

It was an attractive proposition. Probably, the best they'd had
all week. It was a tough one. Zack struggled to glance at his
watch, past a pair of tits he was aching to rub his dick between.
All of a sudden, running around in full battle dress with an
M4A1 carbine was losing its appeal.

'Sorry babe, we're too busy,' he said, half-heartedly.

She could sense that they were wavering. She'd soon have his
pants down, and get below decks.

'What, not even up the bullet hole?'

***

Where the hell were they? Fifteen minutes overdue. Mission
status: delayed. Jesus, it was hot just standing here, even in this

wafer-thin body armour. If Pago got spooked, could he detonate the bomb with some kind of remote? He daren't think about it. Despite the unbearable tension, Bell found his mind drifting. Was Sienna still alive? He hoped so.

Gun metal pressed against Bell's neck, as the back of his shins received a powerful, well-aimed blow. He landed on his back with a thud, followed by a torrent of kicks to his ribcage, which forced him to roll over and eat pine needles. One arm was then twisted sharply up towards the back of his neck.

'No mueva ni yo le mataré!' was whispered into his right ear. A heavy pair of thighs now straddled his back, pinning him to the deck.

'Tu culo es mío!'

Dust filled Bell's eyes, nostrils, and throat as he struggled in vain to escape the textbook wrestling hold.

El Cartero and Manos leant over Bell.

'¿Cuantos guardias?'

'I don't know!' spat Bell.

Manos twisted his arm a little more, and applied an excruciating pressure point to a nerve in Bell's neck. The left-hand side of his body now seemed to have lost all sensation.

'Wait, wait!…I'll tell you,' coughed Bell.

'Mátalo!' ordered El Cartero.

Shit!...whoever they were thought he was one of Pago's! It'd be a bullet in the back of the head at any moment. Steel not lead, in fact. The end would be delivered with the easy swipe of a razor-sharp machete.

'Pago! Pago!' screamed Bell.

El Cartero raised his hand to Manos, just before the steel blade travelled through the air to make contact with the back of Bell's neck.

'¿Está Pago en casa?' asked the harsh voice.

Bell assimilated the question quickly. Pago not at home? Then game over. Mission terminated.

'Si, si, si, Pago en casa!' screamed Bell.

Silence.

Had the trigger been pulled? Was he dead now? Not again!

Zack's Sig Sauer pressed into Manos's temple.

'Easy, buddy…manos arriba!'

Manos released Bell's twisted arm reluctantly. Donnie helped Bell up from the dust. Eight demons, rudely awakened from their crypt, trained their guns on the two Mexicans. El Cartero and Manos now stood a few feet away, with their hands up. Bell nursed his ribs, and tried to rub some life into his poor left arm. He appraised the two Alacrán cartel hitmen carefully. Both were dressed in Telefónica overalls. They were a tight fit on the tubby one. Who were they? Police undercover, CNI agents, or even UOE?

'Thanks guys, I thought you weren't coming.'

'We would have been, but we passed it up to take part in this half-baked mission of yours,' said Brad.

'Yeah, instead of lying between tanned thighs, with red fingernails dug into my buttocks,' lamented Matt.

'Little and Large friends of yours?' said Lee.

'Let's find out,' said Bell.

'¿Hablas bien Inglés?'

These guys looked like they had been held at gunpoint many times before. Bell could see their brains working overtime beneath their swarthy, sullen expressions. They were calculating the percentages; looking for a clever way out of their latest life-threatening fix.

'Un poco,' replied El Cartero in a heavy Mexican accent.

'…of course I speak good English, excellent English, in fact,' he continued, falling into a smooth, Tex-Mex drawl.

Bell glanced at his watch, as the two men continued to glower at him. The mission was now running half an hour late.

'Who are you?'

No reply.

Bell moved forward, and stood before El Cartero who looked back defiantly with cold, lupine eyes and malignant charm. There was no immediate prospect of this pistolero explaining himself.

'¿Quién es usted, por favor?' fired Bell.

Manos continued to stare into space, without emotion, like some hideous reef snake waiting to strike. A wall of silencio. The clock was ticking.

'We are an assault team on a mission to capture or kill Ilya Pago,' explained Bell, carefully.

'Es una artimaña,' whispered El Cartero to Manos, anticipating trickery.

'We have to accomplish our mission by midnight.'

'Es una artimaña.'

'I work for the British government and the EDEA.'

'You are a policeman! Where I come from, we kill policemen, many of them!' spat El Cartero.

'Pago has around twenty soldiers, ex-paratroopers or foreign legion, and some advanced weapons systems. The complex is heavily defended.'

The Mexicans faces dropped. They had not anticipated this, but they were now assessing the valuable intel.

A sudden broad smile from El Cartero.

'We are here to kill him too. We work for the Alacrán cartel in Mexico. This is my associate, Manos.'

'You're a long way from home aren't you?' said Bell.

'It makes a change from Mexico City.'

Bell glanced at his watch again.

'We need to break into the complex in the next five minutes.'

'Those who double-cross the Alacrán cartel will be punished. It is business. Pago is ours.'

Easy decision, if they're up for it.

'Why not join us?'

The military hardware Bell's squad was packing was more than obvious. They were well armed and well prepared. El Cartero turned his sidekick, who nodded. They, in turn, would be able to bring something to the party.

'We will come under your command but under one condition. We are permitted to sever the head and limbs of Señor Pago while he is screaming for mercy.'

'You have my permission,' smiled Bell.

'How are you getting over the wire?'

'With difficulty. We may have to blow the main gate.'

'Si. Six thousand volts AC. Come, we will show you something.'

Bell briefed them at speed, as they stripped off their overalls to reveal linen designer jackets, silk Versace shirts, denim pants, and snake-skin boots. When he explained about the USAF hydrogen bomb, El Cartero drew back his lips, and let out a shrill whistle through his gold teeth.

'I am Julio, also known as El Cartero. This is Manos.'

'The postman?'

'I always deliver.'

The rest of the team eyed up the Mexicans with awe. They were dead pleased that they were now on their side. The big one looked like a barrel on legs. He had a fat, round head, no neck and narrow apertures for eyes. The wiry one had that menacing, cunning look of someone who killed easily and clinically, without remorse. They definitely looked like they could handle themselves.

'Okay, time to get our hair wet,' announced Bell.

Bumped fists and punched Kevlar. As they moved off, Bell was presented with the bizarre spectacle of his guys in combat gear, alongside two Mexican narco-pistoleros, who looked ready to go out on the town for an evening of titty joints and tequila.

Manos and El Cartero led the way to their van, which was hidden nearby. They were all grins again, now that they had been reunited with their Uzis, semi-automatics, and spare ammo. Manos cradled his lethal machete, like it was a long lost lover.

Steve's honeycomb gun continuously dripped a yellow pus-like substance from its nozzle. It was like it was suffering from some kind of virulent sexually transmitted infection. Bell doubted whether he would get to use it, but at least he wouldn't look like a dung beetle.

23 Busting caps

Saturday, 6th August. 22:10
   Sienna scoured the room for anything useful. A sad inventory of basic toiletries, bed linen, towels, and some spare knicks. Nothing that would cut through concrete or steel.

'Anna hates dry skin and beats you if you don't moisturise,' said Amber flatly, 'She'll beat you for doing anything, come to think of it.'

'Outside clothes or proper shoes are forbidden since the other girls escaped.'

'Uh-huh,' replied Sienna.

'The light shaft is at least ten metres up to the glass cover. You seriously think you can do that?'

'What's at the top?'

'Ornamental gardens, maybe.'

'It's square and narrow, so I can keep my muscles braced against the sides as I climb. My yoga and gymnastics will be put to the ultimate test.'

'What if the lid won't budge?'

'We're done for.'

A bed stood up on its end was the best option. It would get her close enough to the low ceiling to start the ascent. A fall would mean broken bones or worse. She had to do this, for both of them.

'Go willingly when Anna comes for you. I'll be suspended up there, well out of view. Don't hang around!'

'Got it.'

'Is she normally on time?'

'Never late, but we'd better hurry!'

Sienna pulled on grippy, rubber-soled slippers. Tight leggings would protect her from the rough concrete sides.

'Should be a doddle,' said Amber.

'Yeah, I'm lighter than you!'

'Bitch!'

Sienna kissed and hugged Amber, not knowing that it would be for the last time.

'I love you sis with all my heart.'

'Love you too.'

'Okay, let's do it.'

Amber steadied the bed frame, as her sister climbed up into position. Sienna then reached vertically into the smooth shaft and cast off. A useful ridge became evident after several feet, a leftover from the concrete moulding process. A great resting spot and a terrific start. She could certainly hold this position for a while.

Amber got the bed frame back into place and put the bed clothes back on. Next, she formed spare pillows into a plausible, foetal outline. The final touch was a balled-up towel, wearing a blonde wig, placed cleverly on the pillow. Alluring wisps of golden hair flowed out from underneath the top edge of the carefully positioned duvet. All set.

'Okay, sis?'

'Yup.'

'Cool.'

'How long now?'

'Two minutes.'

Amber sat on the edge of her bed, nervously moisturising her hands. She couldn't go on living like this.

***

In her private suite, Anna studied her face in the mirror. A seductive, beguiling goddess failed to stare back.

It was true.

Her girlish looks were fading fast.

Taut, fresh skin damaged by blemishes, blotches, wrinkles, and cellulite. She was no longer the elfin pixie she once was.

A decade of muscle-enhancing and recreational drugs had taken their toll. The anti-depressants had probably made it even worse. This was as good as it was going to get, and it didn't look that good.

A decaying dominatrix, at an all-time low.

She would gladly sell her soul to the devil to start over. She loved sex with beautiful young girls, but still wanted to be beautiful herself.

She had resolved to bow out before she decomposed into a poisonous, wrinkled witch.

Her invite to escape on the Valhalla had been politely declined. No need for a broomstick or a senior citizen bus pass, after all. She still had an hour and a half for some final, mouth-watering fun.

There was something delicious that she had always wanted to try. A shiver of anticipation sent tingles through her at the thought of it. It lifted her from her melancholy.

22:28.

She placed a Viagra tablet on her tongue, and knocked it back with vodka. Touch up the black lipstick. Laces, latex, and leather straps all adjusted, a quick glance into the evil mirror.

Queen bitch Grimhilde, cruel, wicked, and vain, pouted back at her.

She threw the empty glass with all her might at her hideous reflection. This is where the story ends. Showtime.

Quick-march to the girls' quarters.

She was late.

***

22:30.

The metal door was levered open, and Anna stepped through the doorway.

'Ready then, my lovely?'

Amber stood up smartly, struggling to contain her nerves.

Sienna seemed to be fast asleep.

Amber headed for the door, but to her alarm, Anna moved further into the room. Amber fought to hide her mounting terror, as Anna appraised Sienna's inert form and approached her bed. Amber tensed as Anna stood right over her snoozing sister. Sienna glimpsed Anna's head passing directly beneath her, as she clung on, muscles squeezed tight and holding her breath.

'Like a baby, eh?' smiled Anna.

'She's been crying a lot.'

'A sob and a little nap will refresh her.'

Fresh meat, more like.

'She's definitely somewhere else,' said Amber.

Anna stroked the hair spread out on the pillow. Surely she would pull back the cover and find a dummy lying there!

Anna turned suddenly, taking Amber's arm, jolting her out of her paralysing anxiety.

'Playtime!'

Amber's enormous relief was expressed by a broad smile.

'Do you know, Amber, I really do think you're starting to enjoy what we do together.'

The door slam was the all-clear. Sienna set to work immediately. She tensed her muscles and pushed on upwards, little by little, squeezing her body against the shaft walls. She could do this! The confined space felt both claustrophobic and strangely comforting. Her spirit soared; freedom beckoned. Don't look down, take it steady, pace yourself!

***

22:16

The Iveco Telefónica van had been convincingly parked by a telephone pole, and close to the perimeter fence. Using a remote, Julio swung the cherry-picker platform round to pick up the first group. After three trips they were all over to the other side, including the heavy armament. The hydraulic apparatus automatically returned to its anchoring resting place, on the top of the van.

'See, Mexican hospitality: no charge!' grinned Julio, pocketing the remote.

Bell looked nervously at his watch. Shit! They'd lost so much valuable time!

Bell had split the assault team into three groups.

The bad-ass Marines, except Richie, would race up to the front of the house and give it everything they had. This would draw all the attention away from the back of the property. Bell, Richie, Julio and Manos would enter the rear using the hopefully unguarded glass doors, and come up behind the defenders at the front of the house.

They would then re-group, and descend to the lower levels and the bomb. The Manchester team would head for the beach,

254

and pick off anyone making a run for it, or deal with reinforcements from the Valhalla. Whatever.

With all the military hardware they were carrying, they should be able to blast the glass doors away easily.

Just as they were about to emerge from the undergrowth, they heard something.

A couple of guards were lazily patrolling the perimeter zone, kicking cones, stripping leaves, laughing and joking. Everyone was bunched up and silent as the goons approached.

'It's just another drill.'

'Merda!' came the reply from the one taking a piss.

He'd got to the second fly button, when Zack and Manos emerged from the shadows, and took them both from behind. No need to urinate now. They dragged the bodies into cover. Two down. Now for the main house.

They fanned out in silence, keeping in formation, moving stealthily, watching for trip wires. Bell knew for sure that they had already been seen. CCTV was everywhere. They were being drawn into carefully prepared killing grounds.

The team took it in turns to obliterate security cameras as they went, each with a well-aimed bullet. Waste of time really, but it kept spirits up and exercised trigger fingers.

22:35

The main control room was full of smoke. Anatoly Kadic liked it that way. It reminded him of interrogation rooms, bright lights, and broken prisoners.

He was sitting at the centre of the spider's web, like a black widow with sensitive, hairy legs, awaiting the slightest tremor along its silky threads.

He took another drag on his Samsun.

They were here, just as he had expected.

Field cameras were continuously being knocked out.

Dark figures approaching the complex.

A military unit who'd easily bypassed the electrified fence. Well-trained commandos, probably. There were at least ten of them.

Adriano and Cesare had bought it, reduced to flat-liners on the display. Four valuable men in two days! Bartolo and Dino in their Mercedes, now Adi and Cesare.

Nearly everyone had been recalled to the main house.

Current status: A squad would snipe from the roof with Dragunovs, fitted with laser sights. The ground floor was sealed on all sides with hydraulically controlled armour-plated shutters. A Ma Deuce fifty-cal was in position upstairs, with boxes and boxes of ammo, ready to take full advantage of all-round, twenty-twenty vision.

He stubbed the cigarette and hunted for a fingernail to bite. The right hand, that had killed and mutilated so many, scratched nervously at his mane of black hair, clasped back in a bun.

All the anti-personnel mines, which surrounded the finca, were now activated. Neat rows of serially-numbered OZM-9s stared back at him on a digital map. Someone would get caught out sooner or later, he chuckled to himself.

Kadic checked the armoured shutter sensors. Condition green. He then tested the controls of the large calibre machine gun mounted on the tower turret. The 0.50 BMG M2 Browning sat on a motorised swiveller on the top of the tower, and had a full 360 degree range. From the main console, he fired a controlled burst of twelve rounds out to sea. Awesome.

He'd only lose the advantage when they got in close, but the OZM-9s would cover the blind spots.

He lit another Samsun, his last one. Shit!

He sucked the smoke deep into his lungs and concentrated on the monitors.

Pago's chopper! Ha! His own evac plan was better!

He looked up at the steel escape hatch above him, and pulled the ladder down smartly with a wooden boat-hook. He shot up the metal rungs into an enclosed space. The narrow escape-ladder was rolled up tightly, ready to be unfurled down the side of the building. He visualised himself jumping to the ground at the base of the tower, and breaking into a sprint across the baked, red earth down to the beach. Not long now!

The Valhalla had weighed anchor, and Pago had flown the roost. Whoever was hoping to slit his throat would be sorely disappointed.

22:36

The three groups had split up. Bell's team of four was concealed behind an old Ibicencan windmill, made of rough bricks and flaking render. Its wood and canvas sail caught the sea breeze, and it rotated slowly on its dry, worn bearings.

The backdoors of Dos Lunas were dead ahead.

The frontal assault would kick off at any moment.

No shot had been fired up till now. The only fright was an ominous and intimidating test-burst of heavy machine gun fire, the tracer rounds flying high up and offshore.

So it begins. Small arms and explosions in the distance. They had to keep low, ducking the red laser dots and accurate high-velocity shells.

The second floor of Dos Lunas was heavily defended, but nothing obvious detected at ground level.

The four of them were now taking cover in the gardens, amongst the sun-bleached statues and ornamental trees. Luckily there were plenty of low walls offering adequate protection, but the last stretch up to the house was an eerie piece of open ground. The last hundred metres to the glass double doors were undoubtedly the killing zone.

Shells stitched along the ground mercilessly, as they came under heavy fire. Then, to make things worse, an HMG came on, firing bullets as big as beer cans, zinging rounds plucking at the dirt like heavy rain. The tracer seemed slow at first, then picked up speed as it whistled past.

The guys inched closer. Snipers on the roof! Hell! Bell concentrated his attention on the crucial backdoors.

It should be just a simple matter of a short burst from an M16 and they'd be in.

Bell took aim and emptied a magazine. The glass shattered alright, but there was something wrong. There was still a solid wall of some kind. Not so easy.

Bell used his night field glasses to see that armoured doors had been drawn across the entrance. All the ground floor windows were the same. No wonder! Bell nodded to Richie who held a M72 light anti-tank weapon.

'Blow the doors, for Chrissake!' screamed Bell.

Donnie pulled the plastic tubes apart. The sights shot up automatically, and he steadied the device on his shoulder. He peeped over the low granite wall and aimed, whilst Bell and the Mexicans took cover as the trigger was pulled. The solid-fuel rocket shot clean and true across the open ground and exploded dead centre. The smoke dispersed quickly in the sea breeze.

Nothing!

The armoured plates were perfectly intact, with barely a dent. The Russian-made multi-mesh armour plating had dissipated the full force of the blast. The guys kept low, the fifty-cal keeping them pinned down with constant fire.

Kadic laughed out aloud, as he registered the impact on the monitors. No chance!

In twenty minutes he could piss off and leave this bloody mess behind. The thought of escaping at thirty five knots in a rigid-hulled inflatable was tantalising. He'd get some more cigarettes on the mainland!

'Try the RPG…quickly!' ordered Bell.

Richie fired.

Bell felt the back-blast as the sustainer motor kicked in, propelling another rocket towards its target. The second explosion was bigger and louder.

Bell checked for any damage. The left hand door was buckled a bit, and a chink of light now shone from the hallway.

Soddit!

'Kill that fucking machine gun!'

He rolled back in despair on the ornate pathway, and called up on his military radiophone.

'Zack, kill the M2! Keep firing RPGs till you do! That's an order!'

Bell knew that they would have to pull off a dangerous skirt-around to get up close, and set a shaped charge. A shitload of C4 might annihilate the back of the building. So be it. Nothing for it. It was the only way in.

They had to blow the doors.

The tail of the first RPG from Zack's group flew across the sky. The aim was too high and it overshot, disappearing off into the night. Zack's second RPG ricocheted off the curved dome of the tower, and exploded wastefully on the roof, illuminating the whole complex.

Kawboom!

By some amazing fluke, it took out two of the Dragunov snipers, who were blown clean off the roof.

Bell and the guys kept up the double taps on the remaining snipers.

They should have been in by now.

An annoying accumulation of delays.

They were running out of time.

Kadic caught a glimpse of a breakaway squad on monitor seven, and despatched Marcel, Pietro and Valerio to cover it. Eugene and Nello would pin the others down at the back doors, as planned.

The last five men.

Kadic tightened his laces and anxiously massaged the RHIB ignition key in his palm.

24 **Bye bye, baby**

S aturday, 6th August.
22:41.

Sienna had carefully varied the load on her muscles on the way up. It had worked. She was now at the top of the shaft, with her face pressed underneath the glass lid. Then disaster struck. Sudden gunfire and a massive explosion startled her.

She lost her grip and slithered painfully back down, grazing her knees and arms. Luckily, her bleeding toes saved her, bringing the slide to a dead halt by snagging one of the concrete ridges.

The rubbing had scuffed her toe knuckles and splintered the nails in the process. She could forget the pedicure. She was pretty well back where she had started.

The friction burns on her unprotected elbows made her want to cry out in despair.

The skin scrapes on her knees were the worst. Her leggings were shredded. The fresh, open abrasions felt like raw, infected ulcers. She cried a little, her eyes watering, getting ready to grind her way back up again.

Tracer fire illuminated the night sky, whipping over the glass like a meteorite storm.

It must be Tom, she thought, it has to be.

It gave her new energy.

Every time she moved now, the skin in contact with the walls stung and abraded. She left traces of blood and sweat as she drove herself upwards.

Finally, she was back up there, exhausted.

She had to work quickly now, pressed tightly into the concave glass dome, and braced across the top of the shaft.

Her muscles were tiring.

If she slipped, it would be fatal.

The latches of the double-glazed unit undid easily. She couldn't believe it! The whole thing could have been corroded solid. In seconds, eight out of eight butterfly nuts had spun off their threads!

Wow!

She levered the glass upwards and away from its aluminium seating, forcing her elbows up and over the metal edges. Her long suffering legs now hung free. She allowed her drained muscles to relax for a pleasurable moment or two before the haul-out on to a bed of fine pebbles.

The deafening rat-tat-tat of semi-automatic weapons echoed around the secluded courtyard.

She lay there recovering, re-focusing her energy. No time to worry about discomfort and grazes. She crawled across to a stone pagoda, and checked out the exquisite Japanese garden.

Abstract stone sculptures sat on finely raked gravel, and waterfalls cascaded into tiered pools full of umbrella grass. There was no one around. The glass door nearby opened into the main corridor. It was unlocked.

***

22:54.

Despite Bell's squad returning fire with their M16s, the remaining snipers on the roof were hanging on in there. Bell had managed to calibrate the mortar, ready to nail those guys. There was a welcome crump as the first shell fired. It fell short, obliterating an expensive marble sculpture. Donnie adjusted the sights. The second shell hit pay-dirt and blew the last sniper away. They fired a couple more on the same settings and waited.

Relative silence.

The fifty-cal in the tower seemed to have turned its attention to the front of the house. Bell considered that it was a perfect opportunity to get a shaped charge ready, and prepare for an exposed dash across open ground. His thoughts returned to grappling with the nuke and its devious anti-tamper safeguards.

It was all down to him.

Down to the wire.

***

Zack, Ben, Richie and Brad were still pinned down at the front of the house. Although they'd blown away the heavy wooden doors, there was constant return fire from the second floor, stopping them from marching straight in.

Richie realised that there was only one highly effective guy left, punching above his weight. Valerio, ex-French foreign legion and experienced in counter-insurgency in North Africa, knew what he was about. He could anticipate the attackers' strategy and planned to take a couple of them with him.

Richie and Ben would divert all the fire over to the right, to allow Zack and Brad to skulk round to the left and get in over a balcony.

Zack and Brad monkeyed straight up the creepers and over the rail like killer-crypt demons. They assessed the veranda area, tastefully laid out with distressed rustic tiles. Just a pair of hardwood sun-loungers and some empty cava bottles. Brad had snagged a couple of Bougainvillea thorns which hurt like hell. They crouched down together, Berettas drawn. Zack produced a laminated map and penlight torch. He pointed at a door at the far end of the seating area. He led the way across, twitchy finger ready.

Before they could complete their dash, the door opened and they were raked with a savage burst of machine gun fire from the inside the room.

Zack automatically fired his grenade launcher to roast whoever was in there. The shells from the MGL M32 flew straight through the door, and the ornate room exploded into a fireball, making the whole building shudder.

Zack had taken a couple of Kevlar hits and lay briefly on his side to recover. No harm done. Just shake it off and get back to the vertical for more incoming.

Brad didn't move.

He lay on his back, gasping, coughing up gloopy bubbles of blood. Brad's first thought had been his girlfriend.

They were soon joined by Richie and Ben, who'd run unopposed in through the front door, and up the stairs. Their high spirits were short lived when they took a close look at Brad.

He'd bought a couple and was haemorrhaging profusely on the terracotta floor. A shower of purple petals had covered him, like some freaky aromatherapy session. His breathing was hoarse and laboured, panting hard. His bright eyes were vivid with terror; frothy blood flowing freely down his chin.

'Hey...Zack,' rasped Brad.

'Take it easy man. We're all here.'

'Where am I hit?'

'Let me get this into you.'

'Is it bad?'

'Yup.'

'...can't feel anything…'

'Easy, pal.'

Ben, a trained medic, rolled the sleeve and pumped in the morphine. Brad didn't flinch.

'Zack…'

'Still here, buddy.'

Brad closed his eyes.

Ben felt Brad's pulse, as he watched the thick, dark blood continue to drain its way out of his side. Internal bleeding had already filled up one of his lungs. He only had only a few minutes left to live. All Ben could do was to make him comfortable. He'd seen it too many times before.

Brad's eyes opened for the last time.

'Ben.'

'Yeah?'

'See that Ellie-May gets the money, tell her I'm sorry.'

'You betcha.'

The gurgling breaths were shorter now.

In shock, skin pale and shiny.

A final, painful breath and he was gone.

'We'll have to leave him here for now.'

'Stay sharp. Let's RV with the CO and take the lower levels.'

'…and nail that M2.'

***

The Manchester guys had followed the rough track, which ran through the orchards and down to the sea.

They were ready to dive into the trees at any hint of trouble.

Presently they came to the cliffs and looked out to sea. The Valhalla was notable for its absence.

Steve was finding that his sticky-gun was cumbersome and uncomfortable on his back. As they prepared to take the incline down to the beach from the top of the cliffs, Steve released the straps with relief and dropped it down. So much easier with just a Beretta. Live rounds! You could get killed doing this!

As they turned the corner and on to the sand, a salvo of bullets ricocheted off the rocks and forced them to hit the deck.

A lone sentry, who was guarding the beach, continued to fire, keeping them pinned. Their team was completely new to all of this, but took to it just like they'd seen it done in the movies, commando-crawling round to take this guy out.

They started firing back as they spread out. Short bursts to start with, then a deluge of bullets. Lee caught the sentry dead centre and below the waistline. The guy was now in the ground, moaning like hell.

Lee finished him off easily with his M16 rifle butt, crushing his skull. The sand turned horribly dark with brain mush and blood. Lee was in his element.

Steve felt sick. His day job in IT hadn't really prepared him for this.

As Bell had instructed, they removed all the webbing of the dead guy, which included his comms gear.

Lee read the new message on his own handset.

'We're ordered back up to the house.'

They all headed back up the gradient.

There were a couple of waveriders moored in the shallows and a serious-looking, rigid-hulled inflatable, with twin engines. Shame they didn't have the keys!

The firefight at the house looked like normal villa fireworks from where they were standing. A casual observer would suspect nothing, other than an exclusive rave in full swing.

Steve pretended that his unusual armament was really heavy, and that he was having trouble with the straps.

'I'll catch you up,' said Steve.

'No jerking off! And watch out for bambi wire!'

They knew really, but disappeared into the night, back to the action like true professionals. There was no hurtful banter. He really appreciated that.

He would hide in the bushes, just off the quadbike track, till it was all over. It was embarrassing and he would have some explaining to do. The 'where-the-fuck-were-yous' would come in thick and fast. This was all in a different league. He would have to live with his cowardice.

He just wasn't up to it.

***

The sporadic crackle of gunfire continued, as the three Mancunians approached the rear of Dos Lunas to rejoin Bell's team.

Dave, the scaffolder, his M16 slung over his shoulder, was beginning to enjoy this. He felt the comforting gunmetal in his palm, knowing that he was fully tooled up with spare magazines, a Glock field knife, morphine, and grenades.

He was ready to kick ass and was getting a bung out of it as well. He didn't blame Steve. Not everyone could handle this crazy shit.

***

22:56.

Sienna walked over to Pago's mahogany desk.

There was a box of scented marzipan balls and dregs of champagne in a sticky glass. She tried all the drawers.

Nothing.

She scanned the room quickly for anything useful.

A miniature samurai sword, about twelve inches long, stood on a nearby coffee table, resting on a black lacquered plinth.

She pulled the blade from its scabbard, gingerly testing the razor-sharp kissaki tip which still managed to nick her index finger.

She could definitely give someone a nasty poke with it. She turned her attention back to the desk and its live CCTV console sitting on one corner. All the outside action was displayed as an eight-grid on the high resolution screen. She sat in Pago's chair and spun the trackerball with her thumb. There were armed combat troops out there, pinned down, trying to get in.

There must be some way to help them. Whoever they were, an enemy of Anna's was a friend of hers.

She ran to the door and out into the corridor.

It got a lot noisier.

The exit which led down to the beach was blocked off by a metal shutter. Explosive debris, glass and scorch marks covered the once pristine floor.

She noticed an almost invisible square panel to her right, set flush into the wall. She opened what looked like an air-con controller unit.

Three main options, 'Auto', 'Remote' and 'Manual'. After playing with the grid of buttons, she got it switched from remote to manual and punched the door-open pictogram. As the shutter started to retract, she retreated to the top of a stairwell, further back from Pago's office door.

The beach exit was now fully open.

She could hear heavy boots approaching on the gravel outside.

Time to make a split-second decision.

***

23:01

Kadic switched the Browning M2 to fully automatic, integrated with intelligent infra-red target recognition. It had plenty of ammo left, and would fire at any moving object that its sensors picked up. It would be the last time that he sat in this room. He was just about to run up the ladder, when an alarm sounded.

The complex rear door! A red warning blinked on his computer display. Manual override must have been engaged!

He didn't care anymore.

He was off.

***

23:01

Anna spun the cap off a half bottle of vodka and held out a Paloma Azul. Amber dutifully took the pill and put the bottle to her lips.

'Bottoms up,' grinned Anna, tightening the straps leading up from her crotch.

Anna had told her to forget the shower, but she still checked Amber's make-up carefully, particularly her lipstick.

The themed video room looked no different, but Anna seemed be in a hurry. They were ready to perform, if a little behind schedule. Amber prayed that Sienna had made it.

Anna wore black.

Amber wore white.

There were four cameras connected to the web feed. They began their routine in the dungeon, standing up.

Anna caressed Amber's breasts from behind, her wrists manacled to chains attached to the ceiling. She was used to it all now, the fondling, licking, penetration, and the fake orgasms. In fact she'd become really rather good at it. They had said that they would kill her otherwise.

Shark bait.

She had to play along, acting up for the cameras as Anna expertly twisted her nipples, causing her to scream out. Amber switched her mind off to it, and dreamed of her sister and freedom.

Get out of here and be in the arms of a man for a change.

The girl-on-girl action progressed to the horizontal, in accordance with the dictates of the script.

Amber now lay on the padded bench, in an unladylike pose, staring up at the white ceiling tiles.

The tickets for the Para Noya concert! They were pinned up in the kitchen back at the villa. All gone to waste now! To compensate, she imagined Michael Kroll performing on stage.

As Michael Kroll sang, Anna licked.

Anna delved into Amber's panties with experienced fingers and stroked the hair under her arms. Amber followed the choreography and parted her legs to allow Anna to seek out her engorged vulva, slick with natural juices. Amber could cope with Anna abusing her body for one last time.

The set progressed in the time-honoured way towards its climax, ticking the change points as it went. Anna had strapped her down like an oven-ready chicken. The white, silk knickers were long gone.

Anna seemed to be working faster than usual with her tongue, the finger-work somehow more impatient. Amber's head had to be turned to face camera number three, in order to film each stage of her arousal.

As Michael Kroll screamed in her mind, so would she.

Anna mounted her helpless charge, kissing her, licking her, joining her on camera three as it was piped out over the web. Amber knew that the finale was fast approaching and that it would soon all be over.

Hopefully forever.

It gradually dawned on Amber that the red light of camera three must be broken. In fact, none of the recording indicators seemed to be on! Then it hit her, they weren't transmitting a signal, the cameras weren't even rolling!

Anna was up to something, but what?

Why are we doing this?!

Blind panic and confusion dawned. Barely had she registered what might be happening, when Anna was upon her, lifting her neck a little, to slip the plastic bag over her head and seal it tight around her neck. Anna continued to thrust her strap-on into Amber, revelling in the violent muscle contractions of the object of her desire lying beneath her.

Amber fought wildly to get free, pulling hopelessly at her bonds, frantically sucking at the rapidly misting bag of carbon dioxide. Anna squeezed her down, frustrating any attempts to break free, relishing these delicious, last moments, as a hot orgasmic rush rose within her, the girl's desperate death-struggle heightening the pleasure of lustful, loveless sex.

The sticky rubber pressure points on the inside of Anna's bolt-on phallus brought Anna to an exquisite climax. Amber's pathetic thrashings had weakened and stopped. As her eyes closed, she lost consciousness and her heart stopped beating.

Anna rolled off the dead girl, unstrapping herself. She wiped the perspiration from her face on to her crumpled singlet, smelling the love juice on her hands.

She left Amber's limp body still in its bonds, looked over it, smiled and left the room, slamming the door behind her.

Let's do that again!

Fresh meat.

25 The bitch bites

2 3:05

They were ready to run across open ground, carrying with them the shaped explosive charges. The granite stonework provided adequate cover, but they had to stay tucked in tight. Three of the Manchester crew had just joined them.

'Where's Steve?' said Bell.

'Trouble with his straps and terrified,' Matt replied.

'I don't blame him. Keep your heads down. Follow us only when we're safely inside.'

If this didn't unfuck the situation, nothing would. Without warning, the back door started to grind open. It sent a bright dagger of light on to the gardens, beckoning them in. Had Zack got through and released the armoured shutters? There was no sign of the Marines. Bell couldn't raise him on his hand-held.

Was it a Kadic trick?

No time to worry about it.

Bell was deeply suspicious of the open patch of flat ground, a clear run to the back doors. The fifty-cal had inexplicably fallen silent.

To avoid what must be a minefield, they would run, like tightrope artistes, along the criss-cross of narrow, low walls.

'Now!' yelled Bell, leading off.

Donnie, Julio and Manos followed.

The Browning burst back into life, like it could think for itself. Bullets pecked the ground as they ran, slow at first, then speeding up like car tail-lights at an intersection.

They charged forward, running precariously along the uneven edges, crouching low and keeping their balance. Bell almost fell into the infinity pool as they arrived at the rear of the main building, and pressed themselves tightly against it.

Manos, who knew how to take a wrestling fall, had lost his footing and had survived a dusty landing. Amazingly, nothing bad had happened. All he had to do was stride back to the wall and take more care. He spared a moment to give them a 'Hey-what-kind-of-fuckwit-am-I?' grin.

Kawboom!

The Czech mine exploded, blowing both his legs off, below the knee. His expression now changed to annoyed shock, as his bulk crumpled back into the red dirt, setting off another mine which blew upwards into the centre off his back, finishing him off. His machete flew up into the air and landed just a few feet away from Julio, who retrieved his friend's killing tool. He adopted it as his own weapon.

A horrible and depressing assortment of dismembered body parts now lay about in front of them. Matt, Lee and Dave had popped their heads up without thinking. No!

Fifty calibre bullets stitched along the ground and killed Lee instantly. A round had disembowelled him, leaving a massive exit wound.

Give death and take death.

Matt and Dave fell back into their safety pit, covered in blood.

'Ma deuce' had eventually found its target.

No time to mourn fallen comrades.

'Dios ten piedad de nosotros!' spat Julio.

'Go!' ordered Bell.

They hugged the wall and poured into the hard-won entrance.

As well as combat boots bursting in at the rear, Sienna could hear heavy footfall running along the corridor from the front of the building. Alarmed and confused, she took fright and ran headlong down the staircase, just as Bell, Julio, and Donnie turned the corner.

She'd just missed him.

Matt and Dave weren't far behind, and they re-grouped in the corridor. Seconds later Zack, Richie, and Ben appeared. Three men down. More resistance possible on the lower levels.

Bell opened the door opposite, and the eight of them grouped around Ilya Pago's desk.

'I want Kadic alive!' screamed Bell.

Bell spread out a plan of the complex over the leather surface.

'We're here; Kadic occupies the security nerve centre, here. Julio and I will go and get him,' said Bell.

The Marines were despatched to head down to the factory and the bomb. The Manchester guys, Matt and Dave would stay and guard this level. They'd left a trail of bloody footprints on Pago's priceless rugs and looked unfazed, menacing, and in full control.

'Where is Pago?' inquired Julio.

'On his yacht,' said Bell.

'So, we have failed.'

'We're not done yet.'

Bell helped himself to one of Pago's marzipan balls.

***

23:18.

The control room was empty.

Just a large ashtray full of cigarette butts and a half-drunk bottle of Pedro Romero.

Bell looked carefully over the video panel, and plumped himself into Kadic's worn swivel chair, glancing up at the array of CCTV monitors. So this was how he'd kept an eye on them. His attention was immediately drawn to the wire escape ladder in the ceiling.

Bell got up there and peered down the side of the tower to the ground. The rope ladder was unfurled all the way. Kadic had escaped from under their noses!

According to the touchscreen display, the Browning M2 fifty-cal was set to automatic. Bell disabled all the systems and cut the power to the electrified fence. They could switch stuff back on when the whole place was secure, and if Dos Lunas hadn't become a radioactive hole in the ground.

A message, meant for Kadic, popped up on the desktop screen.

'ETA 23:40. Immediate evac to the Valhalla'

The Apache attack helicopter was on its way!

Bell knew that the fuselage of the AH-64 had his name etched on it. He felt a joyride coming on.

Marcel and Pietro, two of Pago's remaining gunmen, lay in wait.

Pietro unleashed a short burst from his AK47, but it jammed.

Julio took the initiative and leapt forward. He brought the machete down, with full force, through Pietro's left shoulder, all the way down to his rib cage. Julio whipped his machete out of the wound, stepped back smartly, and beheaded him with one lightning cut into the back of his neck. Manos would have been well pleased. Dios lo tenga en su gloria - God rest his soul.

Marcel appeared and emptied a magazine at Julio, who made a rolling somersault dive into the darkness as bullets ricocheted off the walls.

Julio levered himself up on his elbows, dazed, seeing double, and feeling nauseous. He'd dived headfirst into a wall, smacking his skull, and was now totally disorientated. Marcel stood above him, analysing his Mexican features. Julio's Beretta had skittered across the floor, well out of reach. His gold tiepin was his only weapon.

'You...you are El Cartero, aren't you? You look like the postman to me.'

Marcel raised his Glock a fraction.

The moment stood still. A hundred images flashed into Julio's mind, as he stared up at the gun barrel.

This son of a stinking whore would be the one. After a lifetime of struggle, it would end here. His exploits would enter cartel folklore, and maybe a narcorrido or two. New blood would take his place. He had failed. It would be quick, but there would be no explaining to do back in Mexico City. Plata o plomo - riches or death.

Julio closed his eyes, awaiting the inevitable.

Bell thrust the butt of his M16 hard into Marcel's temple, knocking him sideways, then swung the rifle round smartly, spraying a burst into the ex-legionnaire. Marcel was still alive, and had enough residual strength to reach for his Glock.

Bell was too fast for him, diving on top of Marcel as the shots rang out, just missing him.

Marcel's bloody hands thrashed close to Bell's face, searching for a good hold to tear at his flesh. Bell pressed tightly into Marcel's chest, and rammed his head up into the underside of his jaw. Bell felt Marcel's teeth crash together. The powerful jolt had stunned him for a vital moment. The blow would have snapped the brain stem of a weaker person.

Bell immediately switched to a nutcracker choke. He grabbed the sides of Marcel's collar, and pulled his hands forcibly together, crushing Marcel's Adam's apple with the knuckles of his index fingers. Bell then twisted the dying man's giant pumpkin head with both hands, and wrenched it harshly to the right, snapping his neck and spinal cord with one sharp twist.

He rolled off the corpse, worn out from the exertion.

Julio opened his eyes, gazing at angels. Bell grinned down at him, and helped the mildly concussed postman back to his feet, thrusting Julio's Beretta back into his hand.

'You'll live,' said Bell.

'Muchas gracias, mi amigo.'

***

Kadic ran flat out for the beach, like a springbok on amphetamines. He had the RHIB ignition key, a pile of euros, and a Latvian passport; enough gear to get back to Belgrade.

They weren't going to catch him now.

Steve had been waiting it out with his toxic Jell-O gun, carefully hidden in a thicket of ornamental bamboo.

He'd found it really peaceful, resting up amongst the rows of orange and almond trees. The smell was great and he'd be safe here till it was all over.

The jet nozzle oozed gunk on to the ground, leaving dollops of sticky-foam goop behind. He hoped that the fighting, which he had failed to contribute to, would end in victory. He'd been no use whatsoever. It was evident now that he just didn't have the balls; he was gutted. Hey! There is was again! The pad-pad-pad sound of trainers approaching.

Steve peered around the side of the thicket.

A dark figure raced along the track.

Not one of ours.

'Halt!' screamed Steve.

Kadic stopped a few metres away, and fumbled for his Russian Baikal IZH-79 pistol.

Steve levelled the stainless-steel barrel and slimed him with a thick plume of quick-setting phlegm. The synthetic compound expanded rapidly and wrapped itself around his legs, like frozen chewing gum. Kadic keeled over, face down, in a heap.

Adherent technology in action!

Steve stood over Kadic, deliberately holding the nozzle weeping the foul-smelling chemical mixture, close to his face. Kadic feared that a face-hugging omelette, which would suffocate him in seconds, would be next.

'Wriggle some more and I'll kick your fucking head in!' said Steve, with authority.

'What are you going to do with me?' bleated Kadic.

Steve kicked him hard in the face. Kadic recoiled as best as he could and howled in pain.

'We ask the questions.'

Kadic remained still. He knew that the jig was up. Steve buzzed Bell on his handset, more than delighted with the performance of his anti-personnel foam.

'I got me a runner!'

***

23:00

Sienna had made it down the stairwell to the next level, and started a frantic search for Amber.

The desire to find her was overwhelming. Amber had to be in one of the rooms on this level. Anyone who attacked Sienna would be slashed with the mini samurai sword. She could look after herself.

She stumbled across the Internet server room, with all its computer equipment, packed with pulsing lights and wires. Then the girls' quarters.

She unlocked door number one and surprised a couple of young women she'd never seen before. They cringed back with fear. She calmed them by saying that the police were raiding the place, and that they would soon be free.

Had they seen her sister Amber?

They knew nothing.

'Can we really go now?' the girls asked.

Sienna instructed them to run up the stairs to where armed officers were waiting. She moved on, opening door after door, liberating increasing numbers of traumatised detainees.

But no Amber.

Room number twelve, the last one at the end of the corridor.

She noticed that, strangely, the door was unlocked.

It should have told her something.

Her sixth sense should have warned her.

The surprise discovery that it was her and Amber's room, the room from which she had escaped with such effort, fuddled her judgment.

She pushed the door further open.

The sight of her sister overwhelmed her with joy. Amber was lying there asleep in her bed, curled up like a child, hiding under the bedclothes.

Their holiday nightmare was almost over.

Sienna approached the bed and stopped in her tracks. She had a bad feeling about this, it didn't feel right. Her breathing quickened as she edged closer to the still outline, covered by a sunflower-patterned duvet.

Instinctively, she went for the handle of the miniature samurai sword, as a precaution, but it was too late. Anna sprang from the bed like a screeching harpy, nails clawing and slashing.

Sienna backed up, trying to unsheathe her blade, but Anna was punching her repeatedly, dazing her. As Anna tried to gag her, Sienna bit her hand, only to be rewarded with a further torrent of head blows for doing so. Anna pulled the gag tight, the same type that had seen Dario Hernandez meet his maker, then dragged Sienna out of the room.

Halfway down the corridor, they could hear a group coming down the opposite stairwell. Anatoly Kadic swore incessantly in Serbian, as the guard detail marched past without seeing them.

'Idi Dodjavola!' he yelled.

23:20

The Marines had carried the immobilised Kadic back inside and down to the first sub-level. As they descended the stairs, they just missed catching sight of Anna with her captive.

Instead of using the web room, where Amber's body lay, Anna was forced to change her plan and descend to sub-level 2. Sienna clung on to a door handle in desperation, knowing that friendly forces were approaching. Tom must see her in order to save her, but Anna cruelly karate chopped her hand, breaking several of her fingers. She was wrenched her away before the guys came into view.

Sienna tried to scream, but Anna held the gag tight, as they progressed down the concrete steps. A few moments later, they were beyond the soundproofed security door, and out of sight.

***

They dragged Kadic, kicking and screaming, into the torture chamber. Bell turned to Julio.

'In the chair.'

'Mi placer,' replied Julio.

They strapped the Serbian war criminal into place, using a full set of restraints.

A door clanged in the distance, followed by the sound of army boots running down the corridor.

'You're not going to like this,' hollered Donnie.

'What is it?'

'We think we've found her!'

Bell grimaced, sensing that this was not necessarily good news. Kadic cottoned on quick.

'Your girl was a fine screw,' he teased, from the rigid confines of the dentist's chair.

***

Bell's stomach tightened as he entered the video room. Donnie and Matt stood back, as Bell approached Amber's limp body. He pulled the plastic bag off her head, full of moisture from her final, desperate breaths. He could detect the family likeness immediately. It was Amber, the younger sister that he had never met. It was a pitiful sight.

So where was Sienna? It would have to wait. They only had thirty minutes left.

First Kadic and the bomb.

***

Kadic glared back defiantly, knowing that he would have been approaching the Spanish mainland by now.

Bell stared Kadic in the eye.

'Quick answers.'

'Idi Dodjavola!' Kadic growled, twisting his forehead so violently that the steel bands restraining his head drew blood.

'How do we disarm the bomb?'

'Go to hell, you arsehole! Idi Dodjavola!'

Bell could smell coffee-brandy breath, mixed with strong tobacco and fear.

Bell snapped his fingers.

Julio squeezed the thirty inch bolt cutters shut on Kadic's little toe. Kadic screamed in disbelief as his bleeding little piggy landed on the grubby floor. He had never been tortured before. Now he was beginning to understand all the pain and suffering that he had inflicted.

'Try again?' said Bell.

'Idi Dodjavola!'

Julio had selected Kadic's right big toe this time. The toe joint cracked under the pressure of the bolt cutter jaws, as it was severed clean off. The useless stub bled profusely, as Kadic yelped like a smacked puppy.

The vision of Pago onboard the Valhalla, drinking champagne in the Lapis Lazuli lounge, flashed in front of Kadic's eyes. The injustice of it prompted the Serbian to start talking.

'Kranz is the only one who can disarm the bomb,' panted Kadic.

'Where is he?'

'On the Valhalla, of course. The device is booby-trapped. Tamper with it and it'll blow. Pago bought the USAF bomb on the dark web. Kranz is really a chemist, but Pago forced him to rewire the high-energy signal needed to detonate it, and add special security features. Kranz is very thorough. We're as good as dead.'

The room fell silent. Kadic knew nothing. They were all going to die. Bell bit his lip, then relaxed.

'Can I go now?' pleaded Kadic.

'I don't get it. You were prepared to put your trust in Pago?'

'He promised to send the Apache to pick me up.'

'I know. It's on its way.'

'What! I didn't believe him, so I had made my own arrangements!'

Bell checked the time.

'Anything else you wanna tell us?'

Kadic knew his life's journey would end in this chair. A sniper's bullet would have been better.

'Yeah, fuck you. Is that it? Are we done?'

'I think Donnie wants a word, he'll finish your pedicure.'

Kadic blanched in stark terror.

Julio handed Manos' machete to Donnie.

'Come on, we've got work to do,' said Bell.

***

The team raced down the back stairs to the factory level. The double airlock was easy to blow, and they now stood in the vacated factory complex which had been stripped of its equipment. It wasn't quite as Bell had remembered it.

They ran along the avenue of laboratory cubicles, each triple-glazed and secured with an airlock.

Bell came to a dead halt at the laboratory right next to the one where the hydrogen bomb was located. Through the window, he saw Sienna lying there.

She had been strapped down on a workbench by Anna, who smiled at him while toying with a couple of hand grenades. Anna had deliberately broken the door handle mechanism, and snapped off the security key in its lock. She approached the window and taunted them with a moist kiss against the glass, which left a lasting Cupid's bow imprint. Next, she put her index finger in her mouth, then pointed it at her watch, laughing. A moment later, she had Sienna cruelly gripped by the throat, which was making her gag violently.

Bell pressed his forehead against the window in despair.

The evil witch produced a plastic bag and pulled it tightly over Sienna's head, sealing it around her neck with duct tape. Giving them all the finger was the final insult, calculated to elicit blind rage.

Bell stared helplessly at the spectacle, torn between saving her and disarming the thermonuclear device.

The guys tugged frantically at Bell's combat jacket.

'Come on! It's 23:42…we're running out of time!'

'We have to break in and save her,' replied Bell, robotically.

'Leave her, we're all going to die, anyway,' bawled Donnie.

'We've only got seventeen minutes left!'

Bell pulled himself away, with regret, but it was the right decision. The worst feeling was to see the look on Sienna's face, begging him to save her. Bell forced himself to snap out of it and switch his mental processes back into hyperdrive, issuing brisk instructions.

'Julio and I will defuse the bomb. Donnie and Richie will intercept the Apache and have it prepped for immediate dust-off. Ben and Zack! Have a defibrillator and full resus capability on standby while you break in there and kill that bitch!'

Bell calmly instructed Ben Eulberg, a decorated US Marine combat medic, to draw on all his medical knowledge and experience. He'd be receiving more than a crate of beer if he pulled it off.

'Please save my little girl for me.'

26 Ibiza rocks

Becky had worked a miracle, covering up the bruising on her face with foundation and pancake concealer. It would hold up under poor lighting, but nothing amorous.

She had dropped out of Debs' hen night, leaving them to it. The gals would soon have their knickers down by their ankles, the way they were knocking back the vodka mixers. Wicked! Not that a double gusset was ever going to get in anyone's way. She could get laid any time she liked, now that she'd split up with Lee.

Her last night on the island. Shame she had to fly back to Gatwick tomorrow, but she'd sleep it off in a window seat if she had to.

In the meantime, she was dressed to kill.

She had tickets to get into Manumission at the Labyrinth Club, but what about Para Noya's final tour performance, tonight at Ibiza Rocks?

Shame to miss it, but it was a sell-out.

Where had Tom got to? If she happened to bump into him, it would be straight back to his place and into the sack for a little action.

First stop, the Esclavo bar. A quick look around and a JD and coke in the semi-darkness. She was promptly groped and had her bum pinched by some randy sicko. It was only when they got through to your perineum that you really had to worry.

She dug around in her handbag and found what she was looking for.

The foil blister pack produced her last remaining tablet of Paloma Azul, which was helped down by Jack Danny and flat cola.

She flipped a two euro coin.

Heads.

It was settled then.

Next stop Bar M, then the Mambo bar.

After that, back to the Labyrinth club for the amazing Manumission set. Please, please, Tom, come out of hiding any time you like!

***

Tonight, Ibiza Rocks would host the climax of Para Noya's forty-date world tour, going out live on MTV.

The eyes of the world were on Ibiza.

The other members of the band, who had struggled to keep the profligate Kroll alive for latter stages of the tour, were holed up in the hotel's top floor penthouse suite, nervously waiting for the call to go on.

No sign of their frontman.

It didn't look good.

Johnny Lazzara fretted that, after getting through thirty nine dates, Michael looked like he was going to be missing for the grand finale. Their manager was going mental. Had Kroll topped himself back at the villa? They all knew that unless something incredible happened, Kroll had already sung for the last time.

Who the hell had given him that Beretta, anyway?

***

The news had come through that an ambulance, with a resuscitation team, had been called to the villa. Then the story was that Kroll had overdosed and was in a coma. Another that he'd been found dead in a pool of blood with slit wrists. The rental villa was now completely surrounded by the press, as they waited for a corpse to be stretchered out.

Earlier that afternoon, an unshaven Michael Kroll had lain slumped on the sofa, feeling like shit. He'd been contemplating the patterns made on the ceiling by the jagged piece of mirror glass that he was holding. Then, unexpectedly, his cell-phone had rung, taking him by surprise.

'So, you haven't slashed your wrists yet?' teased Bell.

Kroll pulled himself up and laughed, clearing his throat, delighted to hear his mentor's voice.

'No, but I still have an appetite for self-destruction. How d'ya get this number?'

'Signy has tweeted that she still loves you.'

'She does?'

'Give it something special tonight, just for me, okay?'

'I won't be there,' croaked Kroll.

'What?'

'This is the end of the line,' he replied, mournfully.

The call went dead.

Bell shook his head in despair. So much for reverse psychology.

Kroll lay down again and lit another cigarette. The tobacco smoke snaked and lingered as he wept.

***

Ben and Zack raced back from the medical unit, dragging with them all the kit they would need. They set about dealing with Anna.

She had cunningly disabled the door lock. One sharp kick from her steel toe-capped boot had clinched it. Further merciless kicks to Sienna's body had crushed the residual resistance out of her reluctant playmate. Anna had hauled her screaming prize on to a workbench and strapped her down. It was Anna's lucky night.

More fun with a plastic bag.

After so many girls, so little time left.

She lay astride Sienna, knocking back her last bottle of vodka, whilst dangling two US M67 fragmentation grenades from her index finger.

If one of those blew, it might affect any tilt mechanism attached to the bomb in the next room. Poor Sienna no longer writhed in her bindings. Her body lay there lifeless, with a misty plastic bag over her head.

Anna had performed her suffocation trick once again with ruthless efficiency. She toasted the guys peering through the glass with a cruel smile, and took another swig of triple-distilled nectar. As Anna stared at the empty bottle and threw it at the wall, Ben nipped up and placed a ten second limpet charge on the security glass.

In her drunken state, Anna failed to notice a grey tangerine discreetly adhered to the corner of the laboratory window. The charge blew the triple-glazed pane into the room, causing Anna to fall back off Sienna and on to a fresh carpet of shattered glass.

The shock sobered her up immediately.

Anna thrashed like a wildcat, clawing her way through the razor sharp debris, covered in blood. She reached the nearest grenade and fumbled to remove the pin. Ben was too quick for her. The Marine clinically and accurately pumped three rounds into Queen bitch Grimhilde's head.

She lay there lifeless, the dildo toy still strapped to her, incongruously maintaining its perfect erection. They heaved the equipment through the prickly window frame as fast as they could. A defibrillator, oxygen tanks, tubing, and packs of epinephrine.

'Have the epi ready and plug this in!' shouted Ben.

'Epi?'

'Adrenaline!, knucklehead!'

'But the other girl's dead.'

'I'm the fucking medic, just do what I tell you!'

'Okay, okay! Whatever you say!'

Ben knew exactly what he was about.

Breathing life into a pile of eviscerated body parts was his business. He checked for a pulse and lifted Sienna's left eyelid. The dyke had had enough time to get her kicks and damage the goods. This was Bell's girl and he was going to do everything he could save her. The Brit had good taste for sure. He thought of his own girl, waiting patiently for him back in the US.

They quickly unstrapped Sienna's limp body and got to work. They ripped her T-shirt open, and Ben peeled off the adhesive pads of the resuscitation electrodes and connected them up. They had only a few minutes to pull her back from clinical death.

***

291

Bell and Julio stood in the room where the USAF hydrogen bomb was mounted upon its specially-made, heavy-duty trestle and castors. It was fitted with a model 7 W28 lightweight, class D warhead. It had been lost by the USAF over Palomares, in January 1966.

Bell spotted a small piece of dried seaweed stuck to one of the fins. He looked it over carefully, on the outside chance that there was a blatantly obvious 'on-off' switch.

Worth checking.

Different coloured wires, from various devices with dials and displays, converged on the main section of the bomb. The centrepiece was the trigger transformer, which would deliver the initial, high-voltage discharge when it received the instruction.

Had it really been booby trapped? Liquid mercury, possibly. A severe jolt might set the whole thing off. He couldn't take the chance, despite the urge to start pulling at random wires in the blind hope that the countdown would happily stop.

Julio stood there like a man fighting to wake up from a nightmare. Bell had to keep an eye on him. Julio's eyes betrayed a loosening grip on reality, brought on by a surfeit of life-threatening events. He'd been subjected to too much excitement for one evening.

His complexion was pale and sweaty despite the aircon. He was looking unhinged, probably not helped by head-butting the wall earlier on.

Yeah, they might well be wasting their time playing 'hunt the thimble'.

They weren't even sure what they were looking for. Bell noted the zirconium alloy tubing, lead shielding and dosimeters pushed into the corners of the room like discarded, online purchases. Julio had said that he knew something about security and alarm systems.

'See if you can understand the cabling. We need to know which wire cables trigger and power the primary fission sequence!' instructed Bell, firmly.

Julio inspected the prone device and complex detonation set-up in minute detail. It didn't mean much to him. He was out of his depth. It was far too advanced for him. With no instruction manual, the fiendish rig was way above his pay grade.

The curved outer plates had been cunningly re-welded back into place by Lucifer himself. The shell could be harbouring half a dozen anti-tamper devices.

It was useless.

'Santa Muerta!…Día de los Muertos! It is the work of the devil!' wailed Julio.

Bell looked up from Kranz's desk.

The counter had a kind of mesmerising quality to it, as detonation time drew inexorably closer. The moment when this elderly piece of ordnance would finally strut its stuff. A rapidly expanding ball of gas which would melt the very rock around them at a temperature of tens of millions of degrees centigrade.

Bell felt a small grain of cheer that at least it would be quick and painless. Seeing the room for the second time, he realised how much paper there was. Piles of diagrams, calculations and formulae, much of it in Kranz's Germanic handwriting.

There were a couple of boxes lying around which still contained a few strangely shaped transistors. Bell knew that they were nuclear detonators called Krytrons. Didn't you need a US export licence for them? Bell held one up to the light for a moment. The Krytrons would deliver the arc discharge that would set the whole thing cooking.

It proved to Bell that Kranz had the know-how to rig it up for a successful ground burst. Bell sifted through the loose papers at speed. It didn't help that most of it was scribbled in German, which made it doubly incomprehensible. Bell looked up for a moment and glanced at the counter.

Julio's fearful eyes glared back at him. Bell realised that, without Helmut Kranz, there was nothing they could do. Bell ignored what was happening next door, suppressing the urge to see Sienna.

He'd keep searching till the fat lady sang.

***

Becky cut short her visit to Bar M after a few drinks. In Club K she bumped into what was left of Debs' crew, who were now completely legless. The overhead monitors were playing archive footage of Para Noya performing the songs 'Magic Eye' and 'Pulsar Ulcer', at the London O2 indoor arena.

A lightbulb idea popped up.

There was no sign of Lee, which was good. Tom was not to be found in any of the clubs, which was bad in a sexually frustrating kind of way.

Why not go and meet the band in person, given that they were actually in town?

In the flesh.

Otherwise, what a wasted opportunity! She'd be back in Essex tomorrow, selling knickers. She settled on throwing a sickie – it was her duty to make every second count.

Debs had a guy on each arm.

Blokes! Brains below the waistline and limited in size! Debs opened her mouth, not for the last time that evening.

'Have you seen either Lee or Tom?' quizzed Becky.

'I thought you'd finished with Lee. So who's Tom? Something we should know about? Why not come back with us?'

Becky could visualise a hideous game of nude Twister. No, she had other ideas.

'Not tonight, Debs.'

She decided to ditch the creep who'd been buying her drinks and make a run for it. She shot out of the bar and jumped in front of a taxi.

'Carrer Cervantes, rápido!'

The taxi raced through San An, coming to a halt just a side street away from the big gig.

Becky jumped out.

The front of the building was swarming with fans, press, and security. Entirely as expected.

Becky hoped that Lady Luck was with her.

She marched around the back, and got to the kitchen service door near the bins and the delivery bays.

Armed with a Morse code sequence that a call girl had confided to her in Mambo's, she strode up and rapped on the door with her knuckles.

Nothing.

Louder this time.

A chef wielding a meat cleaver promptly opened the door and waved her in. She was now enveloped by a pandemonium of food preparation.

She was shown to the lift doors, with a knowing wink. A few seconds later the Otis doors eased open and she entered the express elevator to heaven.

Cocaine and Cognac!

The door closed but, to her horror, immediately reopened. Becky held her breath and turned away as a tall figure strode in behind her. Help! In the lift mirror she could see the person removing their motorcycle helmet.

'Michael Kroll!'

Kroll turned in a flash and looked her up and down.

He flicked the emergency stop button, causing the lift car to shudder to a halt between floors.

'B...but I thought that you'd....'

'...topped myself...yeah...I nearly did.'

'You're alive!'

'...And kicking, sshhh, don't tell anyone,' grinned Kroll, pressing his index finger upon her lips.

'So you'll be on tonight?'

'Of course! My guardian angel said he would never forgive me!'

'Wow! This is unreal!'

'Singing 'Cocaine and Cognac', as always. My life coach talked me out of it, made me see sense. He helped me deal with the pain and told me that I wasn't alone. Gave me a new perspective.'

'I'm Becky, by the way.'

Maybe somebody like that could help her get out of Basildon. Kroll moved closer in the confined space and ran his hand through her hair. Becky looked up into his eyes and wondered when she was going to wake up.

'I'm pumped up and ready to perform.'

'Surely, we haven't got time?'

'We don't.'

'You have to give me a nice kiss first.'

'Make it hard for me, won't you!'

27 White island

Ilya Pago supped a malt whisky in Valhalla's palatial Lazuli Lounge.

He savoured the warm glow of well-being as his yacht headed west, creating a safe distance between him and the site of an imminent nuclear explosion. It felt even better to know that he was shaking off the Alacrán cartel. He would make a fresh start somewhere else.

Pago knew that if he held on to Kranz, no one could possibly defuse the bomb. Kranz looked decidedly stressed and uncomfortable, nursing a sweet sherry on the opposite sofa. The elderly chemist didn't drink, but he was seriously thinking of starting now.

As light conversation wasn't up to much, Pago flicked through a rare 1797 copy of De Sade's novel, entitled Justine. He twisted the book around into various positions, as he studied the pornographic illustrations. Finally, he looked at his Rolex and fastidiously returned the volume to the walnut bookcase.

Pago nodded to Kranz and they ascended the spiral staircase to the top deck of the Valhalla.

Kranz felt quite dizzy now from the sherry, hypertension, and the swell of the Valhalla, cruising at twenty five knots towards Gibraltar.

As they appeared on deck, vintage champagne on ice greeted them. Powerful flash goggles had also been provided, along with fresh caviar and toast. Although unmarried and inexperienced in the matters of love, Kranz could think of no worse person than Pago to share such a romantic setting. They took their places on the cushioned teak chairs pointing astern. A perfect balmy August evening to witness the detonation of their salvaged Cold War firecracker. Total destruction of Dos Lunas and all the evidence. It would be like having a good shit.

There would, of course, be a detonation flash and a blast wave to be aware of, other than that, happy days. They would be treated to a superb view of the mushroom cloud, as it sucked up debris and emitted billions of gamma particles.

What an intelligent decision to have Valhalla's twin diesel engines serviced recently.

Pago checked his hand-held GPS and walked over to the champagne bucket. He poured a flute for Kranz and placed it down. The snowy wash of the twin screws could be seen trailing behind them in a straight line, all the way back to the horizon.

'But I don't drink,' bleated Kranz, meekly.

'Nonsense, of course you do,' replied Pago, grinning.

'One mustn't mix one's drinks,' he countered.

'Just a few sips of sherry?!…we'll have you three sheets to the wind yet, eh!?'

'B…but champagne…'

'Come on you boring fart, cheer up! We'll make an old seadog of you yet!'

Pago slapped Kranz's leg hard, in a mock Captain Bluebeard kind of way, which made Kranz's leg sting like buggery. The amateur physicist betted that there would be a crimson welt, in the shape of a hand, to be seen if he were to roll up his trouser leg. Pago glanced at his watch again and raised his glass.

'To your little baby. Not long now. Salut!'

Kranz held the new type of drink by the stem and hunkered down into the comfortable seat covers.

He drifted back to his childhood, when his aunt Magda had looked after him after his parents had died. She had raised him with great love and affection, as if he had been her own, teaching the serious little boy dedication and hard work. She had bought him a toy yacht to sail on the nearby lake in the summer sunshine.

He thought back to his first chemistry set, and how he had experimented with iron filings and copper sulphate. The gift had triggered something in the bright, solitary boy, and it wasn't long before he was producing chlorine gas with batteries, carbon electrodes, and saline solution. He wished he was back by the wood-burning stove, in his auntie's cuckoo clock house, overlooking the Alpine pastures.

Due to ill health, she had been told by her physician to move to warmer climes. Regrettably, she had sold her little dwelling when he went away to Zürich university to read chemistry. She had moved to southern Spain initially, and then had bought a small apartment in Cala Vadella in Ibiza, where she could end her days, painting in watercolour.

Her pulmonary infections had gradually cleared up, and she had blossomed into her eighties. There was no way Kranz was going to let his surrogate mother be vaporised into nuclear particles.

'You look nervous, Kranz.'

'What about all those people?'

'There are too many people in the world.'

'Don't you feel any guilt or remorse?'

'Not at all!' grinned Pago.

Kranz squeezed his eyes shut, gulping the whole glass down in one.

He had disobeyed his master.

There were no anti-tamper devices. Discontinuity in any of the wiring would instantly disable the bomb, but anyone standing over it, watching the clock count down to zero, wouldn't know that.

He prayed that someone was going to find his note.

***

Julio looked on, mesmerised by the dials spinning on the red LED counter. The display helpfully counted down in tenths of a second.

'We only have eleven minutes left!' he blurted, facing certain death for the second time that evening.

Julio's face was white. He looked in vain at his watch, wishing he was back in Mexico with better odds of survival. If only he was in a bar drowning in tequila, with one arm around the waist of a pretty girl.

He whispered a rushed Hail Mary. Preparing to meet his maker, he crossed his heart. Ave Maria. El Mexicano shook his head. What stood before him dwarfed the complexity of any alarm system he had ever dealt with. The shock of losing Manos was superseded by what he was looking at now.

Forcing the vision of Sienna with a plastic bag over her head from his mind, Bell tried to concentrate on the dilemma that faced them.

The hydrogen bomb, with its corroded casing and USAF markings, stood stubbornly before them, withholding its secrets. In eleven minutes time, a small fission bomb would fire, causing the main fusion device to detonate. Things were going to get pretty hot around here. The loud sporadic clicks from the Geiger counter, which indicated gas ionisation as alpha particles passed through the air, were driving them both mad.

Bell noticed a box of RAD badges on one of the shelves. The pair were being bombarded with dangerous radiation just by being there. The sheer balls and demonic wickedness of Pago amazed him.

'You sure it will really blow?' asked Julio.

'Yup. If it goes, the White Island really will be white. An incandescent ball of pure white light.'

'It's too late!' panicked Julio.

'We can't give up…the answer must be here somewhere!'

Julio held Manos's machete in his hand, shaking with fear.

'Let me cut through the fucking wires! Maybe that will stop it!'

Julio raised the blade, ready to hack at the snaking tendrils of insulated copper. Bell lunged forward and grabbed Julio's forearm. He could feel the taut, sinewy muscles concealed by his jacket sleeve, and smelled terror on Julio's dry breath.

'No! It will detonate for sure! We still have time. Help me look through these papers, the answer must be here. It has to be!'

'Can't we just cut the power?!'

'Keep looking!'

Julio dropped the machete, and they both moved over to Kranz's work bench.

They ploughed frantically through the piles of technical diagrams, tables, and illegal downloads from classified US military websites.

Donnie ran up to the other side of the glass window, and signalled that they had hijacked the Apache. Incredibly, Pago had kept his word.

The news spurred Bell on to work faster, scrabbling through the documents which flew in all directions.

'Look for anything unusual or which could possibly be special instructions!'

All of a sudden, something caught Bell's eye.

Under an atomic decay chart.

He fished it out and studied it, motionless.

Julio stopped in his tracks, open-mouthed, hope against hope. O Coatlaxopeuh! Crush this serpent!

Bell stared at a sheet of paper with six lines of Kranz's characteristic, Teutonic handwriting, headed by an exquisite childlike drawing.

No protons or plasma cores this time.

A small boat, with a jib and mainsail, on a lake surrounded by pine trees and cuckoo clock houses. The sun was shining, in a clear bright sky, beating down on snow-capped mountains. Bell read the words out aloud.

'Let it be said
File V to Z
Will indicate to you
That which you have to do
To save this white isle of pines
From thermonuclear mines!'

Bell spun round and looked at the book shelves, A-B, C-E marked on empty box files, then V-Z. Bell hooked the file off the wall in an instant and felt something inside. He opened it to reveal a TV remote with an arrow pointing to the standby button.

Six minutes to go on the LED display.

Not a problem now!

Three hundred and sixty beautiful seconds!

In the rush, the remote fell out of the box file and dropped on to the floor. The plastic casing snapped off the back and the batteries flew out.

Bell retrieved one battery but the other had rolled under a desk. Julio and Bell forced the heavy piece of furniture back with brute force. Bell pressed both the triple-As back into place, squinting at the minute polarity markings moulded into the black plastic.

Julio closed his eyes and crossed his heart.

He thanked the Virgin Mary and the ancient gods of his homeland for hearing his prayer.

Bell pressed the red pulse button on the zapper. Julio and Bell held their breath for a long moment…

The counter stopped.

The LED display had frozen at 23:57:11.

With trembling fingers, Bell warily took out the batteries and replaced the zapper cover.

'Nobody touch fuckin' nuthin'!' warned Bell, through gritted teeth.

Damp patches were clearly noticeable under the armpits of Julio's suit jacket. His outfit had definitely been put through it today.

The Mexican needed a tequila. A large one. Several large ones, in fact.

'Now Pago!'

28 La ley del más fuerte

They raced to the helipad to the waiting Apache helicopter gunship.

The machine, which had cost the US taxpayer over twenty million dollars had mysteriously gone AWOL from its secure compound in southern Afghanistan. As it had forgone daily operations in Helmand province, it was still in perfect condition. Richie could even detect that unmistakable 'new car smell' through his visor.

Richie was seated at the cockpit controls, ready to go. Bell donned a flying helmet and life jacket, and climbed in alongside. The rotation of the blades quickened to a humming blur.

The pilot from the Valhalla, the arsehole who had tried to mow Sienna and himself down in the Cala Comte sand dunes that day, lay stripped naked face down in the dust, with plastic ties around his wrists and ankles.

'She's fully armed and has a three-quarter tank!' shouted Richie, now in his true element.

Bell scanned the rainbow of electronics, as he tightened his webbing and ensured that he was nicely snuggled into his calf-leather seat.

The AH64 lifted off and headed effortlessly south west at one hundred and eighty knots.

Bell looked below to see the lights of Cala Vadella and the fabled island of Es Vedra disappearing quickly behind them. Somewhere down there Para Noya were playing their set with or without the talented Michael Kroll.

Time stood still as the Apache ate up the darkness, cruising smoothly along just above the waves, powered by its twin General Electric turbo-shaft engines. He could discern regular blips of light on the radar, fishing boats or ferries heading to and from Valencia or Denia, on the Spanish coast.

'I have her, fifty three kilometres and closing. ETA nine minutes,' came Donnie over the intercom.

Bell was not going to be sitting in snug comfort for much longer. He switched to forward looking infrared and checked his personal armament.

Two Berettas, extra magazines, Phorox grenades, and a commando knife strapped to each ankle. If he had boobs, he would be Lara Croft.

He thought of Judy briefly, then Sienna. That bitch Anna had got to her first. What bad luck. Was he going to be denied a fairy-tale ending? He felt a surge of anger and adrenaline at the thought, and took a Benzedrine tablet.

Six minutes.

He went to feel the fading scar on his temple but ended up touching his helmet instead. He laughed to himself and checked the quick release latches. He went over the rough layout of the Valhalla in his mind again.

'Hey chief, the Hellfire missiles on this bitch are fixed with depleted uranium warheads!'

'Let's have some of that,' replied Bell, knowing that the DU ordnance would penetrate the hull of the Valhalla like a hot knife through butter.

Somewhere in the distance waited Ilya Pago, in the full knowledge that Kadic had failed. Bell suspected that Pago would want to kill Kadic immediately on touchdown. To all intents and purposes, the passenger emerging from the Apache would be Anatoly Kadic.

***

Pago went berserk when he realised that there would be no nuclear explosion. He ripped his protective goggles off, and threw the bottle of malt whisky overboard, closely followed by the silvered champagne bucket and stand. He drew his handgun from its effeminately decorated holster and pointed it at Kranz.

'I thought you had assured me!...' he spat, through gritted teeth and saliva, holding his gun against Kranz's forehead.

He was about to blast Kranz's exceptional scientific brain through the slats of his teak deckchair, when the bridge buzzed up with an urgent message. The Apache would be back in four minutes.

Pago changed his mind on a whim.

He would deal with Kadic first and kill Kranz later. Whatever happened, they would both be feeding the fishes before dawn. He ordered an armed reception party on to the heli-deck. Both fifty-calibre machine guns, concealed under fibreglass pods on the port and starboard sides were made ready. The Browning M2 was a reliable servant you could trust without question.

Four minutes away from the Valhalla, the radio crackled into life. An F16 pilot from the USS Indianapolis on routine patrol, had pinged their Apache MID transponder. A routine ID confirmation.

'Don't answer!' shouted Bell.

As the helicopter made its final approach to the Valhalla, Donnie unleashed the M230 chain gun, slaved to his helmet mounted display, firing 30mm linkless ammunition at twelve hundred rounds per minute. It cut a swathe through the inexperienced sailors brandishing AK47s on the deck.

The torrent of shells spewed up and splintered the beautifully-oiled teak planking, ripping big holes in the immaculate superstructure. Never mind swim-suited bimbos in stilettos mincing up and down the deck spoiling the pristine woodwork.

Pago looked on in horror at the carnage. As Richie come in for a second pass, two F16 vipers swooped down from nowhere and ordered Richie to identify himself. The jets had checked the MID, and had now remotely immobilised the helicopter armament. Richie had levelled out and had been seconds away from releasing two Hellcat missiles amidships, but the systems were jammed.

'Drop me off on the middle deck and go with those guys. We'll answer questions later!'

The gunship darted in and Bell was in business. Richie peeled off to join his enforced F16 fighter escort back to the USS Indianapolis, with some explaining to do.

Richie's radio crackled one more time.

'Hey, who are you buddy? Your AH64 is meant to be in a concrete hangar in Afghanistan!'

Bell raced past the buckled bodies and limbs, shooting an officer in the head who wasn't fast enough, and charged up the steps to the top deck.

As he flew up the last step, he found himself face to face with the portly master criminal himself.

Ilya Pago stood twenty metres away at the other end, relaxing against the guard-rail. They were now both pointing a handgun at each other.

Glock versus Beretta.

Bell took a couple of paces across the smooth camber of the corked decking and stopped dead.

'So, we meet again. You're a clever bastard Mr Bell. Anatoly was right, I should have killed you when I had the chance. How is the treacherous Anatoly, by the way? Just can't get the staff these days, eh?' Pago pursed his thin, anaemic lips with uncontrolled venom.

'He's all cut up,' smiled Bell.

'So, you spoiled my little firework display this evening. As your name suggests, you delivered.'

'Gee, I'm sawry, Meester Pago,' mocked Bell, in a Bugs Bunny voice.

'I suppose Senor Salazar would still like my head, and I had hoped to cover my tracks so sweetly. How much is the Alacrán cartel paying you Mr Bell? I will double it…if you let me leave the Mediterranean and sail on to pastures new.'

'I work for British Military Intelligence.'

Pago blanched slightly at the revelation, revealing a faint look of amusement on his bleached, puggy face. Bell had him at a disadvantage. They had failed to find out who he actually was. Kadic had been right. Only Bell knew the answer. Pago would just have to play along with the charade.

'MI6? Bit keen, aren't we? So where is the postman?'

Bell grinned.

'Sitting in your office eating your marzipan balls.'

'I like balls,' replied Pago, smiling, 'so what now?'

Bell's expression hardened.

'I want you to turn the Valhalla around and head back to Ibiza Town.'

Pago raised his eyebrows is response. His nostrils flared.

'A U-turn? I'm afraid I can't do that. Aren't you forgetting something?'

'What?'

'That I, too, am a clever, resourceful bastard. You don't think I got where I am today by doing spreadsheets, do you?'

Pago laughed a deep, bellicose laugh, still keeping his Glock M32A trained on Bell's sternum.

Bell calculated the distance across the deck to be about ten metres.

Little prospect of rushing him.

Bell felt the Valhalla lurch violently to starboard.

He fell to the deck, but hey, the ship wasn't listing!

The decking surface had split perfectly down the middle, as the hydraulics turned it into two forty-five degree flaps. Bell stood no chance and he just failed to catch one hand on the ridge. He lost his gun as his fingernails scraped at the polished surface in vain. He slithered out of control over the edge of the starboard side, and into the creamy wash of the Valhalla, some twenty five metres below.

Pago beamed with delight.

It had been an expensive modification, but worth it.

Bell hit the water awkwardly, like smashing into concrete. Torn muscles, compacted ribs, and empty lungs.

He could feel the vibration of the screws, as the Valhalla sped away. What had seemed like a superfluous life jacket now burst into life, dragging him back up to the surface. He had plenty of time to watch the stern navigation lights of the Valhalla disappear into the night.

For a second time on this mission, he was stuck alone in pitch darkness, considering his options.

The trawler had seen the flare. Just good fortune, that far out. Thank God for night fishing!

***

'You were lucky!' smiled Julio.

'We were all lucky,' said Bell.

The two men waited in Sienna's private hospital room in the Galeno clinic. Bell sat right next to Sienna's bed, staring at her face. He held her bruised hand, still chafed and cut from the labours of escaping from her cell. The other hand, with its broken fingers, had been expertly bandaged and set. Anna's hideous lovebites were still visible on her neck.

The sun was setting, just like the first day he had met her. It seemed a long time ago now. Julio had chosen to stand against the wall, looking cool and relaxed in a new suit, fresh shirt, and shark skin loafers.

'She's beautiful isn't she?'

'Yes, I know,' replied Bell, stroking her blond hair, remembering how she had unlocked the rear doors to Dos Lunas.

Footsteps approached and the door opened. The senior consultant, the duty doctor, and a nurse entered. The papers had all been prepared, ready to sign. Bell hesitated for a moment.

'Señor, it is for the best, there are no responses, no vital signs,' soothed the top guy with the grey hair.

Bell looked up, a tear welling in his eye. He glanced at Julio who shrugged, then stared down at the tiled floor. Bell spun his signature across the wad of forms and handed them back. Ben Eulberg had done his best. His desperate attempts to save her with the defibrillator, adrenaline and any other medical voodoo he'd had at his disposal had failed. The nurse in a starched hat leaned over to turn off the life support machine.

'No!' said Bell, with authority.

The room froze.

Bell wished that Sienna would open her eyes and give him a 'So, you're not a doctor, then!', glaring at him in defiant ridicule. He thought back to the short time they'd had together. Love and attraction burned in a crucible at a high temperature. Now there would be no lazy road-trip heading north from Valencia back to England in a silver Ferrari. No sleepy hotels and intimate dinners for two. No more carefree laughter and the chance to really get to know each other. No refinement of the act of physical love. He had broken all his promises to her, to protect her and get her through this. Here is where the story ends, this is goodbye.

'I will do it.'

Bell got up slowly and walked over to the medical box of tricks, and flicked the power switch.

'She would have wanted it this way.'

He sat down again next to her.

'Goodbye Sienna,' whispered Bell, into her ear.

He kissed her on the lips for the last time and then finally on her smooth forehead.

'She saved us…and Ibiza,' said Julio.

Bell released Sienna's hand, placed it back on the bed sheet and stood up.

'Yes,' he replied.

Now she would go and join Amber, her beautiful sister, whom he had only met in death. El Cartero crossed himself. This hardened killer from the favelas had a tear in his eye too.

***

Bell and Julio had returned to the Fenecia Prestige hotel in Santa Euralia. They sat in the gourmet La Vinoteca restaurant, which served exotic Mediterranean dishes. Although it was high season, Bell had paid the manager handsomely to close the restaurant for them.

The two men wanted to eat alone.

They had finished their sumptuous meal and were nursing large Spanish brandies in plush, peaceful surroundings. Each of them sat back and looked into space, contemplating those lost in battle. Fallen comrades. They both knew what business they were in.

Two waiters hovered in the distance in the deserted dining room, well out of earshot. They awaited the slightest hand signal. Julio placed another cigarette between his lips, lit it and dropped his gold lighter back in between the fine crockery. He raised his glass. Bell did likewise.

'Manos and the other guys,' Julio toasted, sombrely.

'Sienna and Amber.'

Julio pulled his lips taut against his teeth, extending his upper lip unnaturally downwards.

'My flight for Madrid leaves in a couple of hours. There are some matters I need to discuss with you.'

He produced a gold trinket out of his pocket, a beautiful and rare fifteenth century statue of Mitlantecuhtli, the Aztec god of the dead.

'This is for you.'

The solid gold skull and body of the king of Mictlan stared up from Bell's palm, its rictus grin and rib cage clearly visible.

'For me?'

Bell looked at the intricate depiction of the deity, fashioned by Aztec artisans hundreds of years earlier.

'This jewel is priceless and I'm deeply honoured Julio, but why?'

Julio waved Bell's riposte away with a shrug. As he did so, Bell noticed a small, black scorpion tattoo located just above his left wrist.

'You saved my life on at least two occasions, and you helped the cartel in its mission to capture and kill its sworn enemy. There is a special bond between men who have fought alongside each other.'

'You didn't need to…'

'El puño de hierro is deeply indebted to you and wishes to express its gratitude. A rare honour. I am sorry Manos is not here also to shake your hand and drink with us.'

The Iron Fist, a.k.a. the Alacrán drug cartel based in the city of Durango. Its influence straddled the Gulf of Mexico to the east and the Pacific ocean to the west. It controlled the supply lines running north up to the US border and, via a series of secret tunnels, on to Phoenix, Tucson and San Diego. It was as dangerous as the neurotoxin barb of a Durango scorpion, its motto: 'Survival of the fittest'.

'But we failed to get Pago, Julio.'

'This is the matter I wish to discuss. He was unusually lucky to get away from me. I failed to deliver. El Padrino, Carlos Salazar, may have me killed for this. Technically, I am no longer El Cartero.'

Julio threw his head back with a laugh.

'You really believe that?' said Bell.

'Yes. If it is to be this way, then I welcome it. I work for a narcorporation, remember.'

'The British Secret Service will continue to search for Pago.'

'Exactly. Salazar has a proposition, if it is acceptable to your people.'

Julio relaxed for a moment as he prepared the words for his next sentence, beckoning the waiter for two more brandies. He grinned and the gold teeth flashed.

'We share information. Together we can still find Pago and kill him. The cartel wants your organisation to consider this idea.'

'How would I contact you?'

Julio handed over an embossed business card of a realty firm with offices in Mexico City, Los Angeles, and Miami.

Bell knew that MIX would consider any method, no matter how unorthodox, to achieve its objectives. MIX didn't officially exist and therefore it didn't have to justify itself. There were no rules. As far as this Mexican cartel was concerned, they had made a tenuous contact with an agent working for British Military intelligence: either MI5 or MI6. They could believe whatever they wanted. An open channel such as this could have its uses in many ways. Bell was sure that Lambda would countenance such a liaison, but it would be a mistake to look too eager.

Bell idly scuffed away some crumbs from the starched white tablecloth, and pointed at Julio's box of Marlboros. He was immediately offered a cigarette. The gold lighter flared…more rules being broken, his own this time. Julio could detect the flicker of doubt in Bell's eyes.

'I am not asking for your Queen's crown jewels, yes?!'

They both fell back laughing. El Cartero's face hardened again, and his eyes drilled into Bell's.

'After you took off in the military helicopter, I searched the place. Salazar had instructed me to find any remains or possessions of his beloved Dario and his companion, Diego. Dario Hernandez was Salazar's nephew, his sister's son. He came here to sign a deal with Pago.'

'Pago killed him, didn't he?'

'Yes.'

'Were you looking for anything in particular?'

'The place had been stripped clean, but I did find something left behind in Pago's office. Boxes of chocolates and Dario's distinctive silver Beretta. Its grip is inlaid with mother of pearl.'

Julio placed the dead man's sidearm in the centre of the table.

El Cartero held Bell's gaze as he stubbed out his Marlboro in the glass ashtray. He then rotated his palm skywards in a relaxed gesture. Bell thought of the metal flight case containing two million dollars. El Cartero twisted the Rolex on his bony wrist. It was time to bring the conversation to a close and get to the airport.

'Did you find anything else?' quizzed Bell.

'No. If the boot was on the other foot, as you say, there would be no traces either. You call me. You need anything, anytime, ser libre, mi amigo.'

The grin returned just as quickly, and Julio offered his glass to Bell.

'La ley del más fuerte.'

'La ley del más fuerte,' replied Bell.

The brandy balloons chimed together.

They both drained away the remains of the smooth, dark spirit and Julio stood up.

'Adiós.'

29 **TfL**

Bell pressed his earphones a little tighter and made his selection: Music, artistes, 'Para Noya', 'Nex Astrum', random-play. He sat back in an empty section of the carriage, and allowed himself to drift away. A late start this morning.

The Central Line tube train bounded along westwards into the City of London: Leytonstone, Leyton, Stratford, Mile End, all the way to Liverpool Street. It was September now, his favourite month. Another day in the orifice.

Mr Knife held his blade up to the face of a young, Swedish language student, now pressed uncomfortably up against the carriage window. She squinted in fright at the Bowie knife's razor-sharp serrations, and hugged her bag of English textbooks for a grain of comfort.

A low-yield target. Just some cash and a cheap ring.

She hadn't heeded the warnings about getting into empty carriages; there are some nasty people about. The crackhead studied her blue-and-yellow clothing, and smiled menacingly into her traumatised Bambi eyes.

He ran his left hand through the greasy ponytail emerging from the back of his cap, and considered how he would terrorise her. A little blood always speeded things up. He split open the front of her shirt in one continuous movement, and accidentally pierced the underside of her chin. Oh, well.

It caused an immediate spurt of blood to run down her blouse and partially exposed breasts. The girl screamed, but Thomas Bell, her guardian angel, the angel of death, was already standing there.

Bell braced himself against the seats across the aisle. His Beretta 92F was pointed at Mr Knife's head.

Bell swayed with the train's movement, as it negotiated each section of points, keeping his aim steady.

Mr K turned slowly and deliberately.

Same clothing as before.

Cap and ponytail, harsh stubble, and crazed eyes which stared at Bell through a heroin and methamphetamine mist. He grinned, revealing a mouthful of rotten, yellow teeth held in place by inflamed gums, nicely diseased with the acute gingivitis.

'Can I help you, pal?'

The girl stared dead ahead like a clueless prairie dog, seconds before the eagle's talons made contact. Mr K noticed the realistic suppressor of Bell's replica gun. He had now lowered the blade away from the girl's Adam's apple.

Next station: Mile End.

Mr K considered his options.

Bell turned to the unfortunate girl, still bleeding profusely.

'What's your name?'

'E...Erica,' she answered.

'Erica, get off at this station. Now!'

Her English should be good enough to understand that.

Incredibly, Erica was permitted to stand up and brush past them to the tube doors.

The agenda had changed.

A dawning realisation had hit Mr K that he had dealt with this pretty-boy meddler before, and beaten him to shit last time.

Let's do it again, except this time, we'll slice off his ears and saw his nose clean off, by starting at the nostril end. Then, cut his gobby tongue out. Why not blind the bastard with well-aimed jabs into both eyes, as a finishing touch? Job done!

The train moved off again.

'You dumb shit, I thought I'd taught you a lesson last time!'

Just a replica firearm, a bluff.

'That's a toy gun, isn't it?'

'Everybody says that,' replied Bell, smoothly.

'I bet you're the filth, a British Transport Police officer dressed in civvies! You guys have to obey rules, you bastard!'

Mr K wasn't worried. He would rush this twat any second now. That was definitely just a kids' airgun that fired harmless pellets. A fucking BB gun!

'I'm your nemesis,' said Bell, evenly.

'My what?!'

'Your undoing.'

'Huh? I should have skinned you alive when I had the chance. You can't shoot me, yer wanker!'

Bell smiled back, unmoved.

As Mr K rose from his seat, Bell fired the first hollow point round into his gut.

No brawl this time.

The next bullet went into the junkie's thigh, bursting open his femoral artery.

Bell was playing with him like a cat with a mouse.

The snot-shot was on its way.

With an instant look of disbelief, he dropped his knife, clutching at the hepatitis-contaminated blood pouring from his body. The ferret eyes widened in horror, a sudden recognition that this suit was the real deal. A player trained to kill clinically and robotically, without remorse, whichever side of the law he was on.

He and his little knife featured somewhere in the lower leagues. This guy was an ice-cool operator in the premier division. Laser blue eyes and a razor-sharp mind fed by pure oxygen.

Bell placed the final bullet into the centre of Mr K's forehead, perfectly bisecting the distance between his dilated pupils.

The back of his skull and spongy, bloody chunks of his addled brain exploded over the windows, upholstery, floor, and ceiling. The greasy ponytail, like some foul, bloody turd, was still attached to a large piece of skin-covered skull fragment.

Now wearing surgical gloves, Bell picked up the hunting knife, twisted off the handle-cap and tipped out the contents. Fish hooks, a compass, and a tight coil of sawing wire fell out on to the carriage floor.

Just as he had suspected.

He dropped the knife on top of its owner and made for the doors, stepping out crisply at Bethnal Green station and taking a deep breath.

The red and silver carriages accelerated away into Central London. Next stop, Liverpool Street, where this train will terminate and be taken out of service due to undisclosed circumstances.

As he made his way to the turnstiles, his phone vibrated impatiently in the palm of his hand. The short greeting caused him to smile and respond spontaneously.

'Judy!'

Also by Richard Gill...

Lebensrune

www.richardgill.uk

Graphic novels out soon

Register for email updates!

Pilot graphic novel chapter for Paloma Azul follows...

Illustrated by Alice Bloomfield
www.alicebloomfield.co.uk

Song references used in Paloma Azul

Lyrics on p. 81 from 'Knowing Me, Knowing You' written
by Benny Andersson, Björn Ulvaeus and Stig Anderson
Lyrics on p. 202 from 'Stairway to Heaven' written
by Jimmy Page and Robert Plant
Reference on p. 206 to 'Champagne Supernova' written
by Noel Gallagher

THE NON-NUCLEAR EXPLOSIVE CHARGES OF TWO DEVICES HAD DETONATED, COVERING A LARGE AREA IN RADIOACTIVE PLUTONIUM, CAESIUM AND BORON.
PU239 HAS A HALF-LIFE OF 24,100 YEARS.

THE US NUCLEAR DISASTER TEAM LOCATES THE 3rd B28 FI BOMB ON THE DRY ALMANZORA RIVERBED. IT IS INTACT, UNLIKE THE OTHER TWO DEVICES.

...A LOT OF TOXIC TOP SOIL WILL HAVE TO BE SHIPPED BACK TO THE US IN SEALED OIL DRUMS...

CAPTAIN E. KURTZ ABOARD THE BRIDGE OF THE *USS PETREL*. AFTER TWO MONTHS OF FRUITLESS SEARCHING THE PROBABLE IMPACT AREA, THE FOURTH THERMO NUKE IS STILL AWOL...

ANOTHER GODDAM FUCK-UP! THEY'RE GONNA HAVE OUR BALLS ON A STICK. ONLY MY CLOSE FRIEND JACK DANIELS IS GONNA GET ME THROUGH THIS....

...THAT BITCH FIRECRACKER MUST BE DOWN THERE ...SOMEWHERE!...

THE PARACHUTE HAD DEPLOYED AND NOW BOMB #4 LAY ON THE SEABED AT A DEPTH OF 80 METRES.

...IT SHOULD JUMP OFF THE SCREEN LIKE A BRANDED MUSTANG! WHERE THE FUCK IS IT?

WEARY SONAR OPERATORS WITH TIRED EYES...

Printed in Great Britain
by Amazon

80827163R00185